FINDING *Dandelion*

LEX MARTIN

This New Adult contemporary romance is recommended for readers 18+ due to mature content.

Copy editing by RJ Locksley

Cover design by Twin Cove Design
Cover image © Shutterstock.com/Linda Moon
Formatting by Polgarus Studio

ISBN 978-0-9915534-3-3

To Matt & my little bears

"If you don't fight for what you love,
don't cry for what you lose."
- Anonymous

PROLOGUE

- Dani -

Goosebumps line my skin as Travis threads his fingers through mine. Closing my eyes, I brace myself.

"You sure you want to do this, Dani?" He sounds nervous even though he's the one who sold me on the idea in the first place. "It's going to hurt. A lot."

Brady laughs. "Man, don't scare her."

Brady is hot, all ridges and taut muscles and menacing tattoos, and I know he's staring down at my naked back right now. He's so out of my league.

Of course this is the only way I'd get a guy like that to touch me.

Swallowing, I nod and clutch my shirt to my chest. "Let's do this. I'm not chickening out."

I've done my homework, researched optimal positioning, pain, methods, everything. Now I just have to take the plunge. *This is going to be my year of firsts.*

"That a girl. I promise I'll be gentle." Brady moves away from me, and the buzzing starts and stops.

Travis's grip tightens as he leans down and whispers, "If your mother knew you were doing this, she'd kill me."

I yank my hand from his and swat my best friend. "What's the matter with you? Now is *not* the time to talk about my mother."

A black gloved hand runs across my shoulder as Brady

lowers the strap on my lacy, black bra. Hell, yes, I wore my sexy underwear.

He lowers his voice. "This is going to be cold."

All of my muscles tense, and he chuckles.

"Honey, relax. This isn't my first time." Brady's voice is sultry and deep, sending chills across me. He rubs my skin slowly, the smell of alcohol thick in the air. "I'll take good care of you. What's in your head is worse than the reality. Trust me. It'll hurt at first, but you'll get used to it, and you'll only be sore for a couple of days."

Shit. I'm really going through with this.

I glance over my shoulder and look him in the eye. Brady smiles, and butterflies swirl in my stomach. He presses a finger into my trapezius muscle. "Right here?"

Nodding, I close my eyes and rest my chin on the back of the chair.

"This is beautiful, by the way." He taps on the translucent piece of paper.

"It's the North Star. To help me find my way." I say this more for myself.

Brady presses the paper against me and rubs. Then the buzzing starts again, and the needle cuts into my skin.

CHAPTER ONE
(THREE WEEKS LATER)

- Dani -

My fingertip traces the lines on my shoulder where my tattoo sits, muscle memory taking my hand to the axis where North and South intersect and where I hope to find balance. A mooring. Some stability.

I can feel it in my bones. Hope. A smile tilts my lips as I start to buy into my pep talk.

My smile grows… until my new co-worker drops a stack of work in front of me.

Laura gives me an empty smile. "I already have plans this weekend, so I'm leaving this for you. As the marketing major, this should be right up your alley."

Our junior year of college hasn't started yet, and she's already bailing on me. Biting my cheek, I reach around to re-stack the documents.

Laura and I are Professor Zinzer's new assistants. We'll be coordinating all of the other work-study students in the art lab this fall while we prep materials for his classes. He always takes on one art student and one business student to manage his office. Because my best friend Travis had Zinzer last semester, I got the inside track on this gig and beat out dozens of other business applicants.

I tuck the pile of work into my messenger bag, not bothering to smile.

"Zin needs it by Monday," she chirps.

In other words, he needs it the Monday of Labor Day weekend. My jaw tightens.

Laura doesn't look even remotely guilty for dumping this on me. As she tosses her hair over her shoulder, she says, "Thanks, Dani." Her not-so-subtle appraisal of me makes me squirm. "You're so… nice."

If I were a cartoon, steam would be pouring from my ears. I've never hated a word so much in my life. If one more person tells me I'm nice, I'm going to lose it.

Nice gets me dumped on. Pushed around. Ignored.

When I was a kid, I thought I merely had manners. What the hell is wrong with being polite? But now I see this characteristic doesn't cut it in Boston where everyone is so much edgier. The Midwest is just a friendlier place. In Chicago, when someone runs into you, the person says, "Excuse me." Here, I get cursed at or shoved. I've gotten used to this faster pace of life, but it doesn't diminish the fact that I can be such a goddamn pushover.

My mother would tell me to "fuck nice." I chuckle to myself. She has a mouth that's worse than half the frat boys at this school.

I guess that's what happens when you almost die of angiosarcoma.

The laughter withers on my lips, and I blink back the sudden onslaught of emotion that comes whenever I think of my mom. She fought like hell to survive, even after she lost all of her hair and both breasts. And she beat it. For now at least.

By the time I get to my dorm suite, I'm still wrestling with what I wish I had told Laura. Why can't I find the words when I'm in the moment? As I stare at the pile of work that sits near the edge of my desk, a tight ball of frustration coils in my stomach. I'm going to be holed up all weekend preparing my professor's brochures instead of unpacking.

My eyes drift to the wall of boxes in the small room I'm sharing with a girl I met last semester. Jenna is a riot. We took a sociology class together. It was such a snooze that to entertain ourselves, we'd write pervy notes to each other to see who could make the other laugh. She always won. And, yeah, my professor hated me. But, come on—when Jenna wrote, "I wanna choke on your thick man-slinky," I couldn't help but bust out laughing.

Her Southern drawl and perfect blonde hair throws you off. First you think she might be an uptight biatch, but then she slings an arm around you and acts like she's known you for ages. I'm not totally sure how she's BFFs with our other roommate, though. I've only met Clem once, but the girl is a glacier. Hello, she rolled her eyes at me when I asked if she liked *The Vampire Diaries.*

On my way out the door to run a few errands, I pause in front of a mirror to smooth back my long hair. My reflection reminds me of my mother.

Everyone tells me I look exactly like her when she was young. I have big green eyes, pale skin, and dark brown hair except for the swaths of pink I dyed last month, and thanks to Victoria's Secret, I have a few well-placed curves.

Opting to skip any makeup, I grab my jacket and head out.

The train ride is quick, and when I step out into the bright afternoon sun, I have to shield my eyes. As I wait for the light to change so I can cross the street, I find myself staring at a guy trying to get what must be ten pizza boxes through the door of a restaurant a few feet away. I walk over and grab the handle to hold it open. Out of the corner of my eye, I see blonde hair streak across the restaurant a second before I hear the girl giggle.

"Hope you and your friends can handle all this pizza," she says, all breathy. I don't know if she's trying to be sexy or if she's out of breath from doing the fifty-yard dash to talk to him.

I roll my eyes while I stand there, still opening the door. The guy's shoulder presses up against the pane of glass, and he laughs.

"I'm sure we can handle it. Thanks, uh—"

"Tamara."

"Thanks, Tamara."

Through the glass, I see her wave a piece of paper. "Here, call me if you decide you need an extra *mouth* for all that... food." The way she says "mouth" tells me she is *not* talking about the pizza. Gross.

Her silhouette disappears briefly on the other side of him. His hands are on the tower of pizzas, and I don't see him reach for the paper, but then his back arches like he's surprised.

When she steps back, her hands are empty. Okay, I think she just shoved her number into the pocket of this guy's jeans.

All righty.

He clears his throat. "Yeah, thanks, doll," he says to the blonde.

When he steps back onto the sidewalk, I get my first good look at him. He's wearing aviators, so I can't see his eyes, but the rest of him is all kinds of sexy. Tall and lean. Skin the color of light caramel like he's been out in the sun. Brownish-blond hair tousled in a devil-may-care kind of way. His biceps, which are corded in muscle, pull at his t-shirt, and I can't help but stare.

An SUV pulls up behind me, and a guy shouts, "Hurry

the hell up, Jax. I'm not going to circle the block again."

Jax laughs and turns slightly. He finally sees me and tilts his head. He clears his throat again.

"Sorry. I'm being an ass, blocking the doorway."

I blink.

He smiles down at me, and I think the heavens part because he's so damn beautiful it hurts to look at him, but before I can get the courage to say something, anything, his friend honks. Jax looks to the SUV and then back to me, smiles again, and walks away.

Ugh! The next time a drop-dead-gorgeous slab of man talks to me, it would be nice to use words.

CHAPTER TWO

- Jax -

Music blares on the stereo behind me, but I'm too tired from this afternoon's workout to lean over and turn it down. I look across the room and snicker. "Dude, your sister is drunk."

Sammy is slouched in the chair with her Magic 8 Ball, staring at it like it has all the answers. Her brother Nick, my roommate, barely spares a glance in her direction before he goes back to his cards. "Don't even think about fucking my sister, Jax."

I punch him in the arm. "You're an asshole. You know there are two kinds of girls I never touch—little sisters and roommates."

Nick's eyebrow lifts. "I've seen your sister's roommates. You've never gotten any of that action?"

"Are you kidding? She'd chop up my balls and shove them down my throat if I ever got close to one of them. She's a little protective." If nothing else, my twin is fierce.

I don't mention that whole fiasco freshman year.

Sammy laughs hysterically at nothing in particular and shakes her Magic 8 Ball. "Is there one guy out there who will love me forever?" She peers into the black triangle at the bottom of the ball. Her face lights up as she reads, "It is decidedly so."

Rolling my eyes, I take a long pull from my beer and scroll through the texts on my phone. *Kelly, Jamie, Emma.* They're hot. *Katie. Lanie.* They're hotter.

My mind wanders to the girl outside the pizza parlor, the one who held the door open for me this afternoon. I don't know why I'm thinking about her. She was beautiful but looked young without any makeup. Kind of innocent and wide-eyed.

Not my type.

I'm debating the larger questions in life, like breast size, but the water sloshing around in that dumb ball distracts me from planning my weekend. I point the neck of the bottle in her direction.

"Sam, I hate to break it to you, but that's all crap. I hope you know that 'cause I like you too much to let you think there's one perfect guy out there." Nick's little sister is a senior in high school, and she's a pretty little thing, but she needs to wise up or some dick like me will break her heart. Only it won't be me.

She ignores my comment and shakes the ball. "Is there one perfect girl out there for Jax Avery who will help him get past his man-whoring ways?" She narrows her eyes as she reads the message that floats to the top. "It is decidedly so."

Nick barks out a laugh. "How much did you drink? Dad is going to kick my ass if you go home tomorrow with a hangover." He goes back to his hand and murmurs, "'Cause you'd have to be drunk if you think that's in the cards for Jax."

Sammy hiccups and then groans like it hurt. She turns to me. "Doesn't it feel empty? Don't you want something with meaning?"

This girl needs to stop watching so many chick flicks.

I take another drink. "It has meaning. It means I get laid with no strings. That's a beautiful thing."

She makes a face like I just took a crap on her dinner. I don't have the energy to explain why relationships are such a bad idea, but if she were to take a two-minute look at my parents, she'd be on my side.

I reach over for a slice of pizza and ignore the hollowness in my chest. "What time is our team meeting tomorrow?"

Nick squints at me. "It's at three, but you should get there early. I hear Coach Patterson is a hardass."

"I can handle it." I continue scrolling through my phone, contemplating how to spend the next twenty-four hours before soccer completely consumes my life. I'm thinking Katie tonight and maybe Lanie tomorrow afternoon.

As I'm about to look up Katie's number, my screen lights up. *Natasha.* Even better. We're friends with benefits. Minus the friends part.

"What are you doing tonight?"

Smiling, I write back. *"Making you scream my name as I fuck you senseless."*

Not a minute goes by before she responds. *"Perfect. I'll be by in twenty."*

Sammy sighs at me from across the table like she knows what I'm planning.

"Some day, a girl is going to kick you on your ass, Jax. I hope I'm here to see it."

Why is a teenager lecturing me about my sex life? "In your dreams, kid. I don't get attached."

I learned that lesson a long time ago. Girls are like beer. Here to bookend the important things.

* * *

I press the button on my phone, and the screen lights up. Only forty-five minutes until practice. Shit. Nick's warning that I should arrive early grates on me. *Why is practice in the middle of the afternoon? My workouts are so much better first thing in the morning.*

I've been in a pissy mood since last night. Natasha and I didn't get into our usual groove. Yeah, we both got off, but it felt like work.

Natasha is almost six feet of Russian model, and she usually knows what I like. We've been hooking up for the last year. Our arrangement works. We meet up, have a drink or two, share a few laughs, fuck and go our separate ways. She's not clingy, and she's rich too, so I know she's not after my trust fund. Why I'm not fucking euphoric right now is beyond me.

My dark mood gets darker as the slurping sound increases. I look down and try not to glare.

"Doll? We gotta wrap this up." I'm not good with names. Doll is just easier. A one-size-fits-all nickname.

Tara or Tammy or Tamara looks up with a mouth full of me and tries to smile.

God, I'm an asshole.

I pull my dick out of her mouth, carefully avoiding the gleaming row of teeth, and tuck it back into my jeans.

"Sorry, Jax." Her eyes dart around. I place my hands on her shoulders and help her stand. Not every girl is good at giving head, but it's something that should be taught in school along with making pancakes. Two very important skills.

"No worries. I didn't realize it was so late. Maybe we could hang out some other time." Or not.

Her eyes brighten. It takes everything in me to smile and hug her before I grab my keys off the coffee table.

When I reach the door, I see it in her eyes. She wants a kiss. Yeah, not happening. And not for the reason you think. This has nothing to do with her deepthroating my junk and everything to do with how she drooled all over my BMW M-5 Hurricane. I could almost see the dollar signs popping out of her eyes. I don't need that shit. I may be pre-law, but I've majored in avoiding gold-diggers.

I lean down to give her a quick peck on the cheek and thank my lucky fucking stars we're at her place before I make my escape.

Once I'm safely inside my oasis of solitude, I crank the music and peel out. The engine purrs, and I revel in my find. This car was a steal at three hundred thousand. My mother didn't think so, but who the hell cares? She owes me, and her kind of debt never goes away.

My baby can go two hundred and twenty-three miles-per-hour in a heartbeat. I can't exactly open her up driving around Chestnut Hill, but I still get to campus in record time. Boston College is only two miles from my place, but it's in the middle of suburban hell. Quiet streets. Manicured lawns. Soccer moms. Strollers and shit. Why BC couldn't be located next to Fenway like my sister's school is beyond me.

By the time I reach the soccer field, I'm wishing I had taken a shower. That girl's perfume is making me gag, especially in this heat.

Coach Patterson is standing in front of the stands, where the rest of my team sits, with his arms crossed over his chest like he owns us. For the next several months, I guess he does. Our old assistant coach ran pre-season until the university finalized Patterson's contract last week.

"Jax Avery, good of you to join us."

I'm on time, so I don't know what his fucking problem is.

As though he can read my mind, he barks, "Be here ten minutes before practice starts or you're late."

I fight the urge to roll my eyes and slide down next to Nick who is wearing a shit-eating grin.

"Told you to be early, asshole," he whispers.

"Had to squeeze in a blow job. It's what gives me my superhuman strength." I lift my arm to make a muscle when Coach blows the whistle.

"Listen up. It's no secret why the school hired me. You guys were a hair's breadth from winning the championship last year. Except what happened? Half of you decided to get tanked the night before."

Not me. I didn't get drunk. I'm not an idiot.

"And the other half of you got caught at two in the morning in an all-girls dorm. Most of those young ladies ended up on academic probation."

Okay, guilty as charged. Who knew girls' dorms had such strict policies?

"I'd like for you to stop thinking with what's between your legs and consider the people you affect. The seniors need to step up and be leaders. When you graduate next May, I hope men cross the stage and not little boys who are too self-absorbed to see straight."

Sighing, he says, "As I'm sure everyone is aware, now that the season is extended, the playoffs are after Thanksgiving break, which means you all need to lie low during those days off. Think earthworm low because if I hear you guys destroyed a hotel room at some resort, you're off the team, plain and simple."

Everyone is silent, but I know the guys are just waiting until Coach walks away to let their guard down. They'll be talking about how this is a fucking joke in sixty seconds flat.

Patterson paces for a minute and stops in front of me and waits until we make eye contact. "No more fuckups. Time to grow a pair and be responsible. If you think I won't kick you off because I'm new, you've got another thing coming. Shape up or you're outta here." He laughs, but I know he's not amused. "I'm not gonna hold your hand and burp you and take your shit. I'm leaving that for your mommas."

Ha. He doesn't know my mother.

Patterson slaps his hand with his clipboard. "I know most of you guys want to play pro soccer, and we have a great nucleus and should be able to go all the way this year if you stay focused on what matters."

That's the question, isn't it? What matters? I wish I knew.

CHAPTER THREE

- Dani -

As much as I'm trying to distract myself by hanging out with Travis this afternoon, the truth is I'll be working my butt off until Monday morning.

I'd like to kick Laura in the shin. I won't, of course, but I need to stand up for myself or she'll take advantage of me all year. Empirically, I know this. But getting the nerve to not back down is the hard part.

And the way I couldn't speak to that gorgeous guy yesterday! He smiles, freaking smiles at me, and I stand there like a block of cement. I'm a junior in college at a great university with a three point five GPA. You'd think I'd have some linguistic abilities.

Travis has been frowning since we left the tattoo parlor.

I have to laugh at this whole situation. When I got my tattoo a few weeks ago, Travis decided he wanted one. Except today, he chickened out, and I emerged with piercings instead. I nudge him with my hip, edging him off the sidewalk. "You're still lusting after Brady, aren't you?"

He turns toward me, his black hair flipping in his face. "What gave me away?"

"Just a hunch. Too bad Brady doesn't play for your team."

"The good ones never do. He seemed pretty into you, though." Travis flashes that trademark crooked grin, and

I shake my head. Travis thinks every guy likes me.

"Brady is, like, a man. He must be twenty-five or twenty-six. At least. I just turned twenty. And he's all muscly and hard and sexy. There's no way he's interested in me."

It's Travis's turn to shake his head and look at me like I'm crazy.

But there's something else. Even though Brady is good-looking, I can't stop thinking about the guy from the restaurant. *Jax*. Damn. Even his name is sexy. One smile from him and my panties almost melted off my body. This is what I get for being so judgmental about that girl trying to give him her number.

Travis bumps me with his elbow. "So were you totally turned on while Brady had his hands all over you?"

"Yeah, until he jabbed me with a needle. Twice." I adjust my bra strap. "Do you think they… look okay?" I can't talk about the piercings without my face turning crimson.

Travis edges around an old lady walking in the opposite direction, and his eyes fall on me, dipping briefly to my chest. "They're hot, and you're gorgeous."

"You don't think they make me look a little trampy?" The words are out of my mouth before I have a chance to filter them, but it's an honest question.

"Hell, no." I love that his response is lightning quick. "So you want to do a little more body modification? It all looks great on you."

I grin. Travis always makes me feel beautiful. He lived on my floor freshman year, and we immediately hit it off. For the last two years, we've been nearly inseparable. He's beautiful with black hair and eyes the color of dark chocolate. My BFF is tall and lanky and a bit of a brooder. All the boys love him. I do too. He was my shoulder to cry on when Reid and I broke up last spring.

"Besides, if anyone is the tramp in this relationship, it's me, remember?" He nudges me again. "You're too pure to be trampy."

Maybe that's my problem. Guys view me as the good girl. The nice one.

I blow out a deep breath. "Do you think that's why Reid lost interest?"

"Reid lost interest 'cause he's a douche canoe. Sleeping with your roommate almost within hours of your breakup is the only proof you need. And you weren't a virgin. You just don't have sex with every guy on the planet."

I get that I'm not ugly, and I'm not the kind of person to fish for compliments, but my girl-next-door qualities don't exactly attract the guys who get my toes curling in bed. More like wham-bam-five-minute-slam. And Reid was no exception. Which is why I was so shocked to see him prance out of Ashley's room an hour after the porno sounds started last spring. Granted, we had broken up a few days before, but still. I'm nauseous thinking about how she screamed the whole time. *"Harder! Oh, God, yes, fuck me harder!"*

I thought she had hooked up with another guy she'd been crushing on. Sucker that I am, I was rooting for her, happy she found someone who was hot in the sack. Except when the door opened, my ex-boyfriend sauntered out, shirtless, with his unbuttoned jeans hanging low on his hips, and his penis still saluting at half-mast through his pants. He didn't even have the decency to be embarrassed. Instead, he gave me a look that suggested I was the problem, not him. Me!

God, I hope she was faking it.

When you see moments like this played out in the

movies, the scorned lover always has clever things to say to hurt the guy and show him it's somehow his loss. Except I didn't. I was speechless. Couldn't say a word. I still want to kick myself in the head for being a mute.

I've barely been able to say anything to the happy couple the half dozen times I've seen them. Of course, I might've been distracted since Reid was trying to massage her tonsils with his tongue. Admittedly, Ashley is tall and gorgeous. I'm a pigmy next to her, so I don't totally blame him for being into her. But do they have to go at it right in front of me? He and I did date for almost a year.

#WhatAWaste

When I ran into them last week, I kinda thought I was over it. But then she accused me of stealing her necklace when I moved out last semester. All I did was stammer and grit my teeth and fantasize about punching her in the kidney.

Travis and I approach a bakery and decide to stop to grab a bite. The aroma of sourdough bread makes my stomach growl, momentarily taking my mind off my asshole ex.

After we settle in a booth and give the waitress our order, I open my journal. "Items number one and two: check!" I take a hot pink sharpie out of my bag and mark them off.

"You wrote a list?" The derision in Travis's voice is thick, paralleled in intensity by his arched eyebrow.

I smirk back. "It's to remind me, so I don't get off track."

"Can I see this list?"

"You already know what's on there, and if you see it in writing, you're going to be obnoxious."

He reaches for it anyway and tugs like a bulldog until I relent. I watch his face as his eyes travel across the page.

"Get a tattoo, get something pierced, have a one-night stand." Travis's eyes turn up. "You should have done number three first. It's more fun. Plus, there's no pain involved. Unless that's how you like it."

That arched eyebrow tilts higher, and I laugh. "Perhaps, but this is about self-discovery, and I'm taking baby steps. Or at least that was the plan."

Travis waits for the waitress to deliver our salads, and as she walks away, he leans toward me. "I wouldn't exactly call numbers one and two baby steps," he mumbles as he reaches for my sharpie and scribbles on the page.

"Hey, you're not allowed to do that." No one, and I mean no one, writes in my journal but me. It's half diary, half sketchbook. Not that there's anything in there Travis doesn't already know.

"Too late." He says it kind of sing-songy, the jubilant tone matching the self-satisfied expression on his face.

I read number four out loud. "Dance on a bar." I shake my head. "Travis, that's so slutty."

He snorts. "You're the one who wants to have a one-night stand."

Glancing around the restaurant, I chuck a crouton at his head. "Could you lower your voice? You know I don't necessarily want a one-night stand. I just…"

He reaches over and grabs my hand. "I know. Your ex head-fucked you, and you need a clean slate. A hot piece of ass will definitely help."

"Uh, I get that Reid's an asshole, but did he seriously have to hookup with Ashley?" The thought of them burning up her sheets together still makes me want to jab them both in the eyeballs with dull pencils.

"Live and learn, babe. See, you never need to worry about the bitches because you already know what to expect. It's the friendly ones you gotta watch out for."

"That's deep."

"I still can't believe you didn't lose your shit."

"What was I supposed to say? 'Ashley, you were a great roommate, right up until you slept with the guy I dated for the last ten months'?" Crumpling my napkin, I shake my head again. "You know I'm not good at confrontations."

Travis puffs out his chest a little. "I'd be happy to kick his weaselly little ass. You're too good for him anyway. He deserves that brainless blonde."

Reid was supposed to be the safe bet, the stable one with the five-year plan and a future of Roth IRAs. So maybe we didn't rock each other's world sexually, but I thought we had mutual respect and friendship. I'm an idiot to think that counted for something.

"Slutty girls who masquerade as goodie-two-shoes suck."

In addition to Reid, Ashley absconded with our other roommates, leaving me to scrounge around at the last minute to figure out another living situation for my junior year of college. If Jenna hadn't asked me to live with her and her friends, I don't know what I would've done.

But that situation with Ashley has left me gun-shy when it comes to living with new people.

Jenna is fun and all, but we don't really know each other aside from the few laughs we shared in class and a couple of study sessions.

And if I'm being honest, Clem scares me a little. Harper seems nice, but we've only spoken for two minutes. Plus, the three of them are seniors and have been friends since they were freshmen. I'm the newcomer.

Around a mouthful of salad, I ask, "Why can't I just

live with you this year? Why do I have to live with strangers?"

Travis sighs. "Because we live in a puritanical society that fears my penis will corrupt you, and apparently vaginas won't."

Salad chunks shoot out my mouth before my hand contains my explosion of laughter.

Travis reaches over and grabs my other hand. "You can always come stay with me for a few days if things get cray-cray. I know West Campus isn't as cool as the brownstones on Bay State Road, but if you get tired of all that estrogen, you can chill in *Casa de Travis* any time."

He and I both have partial scholarships for room and board, but only if we live on campus. I think we'd have a blast living together, but there's no way either of us can afford the rents in this area.

"Thanks. You're the best. I'm sure things will be okay." *I hope.* I flick another crouton in his direction. "Keep next Saturday night free for me, okay?"

"Sure. What's up?"

"Jenna's throwing a party, and since I don't know any of her friends, I need backup. They're headed to Lansdowne Street, and that's your hunting ground anyway."

His uncle's club Cages is one of the hot bars next to Fenway Park, which runs along the Eastern edge of campus. It's been our favorite place to hang out since we hit college. It doesn't hurt that his uncle lets us sneak in for free.

"I'm down." Travis lifts a bite to his mouth but stops midway. "Maybe we can check one more item off your list." He winks at me, and I roll my eyes.

OMG. I hope he's talking about dancing on the bar.

CHAPTER FOUR

- Jax -

The whole time I run the field, it rattles around in my head. Why the hell didn't I get off this afternoon? Who cares that her technique needed more torque? A girl's attention on my dick should equal complete satisfaction. *But things weren't quite right with Natasha last night either.*

I try to shake off the idea that something is wrong. Maybe it's time Natasha and I find other fuck buddies. I remind myself that sex is sex. Fucking is fucking. It's simple. Biological. No need to get philosophical about it.

Sweat pours down my face, stinging my eyes. Coach runs us hard. All the guys stayed in shape with pre-season training, but today's ball-busting practice has everything to do with Patterson wanting to show us who's in charge.

By the time I get home, all I want to do is shower, grab a beer and crash in front of the TV. When my phone lights up with a text, I can barely bring myself to look at the screen. A few minutes later, it starts ringing and doesn't stop.

"Can't you take a hint? Me not answering means go the fuck away," I mumble into the phone.

"Don't be such a bitch, Avery." My best buddy Daren laughs in my ear. We've been friends since birth. He's like my brother. We were next-door neighbors and practically lived at each other's houses growing up. Except unlike me, his parents actually give a shit about him. I figure that's why he's considered an upstanding citizen, and I'm the one gracing the gossip columns on page six of the *Post.*

Yeah, in this town, Daren walks on water. It'd be annoying as fuck if he weren't so likeable.

Only one thing has ever come between us—him screwing over my sister—and I nearly broke his jaw for it. I probably would have, too, if two guys hadn't pulled me off him. It almost did in our friendship, but we both ended up at Boston College, him on a full ride for football, me for soccer, and somehow we got over it. Mostly.

"You going out tonight?" he asks.

"I'm too tired. Just gonna hang out here."

"I was picking up some dinner. I'll swing by, and we can play some *Call of Duty.*" In true Daren Sloan fashion, he doesn't ask.

An hour later, we've got our game faces on as I blow out his guts with my AK-12 assault rifle.

"Fuck!" he shouts at the flatscreen.

Satisfied with my win, I sink back into the distressed leather of my couch and grin. I'm not an idiot. I know my days of being able to hold my own against Daren are long gone, so I take the moment to relish the virtual ass-kicking. I used to be able to go toe to toe with Daren, but since we hit college, he's had to bulk up for football while soccer keeps me leaner.

"Pussy." I can't help but goad him a little.

"Takes one to know one."

"Speaking of, where's your ball and chain tonight?"

Daren exhales loudly, but instead of defending that bitch, he just shrugs. He's been dating Veronica on and off since he broke up with my sister. I keep thinking one day he's going to wake up and smell the fucking coffee and see that Veronica is only after him because he's rich, not to mention the star quarterback for BC. But their last serious breakup was two years ago, and I'm starting to worry he might actually marry that twat. I don't know why. She treats him like shit. If that's true love, keep me the hell away from it.

"Doing anything for your birthday?" he asks as he resets the game with one hand while grabbing his beer with the other.

"I'm headed to a party at BU and then going to Cages on Lansdowne. You should come." I don't mention who'll be there. I'm sure he knows.

He looks like he's considering it for a minute before he shrugs again.

"I can't do shit until the season is over. Coach will lop off my balls if I go out." Daren isn't in the running for the Heisman Trophy for nothing. This guy works out like a madman. I get exhausted thinking about it. "This spring, though, we're doing Maui. My treat. A late twenty-first birthday gift. What do you say?"

"Definitely. Get me out of Boston. If it snows this year like it did last, I'm going to lose my damn mind."

I pause the game to reload my plate with food, and that's when I hear the yelling.

"Shit. They're at it again," I groan. Reason one hundred and one to never get married: Hannah and Greg. I motion toward the adjacent condo. They've been my neighbors for the past two years, since Nick and I moved here sophomore year. "They're splitting up."

When a knock comes at my door a few minutes later, Daren raises his eyebrows. "Dude, I hope you don't have anything to do with their problems."

"Fuck you, man. I don't touch married women." The conversation I had with my roommate last night comes to mind. *Okay, so make that three kinds of chicks I don't touch.*

I may be an asshole, but I'm not a total bottom-feeder.

When I open the door, Hannah is standing there with her four-year-old daughter Chloe, whose face is wet with tears.

"You guys okay over there?" I don't mention that I can hear the yelling, although she must realize it.

Hannah nods and takes the sleeve of her sweatshirt and wipes her daughter's face. "Can I ask a favor, Jax? Would you mind watching Chloe again? Maybe for an hour?"

"No problem." I reach over and swing the little girl into my arms. "Hey, Chloe, guess what? I recorded that show you like. That one with the princess who talks to the animals."

She immediately perks up. "*Sofia the Fuwst*?" She has trouble pronouncing her R's, which makes her even more adorable.

"I think that's the one. Go ask my buddy over there in the living room, and he'll put it on for you."

A small smile breaks out on her face as I set her down on the floor, and she scurries over to the couch.

"Thanks, Jax." Hannah looks relieved. I've watched her daughter a couple of times when she had to run a few errands. She lowers her voice. "I hate that she has to hear us fight. I really appreciate you watching her. I swear I'll bake you more cookies."

I snicker. "I'll never turn away food, but you don't have to do that. She's a great kid. Come get her when you're ready. No rush."

Hannah closes her eyes briefly. "I owe you." Then she turns and walks back to her apartment.

When I sit on the couch, Daren already has cued up Chloe's show, but she's curled up in the far corner of the couch.

"Chloe, baby, are you hungry? Would you like a bite to eat?"

Her eyes widen. "Yes, pweeze."

I grab part of a hoagie, toss it on a plate, and pour a cup of juice, which I put down in front of her. As she reaches for her food, she looks up and grins. I'd be lying if I said I didn't have a soft spot for this kid. She's funny and sweet and sincere, the way I imagine most girls are before they grow up into soul-suckers.

"Chloe, this is my friend Daren."

She takes a bite of her sandwich and waves at him before turning back to me. "Jax, can we make a fort again? After *Sofia* is over?"

"Sure thing. We can even play the princess and the knight. You'll be the princess, of course. I'll be the knight. This time, you can even ride a horsey."

I laugh as Daren realizes my four-year-old neighbor is about to wrap him around her little finger.

An hour later, I hear the front door open.

"What the hell, Jax?" Nick doesn't sound amused.

I call out, "Watch your language. Chloe's hanging out with us."

I peek out from under a cushion as Chloe and Daren come charging out from behind the couch.

"Slay the dragon!" Daren yells as he carries Chloe on his back. She squeals, her laughter amusing me like nothing else can.

Chloe takes her aluminum foil sword and jabs it at my roommate who shoots me a dirty look.

"This is your emergency?" Nick huffs.

"What? We needed a dragon. I'm the knight. Daren's the horse. Clearly, we needed one more person."

Nick leans down to ruffle Chloe's blonde curls. "Hey, sweetie. You having fun with Uncle Jax?"

She grins back. "Yup. We've alweady taken back the castle."

"Good job." He smiles at her, and then he takes a second to survey the damage to our living room, no doubt pausing on the fact that I've used his comforter and pillows to construct our fort.

"Sorry, man." I shrug. "Like I said. Emergency."

I can guess the curse words that are on the tip of his tongue, but then Chloe grabs his pinky and gives him that toothy grin, and I know he's done.

Nick sighs and then leans down.

"'Kay, where's the dragon's lair, Chloe?"

She points toward the kitchen and starts clapping, excited that he's joining her game.

"Do you want me to wear the oven mitts again? They made for pretty good dragon claws last time."

"Yes! Wear the mitts!"

When Chloe takes off to hide in her fortress, I pull Nick aside. "Sorry, man. She was really upset because Hannah and Greg were yelling. I wanted to cheer her up."

He nods. "I get it." He notices that I'm sporting a Batman cape and laughs. "You really went all-out, huh?"

"Go hard or go home," I quip.

"The only girl who's managed to win your heart, and it's a four-year-old." He slaps me hard on the back.

"Yeah, well, what's not to love? Besides, she doesn't deserve the shit that's going down in her life, and if I can make her smile, then maybe I'm not so useless after all."

He pauses and turns to look me in the eye. "You're a good guy, Jax."

"Fuck you."

He laughs as I punch him in the arm before I run off to help Chloe fortify her castle.

"Chloe," I call out, "if anyone can kill the dragon, it's you, baby. Get your horsey to cross the moat, and I'll help chase the beast out of his cave."

I wish understanding all women were this easy. But their motives are never this simple.

CHAPTER FIVE

- Dani -

My mother's words are the last thing I expect to be thinking about as I'm standing in front of a full-length mirror at a boutique on Newbury Street a week later. *No regrets*. But I doubt this is what she had in mind.

"If I twirl, people will see my hooch." My sweaty palms attempt to tame the layers of hot pink tulle that bounce beneath the short black skirt.

Travis crouches behind me and squints one eye. "I don't see the hooch to which you are referring, but maybe I can help." He fluffs my skirt as though he's offended the fabric is obstructing his view. "Sweets, don't take this the wrong way, but those boy shorts are hot." He slaps my ass, and I jump. "Maybe flashing a little hooch is a good thing."

"But don't you think Britney regretted flashing her muff?"

"You're not going commando. You're not even showing any labia."

I whirl around and smack him square on the shoulder. "That's gross!"

He laughs, rubbing his arm. "What? You took all that time for the full-on salon treatment of this area. Might as well flash it a little."

Covering my face, I groan. "Please, let's never again discuss my Brazilian wax again. That hurt like a motherfucker."

He covers his mouth as his eyes widen. "Wow. I got you to say the f-word. Points for Travis!"

"You are no longer allowed to talk me into any more beauty treatments."

Grabbing a long lock of my dark brown hair, he twirls it with a strand of pink, brings it to his nose and sniffs it. He makes a face like he approves of the way it smells. Weirdo.

He raises his eyebrow. "I think you should knock number three off your list tonight. You'll dance with me, and we'll scope out the perfect hottie. Of course, if he's gay, I get to bat."

The thought of a one-night stand makes me nervous. Not like hot-guy-in-my-pants nervous, but creeper-who-slobbers-and-wants-to-put-his-balls-in-my-shoes nervous. Picking up a random guy sounds so hit-or-miss. Knowing my luck, I'll end up with a bad kisser who has a furry fetish.

I motion toward Travis. "How thoughtful of you to stand in if the need arises."

"What are gay best friends for?"

I turn around and push out my lower lip. "Why couldn't you be straight? We'd make such a great couple."

He pulls me to his chest. "I know. We'd be perfect. We could even color-coordinate our outfits when we go out for dates."

"Oh, that'd be fun!"

"Right?" He flips his hair out of his face. "By the way, tonight, don't ask the guy's name or you'll get attached, and you don't want to get attached." He makes it sound so simple. Travis lets go of me to grab a shirt off a hanger. He holds it up. "Here, try this on."

After pulling off my shirt, I slide on the tiny spaghetti-strapped tank top. He reaches for my shirt and tucks it into my skirt before he kisses the top of my head.

"Total hotness. This pink push-up bra makes your hooters look huge."

"It's an optical illusion. I'm tiny, so proportionally, they look big." I used to hate having boobs when I did gymnastics. Now, they're not so bad.

As I change out of the clothes and back into my jeans and t-shirt, Travis holds the skirt up to his waist, and I start laughing.

"Are you thinking of going in drag?" He'd make a gorgeous girl because he's a gorgeous boy, but I know he's not wired that way.

He rolls his eyes and hands me my clothes.

When I finally check out the price tag, I wish I hadn't. "Crap. This is expensive. Which reminds me, thanks for snagging the art lab job for me. Professor Zinzer is amazing, and working there will force me to do something with my journal of ideas. I think I'm going to love that gig." Except for my stupid co-worker who thinks I'm a pushover already. But I'm excited to hang out and soak in the creativity in the art department.

"My pleasure. If I can't get you to switch majors, maybe I can try to brainwash you. Why you'd rather hang out with suits all day is beyond me."

Nobody gets my business major, not even my best friend. Hell, I don't even understand it some days. While I do okay in those classes, they don't rock my world like art does. But what the hell am I supposed to do with an art degree?

With a business degree, I'll be able to do things for myself.

I watched my mom implode after my dad left us. No, thanks. I'm all for dating and love and hot sex, but there's one thing I have to do for myself and that's make my own way.

* * *

Several hours later, as the pounding beat of music vibrates all of my internal organs, I wonder what the hell I was thinking. Travis keeps saying no one really watches, but I'm sure that's so I don't back out and hide under a table. Somehow this activity went from dancing on a bar to writhing in a cage, and for the last twenty minutes, I've been trying to psych myself up for this.

"You look stunning, girl." Travis's breath smells like orange juice and vodka. "I love the garters." He reaches down and tugs on the ribbon holding up my tights, and I swat his hand.

"I look like a hooker." In the quiet of my friend's apartment as I was getting ready, this seemed like a good idea—dress up, dance my ass off wearing a crazy outfit, and get out of myself for a little while—but now I'm not so convinced. Aside from the leotards I used to sport when I did gymnastics, I've never gone out flashing so much skin. But I have to admit I like the Mary Janes that give me a couple of extra inches on my five-four frame.

"You do, and it looks fucking fabulous," my girlfriend Margo shouts in my ear, making it ring. "What time are your roommates coming?"

"I'm not sure," I yell. "I haven't seen them yet."

After a few back-and-forth texts with Jenna, I finally realize that tonight's outing is to celebrate Clem's twenty-first birthday. All of their friends are meeting up for a few drinks before the club, but since I only really know Jenna, I opted to skip the party and spare myself some awkwardness.

"This bra hurts," I say, tugging it down.

"But these babies are going to make some guy so happy." Margo's hands wrap around my boobs and squeeze, making me wince.

Why my friend thinks she can grope me, much less in the middle of the dance floor, makes me shake my head. Laughing, I look up and lock eyes with… the most beautiful guy I've ever seen. Holy sweet Jesus.

He's tall and lean but muscular. His hair is short on the sides and a little longer on top, flopping into his eyes and drawing my attention to those high cheekbones and some seriously pouty lips. He's wearing a fitted long-sleeved black Henley and jeans. Judging by the smirk on his face, he clearly saw Margo feeling me up.

God, there is something so familiar about him.

I stare. He stares back.

My heart stops beating.

"I need a drink. A very, very strong drink." I turn and beeline straight to the bar where Travis's Uncle Joe bartends. Yes, when faced with a total hottie, I run like hell. #SoSmooth

The plan for tonight? Drink. Heavily. Dance. Pretend Hot Guy didn't see Margo clutch my boobies. And hopefully live to see tomorrow.

"What'll it be, Dani?" Joe wipes condensation off the counter and reaches for a martini glass. "The usual?"

"Yes!" I have to shout over the music so he can hear me.

Even though none of us are twenty-one yet, Travis's uncle knows we won't do anything stupid, so he gets us in and lets us have a few drinks.

He hands me an apple martini and waves off my money when I try to pay. "You're cage dancing. Booze is on the house."

I grin and lean over the bar to grab a cherry off the tray of garnishes.

Crossing his burly arms over his chest, he shakes his head. "It's only 'cause you're so cute that I don't kick your ass for that." His mouth twists as he tries to look tough, and I wink at him and head back to my friends.

When I find Margo and Travis, they look pissed.

"What's wrong?" I ask, taking a swig of my sweet concoction.

Margo bumps me with her elbow and nods her head across the dance floor. "Asshole is here."

That can only mean one person. My ex. Reid.

"He hates clubs," I mutter.

It's ironic that he was always calling me uptight because he's the one who never wanted to go clubbing, and yet here he is, twenty feet away, looking all preppy in a dark polo. Damn. He looks good. A second later, Ashley sidles up next to him and plants her mouth on his. I actually see her tongue extend before their lips connect. Gross.

I chug the rest of my drink, hoping the booze will ease the ache in my chest, and turn back toward my friends.

"I've had two drinks. Let's do this before I lose my nerve." Because nothing distracts a girl from her former lover like writhing around in a cage.

When I get to the platform, I turn around and bump into Travis, who has to grab me to keep me from falling over. Once I'm steady, he holds me by my shoulders and leans down.

"Dani, I know I put this on your list, but if you're not comfortable, you don't have to go through with it."

"I'm not backing out. Not with dickhead down there." I put my mouth against his ear and whisper, "Do I look okay?" I brush down my skirt. Man, it's short.

"You look like sex on a stick, and he's going to be blue-balling himself all over the club when he sees your hot little ass up there." Travis pats me on the bum and shoos me up the small steps. Thankfully, there are five other cages, so it's not like I'm the main attraction.

When we got here, Travis's uncle said one of the girls called in sick, so my best friend kindly suggested that I take her place. I've been here enough times to know how the girls move, and if I don't think too hard about it, I should be okay.

As I get to the top of the stairs, I turn back to give Travis a nervous smile. It's now or never. I gulp, wishing I had another drink, and strut into the cage before I can rethink this.

Closing my eyes, I feel the beat in my chest, and I let my hips move while I grip the bars like my life depends on it. *The crowd is busy. No one will notice you.*

I've always been a decent dancer, probably from years of gymnastics. Hopefully, I'll check off item number four on my list without making a total ass of myself.

I start to let myself go, and the pounding in my heart subsides and is replaced with the driving rhythm of music. The lights pulse above, and I swirl my hips and thrust my chest and move. Heat flushes my cheeks. Sweat beads on my skin.

Feeling braver, I open my eyes. At first I just look at the floor of the cage. It takes another few minutes before I brave looking out into the crowd. And then I wish I hadn't.

Because staring at me is Hot Guy.

I'm not good at being coy. That's Margo's game. She can lure them in and chew them up before they realize what's happening.

Somewhere in my alcohol-addled brain, I decide to

pretend I'm her. Why didn't I think of this sooner? This is just a game. No biggie. Why am I so serious all the time? See, this is what my mother is always talking about. I'm too structured. Too rigid. *Too damn nice.* Anger starts to pound through my veins as I think of all the times I've been called that word. Reid called me nice. Screw nice.

I wink at Hot Guy and decide I definitely need more alcohol. Looking to the side of the cage, I see Travis, and I make a drinking motion, and he nods.

I continue to dance until he steps into the cage with my martini, which I chug.

"Damn, girl. Take it easy."

"I'm not drunk enough to do this."

He pushes up against me and smiles. "Move over. You're hogging the limelight."

Travis grabs my hips and spins me so I'm facing the crowd. Then he pulls me tight and grinds against me, making me gasp.

"I thought you weren't into girls," I yell.

"As much as I'd love to say this boner is for you, I was dancing with Evan a few minutes ago."

I laugh and dance with him until we're both hot and sweaty. I thrust my hips back against him and wrap my arms around his neck as his hands wind down my body.

He spins me around to face him, and he dips me back, grinding his hips into mine. *Okay.*

When he pulls me up, he laughs at my expression. "Was that too much?" he whispers in my ear.

"I don't think I've ever had this much foreplay before with a *straight* guy."

He laughs again and kisses my cheek, turning me back to the crowd. "That's a shame, honey."

When I turn back, Hot Guy is gone. Damn.

I search for him, my eyes scanning the crowd, but

after half an hour, I finally give up.

My insides feel deflated from the lost potential of tonight as I descend the stairs onto the main dance floor. But who am I kidding? Even if I had talked to that guy, he probably has a girlfriend. Or ten. He's too gorgeous to be here by himself.

Spotting an opening in the crowd, I decide to head for the bar and drown my disappointment in vodka.

And as I turn, I run straight into Reid and Ashley.

CHAPTER SIX

- Jax -

I've been peeling heart stickers off my shirt since I got to Cages. You'd think I'd like kissing all those girls to earn my birthday gift. A weekend skiing at Sugarloaf in Maine can't be beat. The guys know I love skiing. It takes my mind off all the bullshit at school. But by the third girl, I was done. Kissing that many chicks skeeved me out. Even without tongue. It shouldn't have—some of them were hot, but after the first few, the thrill was gone.

Looking around the pulsing floor, I don't see any of our friends yet. I get the distinct feeling Nick has abandoned me for that tall sorority girl we saw on our way in. I'm wondering whether I should wait around for the rest of our friends or take a cab home when I see a girl look down at her bare shoulder.

I take a few steps closer to see the tattoo on her back. It's a blue star. She turns slightly, and my eyes travel up the length of her. She's gorgeous, petite with long, dark hair, smooth pale skin, and the face of a fucking angel.

My heart hammers in my chest. Actually hammers. Shit.

Her girlfriend grabs her tits, and she swats her away, laughing.

Then her eyes tilt up toward mine, and she freezes. I can feel the smirk on my face. I can't hide my amusement from watching her get felt up in the middle of a club.

But before I can talk to her, she turns and bolts the

other way. Hmm, wasn't expecting that.

A slap on my back makes me flinch.

"Hey, man. Gonna head out with Tracy," Nick says, pointing toward a leggy brunette. "You gonna be okay?"

"Yeah. I'm sure everyone'll get here soon." I motion toward his chick. "Have fun."

The side of his mouth tilts up. "Don't wait up for me, Mom. You know I like my BU girls."

As long as he stays the fuck away from my sister, he can go to town. "No doubt. I'll see you tomorrow."

I head over to the bar that runs against the back of the cavernous room. I've already had several shots, and I don't want to push my luck tonight, so I grab a beer and lean back against a pillar while I scan the crowd and look for the girl with the tattoo.

After a few minutes, I spot her with her friends before she heads toward the platform that runs opposite the bar. Five cages hang down from the ceiling. The one in the middle is empty, and that pretty girl walks up the steps and saunters into the cage before she starts to sway and move.

God, she's stunning.

The cages are bathed in a bright light, and she's dressed in something that looks straight out of a burlesque with garters, a short gauzy skirt and a skin-tight shirt that puts all of her best assets on display. She's slender but stacked. I get hard just watching her. I guess that's the point.

She runs her hands through her thick hair that runs halfway down her back. She's like a pinup, posing and moving like an erotic fantasy. She has streaks of color in her hair, but I can't tell what it is from here. She finally opens her eyes, and behind the sultry makeup, I swear there's a flash of innocence on that gorgeous face.

Something about her seems so familiar, but I can't place her.

A couple of the girls up there look downright stupid, but she's a great dancer and owns it, grabbing hold of the bars and dancing to the beat. I feel a little like a stalker, standing here, watching her every move.

The music fades away into the solitary beat of a drum. That's when she looks up and sees me. At first, she glances away. Is she shy? But then, a minute later, she stares back and winks before she twirls away and shakes her hips. Okay, I think my mouth just watered.

When a tall guy walks into her cage and grips her to him, I worry for a second that they're together, but I think I just saw him grinding up against some other dude ten minutes ago.

But it's obvious they're close. They move together like they've been partners for a while because she doesn't seem to mind that his hands are all over her. Fuck, let him be gay.

A couple of my buddies arrive, and I talk to them for a while, but my eyes always gravitate toward her cage.

She finally takes a break and walks back onto the dance floor, and I'm closing the distance between us when two people step in front of her. Her expression looks like something between hurt and disgust.

Thinking fast, I move to her side and wrap my arm around her tiny waist. She jumps, but when she realizes it's me, her face lights up. "There you are," she says like she's known me her whole life.

And then she does the damnedest thing. She reaches up, running her hand along my jaw and into my hair, and draws my face to hers. When her lips reach mine, I think I've died and gone to heaven. They're soft, and when she pulls away a second later, I taste apple on my lips.

"Hey, babe," I say loud enough for her audience.

Her eyes twinkle back. She's clearly enjoying our little game. She licks her lips like she's trying to taste me too before she reaches around my waist and turns to the guy and his blonde.

My girl tilts her head and smirks. "Reid, I have nothing to say to you and Ashley. I don't have that necklace. I've told you this." She has to yell to be heard over the music.

"Danielle, you were in my room the last time I saw it," Ashley screeches.

Her name is Danielle.

"Just because you can't remember what you did with it doesn't mean you should blame me."

"You're just pissed he gave it to me instead of you." If the venom in Ashley's voice didn't tell me this girl is a bitch, the way she looks down at her fake nails and snorts does.

Danielle shrugs and leans into me, and I wrap my arm around her shoulder. Her little body fits perfectly against me.

"Ashley, I think you're forgetting that Reid and I had already broken up, but you're welcome to the sloppy seconds. Besides, between your small brain and his small dick, I'd say you're a match made in heaven."

I chuckle, and Danielle looks up and grins. Then I can't help it. I lean down and kiss her again.

CHAPTER SEVEN

- Dani -

Reid and Ashley disappear as I get lost in his kiss. We stand there while bodies crash around us to the music, and I'm caught against him like a wave breaking on the beach.

I don't know what possessed me to kiss this guy out of the blue and pretend we were somehow together. Right now, I'm blaming the three apple martinis. I just couldn't stand one more interaction with Reid where I stammered like some kind of loser.

Am I imagining it or did I just tell off my ex? It's hard to think clearly when I'm pressed up against this beautiful creature. I trail my hands up along his tall frame, dipping the tips of my fingers against the hard ridges and planes of his chest. He looks good in clothes, but the thought of what he looks like *without* anything on does delicious things to my body. I try to burn the sensation of what he feels like into my memory.

When we finally pull back for air, we stop to look at each other. And then we laugh.

"Holy shit." I put my hand to my mouth, for the first time embarrassed that I've been trying to swallow him whole for the last five minutes. "Hi."

He grins back. "Hi."

I don't hear him so much as read his lips, which I can appreciate now that my mouth isn't sealed against them. His head slants as though he's pondering some deep thought, like maybe how he spent the last few minutes locking tongues with a crazy girl who doesn't even know him.

And then my world slows down as I realize who he is.

Holy shit. It's the sexy guy from the pizza place.

Jax.

I was excited before I recognized him, but now my heartbeat outpaces the driving rhythm of the music.

If I'm honest with myself, I don't really know how to talk to guys this gorgeous. I'm not a big flirt, and I don't think I'm particularly eloquent.

What the hell would Margo say right now? Something funny. And she'd look sexy while being funny.

I cock my hip and tilt my head, so all my hair tumbles down my shoulder. This is me, trying to be sexy, hoping I don't look stupid.

I start to talk, but the music is too loud, so he lowers his head to mine, and I say, "How did you know I needed you to save me from my ex? Are you some kind of knight in shining armor who rescues girls from assholes like Reid?"

I'd never say anything quite that cheesy in the light of day, but I'm buzzed. I expect him to be all smiles and charm because he clearly has that in spades. Instead, his brow furrows.

"I should probably warn you." He brushes my cheek with his thumb. "I'm no knight. More like the big bad wolf." He looks away for a moment. "Maybe you should run while you can."

I watch him to see if he's serious, and my stomach plummets because he is.

Trying to regain some of my earlier bravado, I press my shoulders back. I use this opportunity to stare at him up close, allowing my eyes to travel up and down his body. When my eyes reach his, I go for broke.

"Maybe I'm looking for a wolf." I swallow down a crazy surge of insecurity that makes my insides do flip flops. "And maybe I can handle bad."

His eyes widen, and I wonder if that was the wrong thing to say when he utters, "Fuck." And then his mouth crushes against mine.

His tongue licks and strokes mine, and I'm on fire. My arms lock around his neck, and I kiss back like he's the last guy I'll ever touch. He's tall so when his hips press against my stomach, I get my first introduction to his degree of interest in me. Hell, yes!

When someone bumps into us, breaking our connection, I look around. The dance floor is packed. I have no idea where my friends are or if my roommates ever arrived. All I know is I have to be alone with Jax. Now.

I spot Travis's uncle close the door to the green room where the DJs usually hang out before their set, and once he's back behind the bar, I lace my fingers through Jax's.

"Follow me?"

He gives me a flirty grin. "Anywhere."

A smile erupts on my face. I turn, pulling him behind me as we weave through the crowd and down into the dark hallway.

Please let it be empty.

When I open the door, the only light shining comes from a couple of lava lamps in the corner. The room is small, sporting a retro 60s-looking leather couch, a coffee table, and a small row of lockers in the back where the bartenders keep their stuff.

I tug Jax in behind me, hoping he's as into this as I am. He kicks the door behind me and scoops me in his arms, making me laugh. Yeah, he's into it.

My legs instinctively wrap around his waist, my ankles cross behind him. "Lock the door," I instruct, eager to make sure this is private. He turns and reaches up to the door and latches the silver metal lock.

Jax's mouth is instantly on mine. We kiss, frantically trying to get closer, and when I suck on his tongue, he groans. Then air rushes around me, and we're falling onto the couch, laughing. Jax kisses along my neck, and I'm so glad he can't see my face because I'm grinning like a lunatic.

I honestly don't remember the last time I had this much fun. For the first time in so, so long, I feel alive, each cell in my body awake and electrified.

He pulls back onto his knees and stares down at me. I realize my skirt is hitched around my waist, revealing my garters and black boy shorts. Everything pauses as I think about what I'm about to do. I've never been in this moment before—about to have sex with a guy I don't know.

I want to pull back and withdraw as the fear grows, but then I remember Reid, who was supposed to be my safe and steady and everything I thought I needed. All that relationship did was make me doubt myself and leave me empty.

Jax interrupts my thoughts.

"Goddamn, you're beautiful." His smile is gone, and the look on his face makes my whole body thrum again with a desperate need for him to touch me. "I couldn't get my eyes off you tonight."

The music beats through the walls, and it feels like we're nestled in a cave, making his words sound like something out of a dream.

I want to tell him I'm thinking the same thing about him, that he looks like some kind of gorgeous mythological god, but that sounds ridiculous in my head. All I know is that I want his body on mine.

"You're too far away. Why do you have so many clothes on?" I tug on his shirt, and he rips it off and grins at me.

Holy shit balls. This guy is ripped. I knew he was muscular, but now I can see every inch of those washboard abs as they trail into his jeans. I stare, trying to soak in all of his deliciousness.

He chuckles. "Your turn, baby." He gives me a wolfish grin as he reaches down to lift off my shirt, revealing my hot pink lace demi-bra.

I lie back down, enjoying the fact that he's nestled between my thighs, and I reach down to the front of my bra. I take a deep breath for the courage to unclasp it. *No guy I've been with has seen me like this before.* I'm not sure how I stand it, but I watch his face as I pull the fabric away from me. It's freezing in here, and my skin pebbles even tighter against the rush of cold air.

The look on his face is priceless.

"Fuck." He closes his eyes briefly, and when he opens them, I see the lust behind his dilated pupils. "You're pierced?"

He doesn't need to ask the question because his hands are immediately on me as though he needs proof. My nipples are still a little sore, but having him touch me sends an instant jolt to my core.

"You're a devilish little angel," he whispers before he lowers himself onto me. "I think I might need to explore every inch of your body with my mouth."

Yes, do that! A lot of that!

I groan as his body fits tightly against mine, his hardness between my legs finally putting pressure where I need it most. Feeling his chest rub against me has my eyes practically rolling back in my head. *Oh dear God, the piercings rock.*

He starts to slide down me, sucking and kissing his way down my body. When he laves my nipple with his hot tongue, I moan, threading my fingers through his messy thick hair. He tugs the ring with his teeth, and I gasp at the sensation.

Jax mumbles against me, "Babe, you're so hot." He moves to my other breast while his fingers flick at the ring, and I think I could come right here, right now, without any other stimulation, which would be nothing short of miraculous.

His head starts to disappear between my thighs, but he pauses and looks up at me. The question hangs in the air between us, and I nod, giving him permission.

My undies slide down my thighs, his fingers scoring into my skin.

He groans, and I look down at him. The smile on his face is breathtaking.

"You're fucking perfection."

I laugh, realizing he's appreciating my Brazilian wax. "You like that, huh?"

"You have no idea." His head lowers, all the while our eyes are locked. I start to turn away, but his grasp on my thighs tightens. "No, babe, watch."

He smirks, and I wonder why he called me devilish because he's the one who wants to put on a show while he goes down on me.

I hold my breath as his tongue dips into me, my hands gripping the couch. His hot mouth on my most delicate, bare skin has me writhing on the edge. Watching his lips connect with my body makes me painfully aware of how wet I am, but he seems to be enjoying it.

Jax brushes his nose against that little bundle of

nerves, and I shiver, wondering how long I can hold on. He reaches between my legs and slides his finger into me, and I feel all my muscles constrict, the pressure at my core building. It takes a single flick of his tongue, and I come apart, light sparking behind my eyes as my back lifts off the couch.

I ride the high, tangling my fingers into his hair. My chest is heaving when he crawls back up.

I open my eyes, and he stares down, grinning.

"That was hot." I giggle, amused that I just admitted that out loud.

"That was." He licks his lips, and I blush knowing that he's tasting me. I try to push that thought out of my head and focus because I want him to fall apart now.

"Your turn." I start to get up, but he places his hand on my shoulder.

He shakes his head and closes his eyes for a moment. When he opens them, there's a seriousness that catches me off guard. "You… you don't have to do anything you don't want."

I laugh. "Who says I don't want to do this?" I grab the waistband of his jeans and pull him to me. I sit up so that my thighs are wrapped around his and we're nose to nose. "Why don't you tell me what you'd like?"

He gently brushes the hair out of my face, and it's a tender act that makes me melt. His arms wrap around my waist, pulling me tightly to him, and he exhales on my neck. "I want to bury myself in you." He says it like an apology, and I want to ask why he's hesitating, but I don't.

I bite his shoulder. "I'd love nothing more."

CHAPTER EIGHT

- Jax -

I don't know what the fuck is wrong with me, but I can't do this. I want to have sex with her. God, do I want to, but she's beautiful and luminous, and I think if I fuck her, I'll somehow tarnish her. Because that's all this'll be, sex in a dark club, and she's not the kind of girl I want to use and abuse for one night.

Shit. I sound like a chick.

I've never, *ever* turned down sex before, but I know how I treat women, and I don't want to do this to her. She doesn't even know my name.

"Babe, really, we don't have to do this," I say against her mouth, unable to peel my body off of hers.

I'm trying to think of a way to stop our momentum when the door rattles with a knock.

Danielle jerks back as someone yells, "Open up. I gotta get my shit."

Danielle leaps off me and races around the couch, grabbing her clothes. Her long hair is tangled around her, and the only thing I can do is sit here and watch. Her pale skin looks radiant against the black of her clothes.

"Hold on a sec," she yells as she flings my shirt at me. She sees my expression and stops. "You okay?"

I clear my throat and nod as I stand to tug on my clothes.

When she's dressed, she turns to see that my shirt is on, and she unlatches the door. The blonde on the other side looks pissed. I think she's one of the bartenders.

"Sorry," Danielle says, looking genuinely remorseful.

"It's about fucking time." The girl checks me out, her eyes traveling slowly up my body. She smiles seductively, apparently not caring that I'm here with someone else or that Danielle is watching her flirt with me. The woman unwraps her black apron from her waist as though she's doing a striptease, and I can see the tension in Danielle's body.

I walk up to my little angel, throw my arm around her shoulder and kiss her forehead.

"Yeah, sorry. My girl and I got carried away."

The blonde rolls her eyes. But the smile on Danielle's face damn near breaks open my chest.

It's crazy that I'm feeling like this because I don't know anything about her except that we have volcanic chemistry, but I'd like to know her, and for that I need more time.

Yeah, I definitely need her for more than one night.

* * *

My biggest problem at the moment is my raging hard-on. We walk slowly back through the dark hall, and I rack my brain to think of something to lose the boner before we make it to the bar.

Then it comes to me: Will Ferrell.

Better.

The moment we reach the dance floor, Danielle pulls away. "I need to run to the bathroom. Can we meet up at the bar in ten minutes?" She looks unsure, and there are a thousand things I want to tell her, but the music is deafening.

I nod. I know I should kiss her. Reassure her. She

must think I'm a dick. Most girls do after we hook up. Or they want more. I can never find the happy medium except for Natasha, but a steady diet of her is like eating Starbursts for every meal.

I'm about to ask Danielle for her number in case we get separated, but she turns and darts through the crowd.

When she gets back, we'll make plans for dinner tomorrow night. I want to know more about this girl.

I watch her disappear into the darkness. It doesn't escape me that I've been calling her baby all night. There's only one other girl I ever called that.

"Jax!" I turn to find Jenna, my sister's roommate. "Where the fuck have you been?"

She's drunk. She's hysterical when she's sober, but when she's drunk, my friends piss their pants. Her boyfriend Ryan sidles up to her and drapes his arm around her. If I was dating Jenna, I'd want the world to know it too. She's gorgeous. But don't let the blonde hair and hot bod fool you. She's smart as hell.

"Thanks for the party, man," I tell her boyfriend. Ryan had a shit ton of people over at his house to celebrate before we came to the club.

He grins. "My pleasure. Dude, you should come over next Sunday. We're watching the Notre Dame game, and the girls are making us lunch."

"Sounds great. I'm there."

Ryan is the lead singer of some indie band. I can never remember their name, but I heard them play once. They're really good. By the end of their show, girls were tossing their clothes on stage.

He and Jenna have been together a while. At least a couple of years. I never understood it before now, how he could have girls lining up for him after a gig, but he always went home with his girlfriend. He deserves some kind of medal for his commitment. But these days, I kind of get maybe wanting something more. No doubt it's a sign of the apocalypse.

My phone buzzes in my pocket, and I pull it out to see a text from Hannah.

"I need your help! Got locked out. Chloe's inside. Left something on the stove. Where are you? I'm freaking out."

Shit. Hannah is a great mom, but she can be a total space cadet. Chloe is probably asleep, but this isn't good.

Her texts keep coming.

"Can't get hold of building manager."

"What if food on stove burns?"

"Chloe's dad went out of town."

"What do I do?"

Goddamn it, Hannah. She and her husband argued all week, and he leaves just in time for this to happen.

"Dude, I gotta go," I tell Ryan. "See you next weekend." I do the dude slap on the shoulder and head toward the exit.

My phone lights up again. *"I can hear her crying. She's afraid of the dark."*

Ah, hell.

I text back. "I'm on my way. I'll be there in fifteen." Even though she's a good twenty-five minutes away.

Once I make it on the street, I'm about to hail a cab when a red Mustang pulls up. It's Natasha. I told her to join us if she was around.

"I need a ride home. It's an emergency." I hop in the car. I don't even have to explain. Her wheels screech, and she honks, making a dozen people jump out of her way.

And then I remember Danielle.

Fuck!

CHAPTER NINE

- Dani -

Half an hour ago I had the most intense sexual experience of my life with Jax, and now he's gone. I see some friends and a couple of my roommates at the bar but no Jax. I've been scanning the crowd like my life depends on it, and he's nowhere to be found.

I fight back tears.

This is stupid. I knew this was just sex. Shit, he didn't even ask my name. Why would I be dumb enough to think he'd somehow want more with a girl who gave it up without even a proper introduction? He probably thinks I'm a tramp who puts out every weekend.

Wait. He tried to stop me from going all the way. Maybe he wasn't into me after all. How embarrassing. God, I feel like a total loser.

I find Travis, who looks around me like I'm missing something. "Where'd he go?"

I shrug, biting the inside of my cheek to keep the tears back. Travis's head tilts down, and he scrutinizes my face. All of a sudden, he looks pissed.

"Did he hurt you?"

"No! Of course not. He was amazing. I came like a fucking category-five hurricane."

Travis laughs so loudly that people around us stop to stare. "Okay." He says it as though it has five syllables. "So why do you look like someone peed in your Wheaties?"

"Can we go? I'll explain if we can get out of here."

He makes a sad face, like he's humoring me, and I give him the finger, making him laugh. He throws his arm around my neck, gives me a noogie, and drags me out to the street. Because I look miserable, he decides the only proper way to dish is over pancakes, so we stop off at the I-Hop around the corner, and once we're safely in a booth, I spill my guts.

When I'm done, Travis raises his eyebrows. "Let me get this straight. He tried to talk you *out* of doing the deed?"

I feel mortified, but I answer the question. "Yeah."

"But then he acted like you were together when that girl came in?"

"I guess."

"And you had a screaming orgasm?"

My face burns ten shades of red. "Yes."

Travis grins widely and runs his hands through his hair. "Shit, girl. I think he likes you."

I snort in disbelief. "Did you miss the part where he didn't ask for my name or phone number and then ran like hell when we were done?"

Travis frowns. "That is a tad confusing."

"No shit."

He takes a sip of his water and then runs his finger over the condensation. "Okay, this may not be what you want to hear, but the whole point of the down-and-dirty one-night stand was to get your mind off of Reid. Did it work?"

That's an easy question to answer. "Reid who?"

He laughs and then takes another swig of his drink.

I shake my head. "The thing about Reid is he couldn't find my clit if it had a neon sign and balloons attached to it."

Water shoots from Travis' mouth, and I have to reach around and pat him on the back to keep him from choking.

By the time our food comes, Travis is no long in danger of aspirating. We eat our stacks of pancakes in comfortable silence. When we're done, he pays the check. It's pointless to try to give him money. He'll just stick it in my dresser or purse or closet when I'm not looking.

Travis nudges me with his elbow. "Wanna come back to my place?"

"Yeah, is that okay?" I feel weird about going back to my room after I told Jenna we'd hang out tonight. I didn't even try to find her. I know I'm being a sucky roommate.

"Course. I'll even let you spoon me, and you know I hate to be the little spoon."

I laugh. "Thanks. You're my teddy bear. What would I do without you?"

He pulls me into another head lock. "I know this was tough, sweets, but in a week, you'll be over it. Look on the bright side. You totally told off Reid and that bitch. You had this major breakthrough, a hot little hookup, and a fab meal with yours truly. In my book, this was a great night."

I smile up at him. "You're right."

CHAPTER TEN

- Dani -

In my head, it was so much more than oral sex.

Jax looms larger than life in my fantasies. I can see every erotic moment play out in the low light of the lava lamps, but in my mind, we do it on every surface in that room.

I've always liked sex okay even though no one ever really did it for me. Until last Saturday, my best orgasms came courtesy of my battery-operated buddy. It was like I was batting clean up for the home run. I'd just go home, break out my vibrator, and finish it off properly. And the guy was none the wiser.

But with Jax… I clench my thighs just thinking about him. I groan at how pathetic I'm being. Our hookup was so, so hot, but then he was gone. I'm still kicking myself for running off to the bathroom, but I can't justify why he disappeared the moment my back was turned.

As much as I want to pretend it didn't mean anything, that it was all for recreational purposes, my chest aches as I remember standing there like an ass, looking for him in the crowd.

It doesn't help that Reid never went down on me. He seemed offended if I ever suggested it, and he didn't seem to like blow jobs, which I never understood. I thought all guys liked that.

"Danielle. Are you listening?" My mother's small voice breaks through my thoughts.

"Sorry. I've got a lot on my mind," I mumble into the phone. Like how I can't stop thinking about the guy I hooked up with this weekend who took off like Vin Diesel in *The Fast & The Furious* before I could tell him my name.

#SoFuckingEmbarrassing

My mom tsks at me. "Honey, stop being afraid. Live a little."

How does she arrive here from my one comment? I told her I was worried about her, and this is where the conversation ends up. I call it the "Life Lessons 101" convo. The one where she tries to jam in every piece of wisdom she's ever learned in a ten-minute chat.

"Danielle, if I've learned anything, it's that you need to live without regret."

My stomach churns.

I thought that's what I was doing. I thought that's what Jax was all about. Taking a chance. Shedding that good-girl persona for one night. *Then why do I feel so miserable?*

"I should be closer to you," I say under my breath.

What if she gets sick again? What if she needs someone to take care of her? But she won't even entertain the idea of me transferring to a school near home.

She laughs in my ear. "I'm in remission. I'm great knowing that you're where you need to be, and now that you're taking some art classes, I think you're going to be happier. I never thought business was right for you. Stop trying to fit your square peg in a round hole, dear." She laughs again, making me wish I could see her, only her laptop camera stopped working last week so we can't Skype.

I don't have the heart to tell her that I couldn't work

the art class into my schedule.

She sighs, and I know there's more coming. "Honey, you should curse more. It feels fucking good every once in a while."

"Mom!" I know cancer changes you, but my mom dropping F-bombs is something I'll never get used to.

"What?" She feigns innocence. "Dance in the rain. Fool around with a good-looking boy who's not your type."

My face flushes again. Oh my God. *Been there. Done that.*

"Mom, stop. You're embarrassing me." Nothing freaks me out more than talking about guys, kissing, or sex with my mother. I used to think she was shy too, but since the cancer, she lets it all hang out.

"Don't feel ashamed. Embrace it. Stop feeling sorry for me. Figure out what you want, and go after it. That's what college is for. If you find you don't like your major, change it. But don't live quietly. No regrets, okay? Promise me."

I'm surprised when fat tears roll down my face. Knowing that my mother, the only person I have on the planet, almost died reaches into a part of me I didn't know existed. I never cried when she was sick. I thought she needed me to be strong. I held it in until we got word she was in remission, and then I bawled until my eyes nearly swelled shut. I was never a big crier before that, but I've had a hard time shutting down those floodgates since then.

I sniffle. "No regrets. I promise." I pull the phone away from my face to take a deep breath. "Mom?"

"Yeah, baby?"

"I love you, and I'm really proud of you. You're the best parent I could have had."

Fortunately, she skips the joke about how she's my only parent. Which isn't true, of course. I have a father somewhere. Or at least he's the one who deposited sperm, played house until I was ten and then took off because he "couldn't handle the stress." Whatever that means.

"Sweetheart, you've made it easy. I love you."

* * *

Despite the pep talk from my mom, the week starts out painful, every class a drag, every shift at work irritating.

By Wednesday, though, I no longer want to dropkick Laura. She seems to be picking up her end of this partnership and is actually helping around the art lab. She's a techie and can solve any student's software issues in the time it takes me to identify the problem.

Since we coordinate everyone else's schedules, we get the choice spots, so I take a few midday slots each week. I use my time to finish some new designs for Professor Zinzer, who stops by on his way out each day.

Zin is cute. He's older, maybe in his late sixties, and wears a different-colored bow tie every day of the week.

"Ms. Hart, now don't be offended by this, but are you sure you're a business student?"

His question surprises me. I brace myself for what I'm sure will be some kind of insult because I know my grades haven't always been great. My business professors are so nitpicky and annoying. They'll love my presentations but dock me a full letter grade on projects because of my clothes or the streaks in my hair. They want me to wear conservative clothes and tie my hair up in a bun. #HellNo At least I look pretty normal when I'm hanging in the art department.

"I'm sorry, sir, what?"

"Your work for me is spectacular. I'm wondering if you're not a pro masquerading as a student."

Exhaling in relief, I smile. "You're too kind, but I can assure you that I'm very much a student."

Zin drags a nearby chair to my desk and sits. He glances around the bustling lab and then lowers his voice. "I don't say this often because the kids around here are usually full of their own virtue, but I wanted to let you know that you have a lot of natural artistic talent. Your drawings are spectacular and your graphic design top-notch." He scratches his chin. "You know, if you ever want to audit some courses in my little nook of the universe, I could make that happen."

I knew he was happy with my brochures, but I'm a little floored by his compliment. I rewrote his marketing materials, drew some original artwork, scanned them in, tweaked the colors in Photoshop, and had everything printed out for his approval before he asked. But I figured that's what the job called for.

"Thank you, Professor. I'd really like that." Actually, I'd love it.

After only two weeks of business classes, none of which have been particularly inspiring, I'd be crazy to pass up his offer even if it means my schedule will be jam-packed. *Then I wouldn't have to lie to my mom.*

He reaches for a laptop and pulls up a screen of class listings.

"Some of these are full, but take a look and see what catches your eye. See me tomorrow with your top three choices, and we'll go from there and figure out what we can work into your schedule."

My day gets better when I bump into Jenna on the way home. We grab some mochas, and she surprises me when she loops her arm through mine as we walk down the street like we're the oldest of friends.

"Okay, girl. I know we haven't had a chance to hang out, and I want the scoop. Dish."

"That's a little broad, Jenna." I laugh. "What do you want to know?"

"Any hot men in your life? I love Ryan, but sometimes I need to live vicariously through my friends. Plus, I'm taking this romance writing class this semester, and I'm out of ideas."

"I don't think I have anything juicy enough for your class."

"Weren't you dating that guy last semester?"

"Pshaw. That's over. Way, way over."

She frowns. "Bummer."

"Not so much. He's an ass." We walk in silence, and I bump her with my hip. "I can't believe I'm telling you this, but I did kinda hook up with someone last weekend."

Her eyes widen like she's won the lottery. "Shut up! When?"

"At the club. When I was blowing you off, I was busy with this beautiful guy in the green room."

She squeals like a teenager, and a few people on the corner turn to watch us.

"He made my toes curl. He was so gorgeous. Tall, totally ripped, messy brownish-blond hair. The best kisser."

"Yum!" She shivers dramatically, and I laugh again. "Are you going to see him again?"

I shake my head. "No. It's not like that." Although I wish it were.

She frowns again but then sighs. "At least you have some good spank bank material, though."

I don't bother fighting the smile that peeks out on my face. "Definitely."

"Speaking of tickling the taco, my sister threw a sex toy party, and she said it was a blast." A snort of laughter bursts out of me. *Tickling the taco?* Jenna smiles conspiratorially. "I'm thinking of throwing one later this semester. This company demos all their stuff while we get trashed. Sound like fun?"

Still chuckling, I nod. "Count me in."

"Good. Now maybe you can help me talk Clem into it. She's too hermetically sealed. I want to help her loosen up."

I tense. I've said hi to Clem all week, and she barely mumbles any kind of greeting in return. I even asked if she wanted to watch *Glee*, and she rolled her eyes at me. Again.

"What?" Jenna asks.

Maybe I shouldn't say anything, but I can't seem to help my diarrhea of the mouth. "I know you and Clem are really tight, but… I don't think she likes me."

She pulls me to a stop. "I know Clementine seems like a total bitch on a good day, but give her time to get to know you. There's no one more loyal. She's just been through a lot of shit, so she doesn't trust people, and she's kind of in her own world, but once you get to know her, you'll love her. I promise."

I nod hesitantly.

"Okay."

Jenna laughs. "She's going to kill me for saying this, but you should ask to read her book. She's this amazing writer, and no one knows 'cause she writes under a pen name. She's super private. But if she lets you read it, you'll get a whole new insight into her. The book is really about what happened to her in high school with her ex and her asshole parents. Clem's life is a soap opera, but you'd never know it."

Now I'm intrigued.

Jenna turns me to her, a serious expression on her face. "I'm only telling you this because I trust you. Being friends with Clem is hardcore. You can't screw her over."

My spine straightens. I'm not sure if I should be afraid or offended.

Her eyes soften. "Sorry, I don't mean to freak you out. I love her like a sister, and if you knew the shit she's gone through, you'd be protective of her too. And I want the two of you to be close, which is why I'm putting this out there."

I get it. Jenna is Clem's Travis. He'd walk through fire for me. "It's cool. I understand."

* * *

On Sunday, I finally get a chance to hang out with Clem. She's gorgeous with long blondish-brown hair and big blue eyes. I know she works out like a maniac because every time I see her, she's headed out for a run. She looks amazing even in sweats, which is what we're all wearing.

I drank a little too much with Travis last night, so I'm fighting a hangover, and I'm sure I look like hell. My hair is pulled up into a ponytail, and I didn't bother with any makeup. Whatever. We're just doing laundry at Ryan's and making lunch.

I'm stuffed in the back seat of a Honda Civic, squished next to Clem, bags of dirty laundry at our feet, when her book comes up.

"I don't know what I'm going to do," she says, complaining about her book cover. "I don't really want to deal with hiring a designer."

"You don't need a designer. I can do a cover for you." I reach into my purse, hoping I can find some gum so I don't kill her with my hangover breath.

Her face lights up like I just told her Henry Cavill wants her to have his baby. "That would be huge! I will totally pay you."

I shake my head. "No way. You're my roommate. It's, like, against the code or something."

She pauses to look at Jenna and then turns back to me. "Okay, if you're not going to take my money, let me buy you some art supplies because I know that shit is expensive."

With that new art class I'm auditing, I could use some supplies. I offer her a stick of gum. "Deal, but I want to read your book. Jenna says you're a great writer."

She kicks Jenna's seat and then pauses. Silence fills the car. I'm about to say it's not a big deal and to forget it when she says, "All right, but you're sworn to secrecy. I write under a pen name, and I don't want that getting out. And when I say secrecy, we're talking blood oath or I get your first child."

I laugh, but I know she's being serious.

Once we start talking about designs and concepts, she lets her guard down, and the conversation flows easily. When Clem isn't scowling, she's downright captivating with a natural kind of charisma. It makes me wonder what happened to her that has her so closed off, which makes me more eager to read her book.

When we reach Ryan's house, we lug the laundry up the stairs. I trail behind, too tired to keep up. Inside, I hear Ryan call my roommate Clemster. I'm surprised she doesn't punch him, but Ryan seems to be able to say things no one else can.

I drop the laundry in the hall and duck into the

kitchen to put a few groceries in the refrigerator. Jenna pops in behind me.

"I should warn you," she whispers. "Have you met Clem's twin?"

I turn to look at her. "No."

"He's here, and he's totally beautiful but kind of a man-whore. Don't let him charm you. Clem kinda hates when he tries to hookup with her friends." Her Southern accent is soft with a musical quality to it, but I know she means business.

"Good to know. Thanks for the warning."

This is what I need. Girl bonding. I haven't thought about what happened last weekend all morning. Thank God. Maybe I'm over it. Over him. Who needs hot hookups in a club when you have good girlfriends?

Jenna winks and hands me a beer.

I wander into the living room, which is full of guys. The Notre Dame theme music is blaring from the flatscreen that's mounted on the wall, and I turn to try to figure out the score.

"Cool. Who are the Irish playing?" I ask no one in particular. Ryan comes up and hugs me.

"Hey, gorgeous."

"Hi, Ryan." I grin. Jenna's boyfriend is awesome. I met him for twenty minutes last week, and he immediately treated me like one of their inner circle.

"They're playing Stanford. I didn't know you were a football fan."

"Yeah, I love football and basketball, but really, I like anything that includes mascots, beer and brats."

"I knew I liked you. Hey, I don't think you've met my band." He turns me to face everyone and starts to introduce me to his friends.

But I don't hear anything he says because sitting there,

at the end of the couch, is a familiar face. A very familiar face.

My breathing stops, and sweat breaks out on my forehead.

Finally, Ryan's words break through my fog. "And this asshole here is Jax, Clem's twin. You'll want to stay away from him," Ryan jokes. "He's a slut."

Yeah. I caught that already.

Shit.

CHAPTER ELEVEN

- Dani -

What's worse than learning you almost slept with your new roommate's brother? Um, that would be him not remembering you.

I wait for the recognition, the look in his eyes that says, yes, I went down on you and lapped you up like a Slurpee, but it never comes. In fact, he barely glances in my direction. Finally, he yells, "Down in front, girls."

Oh my God.

Was he that drunk last Saturday night? I swear he seemed fine. I was more buzzed than he was. So not only did he stop us from doing it—which is totally offensive now that I know he sleeps with a lot of girls—but then he ditched me. And now doesn't remember me.

#Asshole

I would scream right now if I weren't in a room full of people.

Instead, I chug my beer, ignore the game, and try to busy myself in the kitchen with Jenna and Clem as they make lunch. But I can't look at my roommate. If Clem finds out I screwed around with Jax, she'll hate me. Isn't that why I hated Ashley? Because she violated the roommate code. I've always honored those unspoken rules. Until now.

Damn it. Jenna *just* told me to stay away from Clem's brother.

I fight back tears and excuse myself to run to the

bathroom where I pull out my phone. There's a message from Travis.

"Guess who I saw at the art lab? You're going to die! And he asked about you…"

I ignore his question and start a mad flurry of texts. Two minutes later, my phone lights up.

"Oh! My! God! What are you going to do? Did you know he was Clem's brother?"

I write back. *"Of course I didn't fucking know!"*

Eventually I realize I can't hide next to the toilet forever, and I open the door and peek down the hall. Everyone seems to be crowding in the living room. I step out slowly, wondering if I should bolt for the front door and never look back.

Someone's arguing. I hear Clem's voice. After a minute, I duck into the kitchen right as Clem races down the hallway to the back stairs. Jenna joins me, shaking her head.

She leans into me and lowers her voice. "One of the guys said shit to Clem about her ex-boyfriend Daren who plays football for BC and was just on TV, talking about his fiancée. If you read her book, you'll learn the whole story." She motions toward the now empty hallway. "Clem's dying that a room full of people heard the whole thing."

That sucks.

"Do you need to go talk to her?" I ask.

"No, she'll want to hide in a cave for a little while." Good to know I'm not the only one who runs for cover. "I'll give her half an hour, but once lunch is ready, I'm going to haul her ass back up here. My guess is she's doing laundry right now. Or killing someone's pet."

Jenna laughs. I think she's joking. I hope.

- Jax -

How do I know this girl?

My sister's roommate stares at me like we've met, like we're friends. Hell, like we're more than friends. But all I draw is a blank.

Her expression is a cross between excitement, fear and horror. Yes, that's what I do to women.

In sweats and a black t-shirt that hugs her small frame, she looks like she's sixteen, especially since she's not wearing makeup. But she's beautiful. Delicate.

I start to worry that I slept with her in some drunken state, but nothing about Dani makes me think that's possible. First of all, her tits aren't hanging out like Christmas ornaments. Strike one. Secondly, she lives with Clem. Strike two. Thirdly, she looks too innocent to be interested in me. Strike three.

Nothing in that equation puts her even remotely in the fuckable category.

So then why do I have an immediate boner? And why does she keep looking at me like that?

Fuck. I rub my temple, the pounding nearly unbearable.

Concussions suck. The doctor said the headaches should go away within a week, but a week has gone by, and I'm still miserable.

I had to fucking scale Hannah's balcony to get into her apartment. Or at least that's what I'm told since I don't remember any of it.

I leapt over the railing, something I've done all the other times she got locked out. Except this time I slipped, slammed my head on her grill and blacked out. Good thing the building manager arrived to unlock the door.

Chloe saw the whole thing through the sliding glass door, me wiping out. It scared the shit out of her. I woke up to her screams.

As it turns out, the soup Hannah left on the stove had burned to a crisp, so even though my coach thinks I got a concussion because I was out partying on my birthday, I know the truth.

And I'd do it again. Chloe reminds me of Clementine. It's the way she looks at me like I can fix anything. It's been years since my sister looked at me like that, and it sucks that we've grown apart. It's my fault. I can't do anything about it now, but when I look at little Chloe, it makes me want to protect her.

Of course, no good deed goes unpunished. I'm on probation because I had to miss several practices. Coach says one more screwup and I'm off the team. Happy fucking birthday to me.

CHAPTER TWELVE

- Dani -

I spend the rest of the day avoiding Jax like he has the Ebola virus. After lunch, someone knocks on the front door, and an Amazonian-looking supermodel saunters in. She doesn't bother telling anyone hi. Instead, she heads straight to Jax and drops into his lap, making a point to tongue him up in front of a room full of people.

The guys love the show, and they hoot and holler like she's doling out free lap dances. Clem, who seems to have recovered from her earlier embarrassment, rolls her eyes and makes a gagging sound. I'm starting to like her more and more.

And, yeah, I'm painfully and ridiculously jealous.

On the way home, I close my eyes and let my head fall back against the seat. The purr of the car is strangely soothing. I can't wait to get home so I can die an appropriate death alone. All I can think of is how he kissed that girl back and how his lips must have felt.

"Can you believe my brother?" Clem asks, breaking into my misery.

I stiffen immediately. I don't think I'm in a position to say anything so I keep my mouth shut.

She continues without any encouragement. "Why can't he grow up and stop being such a slut? That girl was skeevy."

"I think I've seen her in a Calvin Klein ad," Jenna says.

Ugh. That's where I recognize her from.

If I ever thought there was a chance in hell he'd be interested in me, today shot down that delusion. Of course he loves bombshells. What guy doesn't? I'm Midwest and corn-fed. She's runway and underfed. She probably survives on two carrots and a twig a day.

Tears brim my eyes, and I blink them away quickly. I don't know why I want to cry. I set out for a one-night hookup and that's what I got. The problem is I know this guy, and I'll probably have to see him around.

At least he goes to Boston College. That's far enough away. It's better than seeing him around campus. That's another freakish twist of luck. On the night of his birthday, he was hanging out in BU territory. Under normal circumstances, our paths would probably never cross.

Except I did see him at that pizza place first.

I talk myself in a dizzying circle, trying to make sense of the whole situation.

Eventually, I come to a conclusion. I'll avoid him. Plain and simple. How hard could that be?

* * *

The next afternoon, Travis is waiting for me at work with a mocha and a bear hug. I throw my backpack behind the desk and collapse into a chair.

"Thanks for the drink."

I take a sip and let the caffeine settle into my body. I'm exhausted. Although I went to bed early last night, I tossed around for hours before I finally fell asleep.

Travis nudges me and motions toward the computer screen in front of him. I roll my chair closer to his cubicle.

"I think you need to see who you let lick your lady garden."

I close my eyes, hoping no one heard us, but some guy next to us chuckles. I smack Travis in the arm, and he laughs.

Finally, I focus on the website he's pulled up. Staring back at me is the object of my contempt and affection.

Jax Avery.

"What is this?" I'm glad I'm sitting down.

"Gossip website." Travis pokes my knee. "Did you have any idea he's, like, a bazillionaire?"

I shake my head, still trying to process the image in front of me. In the photo, Jax is walking up to a red sports car. The marquee for Cages is in the background. "It was taken last Saturday."

The caption reads, "Playboy and heir to the Avery fortune parties it up at Cages before some fun on the town with Calvin Klein model Natasha Kozlov."

"Oh," Travis says as he scrolls through his phone. "It's all over Twitter too." He shows me the screen.

Dear God. The man went down on me and then ran off to hook up with a supermodel. No wonder he didn't want to sleep with me! Why have a hamburger when you can down steak and lobster with a side order of shrimp?

I burrow my head into Travis's chest, and his arm wraps around me.

"This is so fucking humiliating," I mumble against him.

Travis strokes my hair. "No one knows. It's fine. Next time you see him, keep pretending you don't care because as far as he knows, you don't."

I nod because I can't bring myself to talk. After a while, Travis releases me from his embrace, and I look around to make sure no one is paying attention.

Fortunately, everyone is working at their cubicles.

Travis bumps me with his elbow. "I have one word to get you over this Jax bullshit: Brady Shepherd."

"Those are two words. And who the hell is Brady Shepherd?"

He gives me a look. "Uh, hello, hot tattoo guy, the one who got you half naked to pierce your nips."

"Shhh! I can't take you anywhere."

Apparently, I shush too loudly and a few people shoot me dirty looks.

Travis chuckles. "I saw him here yesterday evening. He totally asked about you, and I might have mentioned you work here."

"Okay." I'm confused why that guy would care where I work.

"My point being that Brady is every bit as hot as Jax. And you might see him here." Travis pauses. "Or he might call you." His mouth tilts up into a wide grin.

"Travis, how would he have my number to call me?" Not that I'd necessarily mind because, yeah, Brady is hot, but I hate being set up, and my head feels too jumbled to go out on any dates.

"A little birdie might have given him your number."

I roll my eyes. "Fine. Whatever. I just want to say that it was this very thing—trying to get over Reid—that got me in this predicament with Jax." I log on to my laptop. "Maybe I should lay off any overt attempt to fix my life and just be."

"Or instead of laying *off*, you get laid *on*." He laughs at his own joke.

"You're such a gossip whore. You want juicy details so you can get your jollies off some hot boys."

He feigns offense and then laughs. "As long as someone gets a hot boy."

Although I smile at Travis for trying to make me feel better, I'm thinking I'm done with guys for a while, and I'm definitely done with Jax. I can't think of one thing that would persuade me otherwise.

CHAPTER THIRTEEN

- Jax -

My sister clearly isn't expecting me, and she looks like I grew horns and a tail for trying to save her high school crap from the dumpster. The last time we spoke, she told me to toss it, but deep down I thought she'd want it someday, so I packed up her yearbooks and photos, which means we'll have to talk about Daren, a conversation we've been avoiding for too long.

Clementine hasn't spoken to our mother since her freshman year, so our mother is converting her room into a storage area. I'm not sure what initially pissed her off, but Clem refuses to call her. As much as I hate to admit it, my sister and I are a lot alike. If we're worked up, it can take a while to talk us off the ledge.

Clem paces in her small bedroom, eyeing me like I'm the enemy.

So maybe that wasn't the smartest thing to say, asking if she was still in love with Daren to explain why she never dates and hardly has any friends, but I'm tired of her deflecting me. It's probably unfair to say this now since I think she's seeing that guy Gavin, who's sitting in the living room, but he's the first person she's dated in three years.

The moment the words are out of my mouth, she looks like she wants to rip my heart out of my chest.

"What do you even know about me, Jackson? I *lost* my track scholarship, so I've had to work my ass off for the past two years to pay for my tuition. My professor attacked me when I was a freshman. I'd say I'm doing pretty damn well considering."

The air thickens in the room, pressing against me as though gravity has intensified somehow. My head tilts. My eyes close.

Someone hurt my sister?

I swallow. And then swallow again.

"What do you mean your professor attacked you?" My jaw tightens so hard it hurts. At the beginning of her senior year in college she decides to tell me someone did this to her as a freshman. I stand in the doorway of Clem's bedroom at a loss for words. "Fucking hell, Clementine. Who is this asshole?"

She shakes her head. "Forget about it. There's nothing you can do. I'm fine. *Now.*"

I don't miss the jab.

"Why didn't you tell me?" Growing up, Clem and I were inseparable. Even if our parents were the most self-absorbed jerkoffs in the world, my twin and I were close. Until she broke up with Daren. My relationship with my sister has never been the same.

The hurt in Clem's eyes is unnerving. I'm so used to my sister being made of steel.

"You didn't back me up with Daren." Having her say that out loud is more painful than I thought it would be, but she doesn't know the whole story. "Why would you care about this? Besides, Mom and Dad didn't seem to care." She stares at me like she might bore a hole through my body. "You know, they don't pay for my shit like they pay for yours."

Did she call them and they didn't do anything?

A familiar bitterness clenches my stomach. Of course our mother didn't do jack shit. Because it didn't affect her. Why would she bother? Our father, though… Just because he spends most of his time in Europe on business doesn't mean he wouldn't care. That he wouldn't want to protect my sister.

But at the end of the day, Clementine felt alone.

Fury sweeps through me. Had I known, I would have done something. I don't know what, beat the shit out of her professor, cut off his balls—something. And what the fuck does she mean our parents don't pay for her stuff? They're multi-millionaires. They could wipe their asses with hundred-dollar bills if they wanted.

"Jax, if you think what happened with Daren is what broke me, you don't know me at all."

I rub just above my hairline where I can feel the tiny bumps the stiches left. I still can't remember what happened on my birthday aside from jumping in Natasha's car and staring up at Hannah's balcony. But if I could choose one night to forget, I'm thinking this one would be it. I'm never up for full-out confrontations with my sister.

We go in circles rehashing the past, each minute more painful than the last. *Yes, I knew Daren was cheating on you with your best friend. No, I didn't tell you. Yes, I hoped you'd both get past it. Why? You and Daren are the only family I've ever really had.*

Her body shakes with rage. "Did you ever wonder how I lost my state meet after I won all the others my senior year? How I barely eked out a fifth-place finish when my practice times could've beaten all those girls that day?"

I should know this, but I don't. I was too busy dealing with my girlfriend. Yes, I had a girlfriend at the time. It only took one to show me why I never wanted another.

Clem blinks quickly. "Mom found out I had broken

up with Daren that morning. I was walking out the door, and she told me it was my fault Daren cheated on me because I should have slept with him months ago. She asked, 'Why do you think I put you on the pill?' Then she said she was late for a meeting and left."

What. The. Fuck.

I can barely keep up as Clem drops one grenade after the next. Finally, she grabs her running shoes and starts lacing them up. What the hell do I say? My throat is tight, and even though I'm breathing, my lungs don't seem to fill.

"Clementine, I'm so sorry. For everything, I—"

She ignores me and storms out. I vaguely hear her talking to her roommates and then the front door slams.

I don't know how long I stand there pressing my palm to my throbbing temple.

God, I'm such a fuckup.

I'd like to say I brought the box tonight because I'm trying to be a good brother, trying to right a few wrongs, and yes, I do want to be close to Clem. That conversation was long overdue. But the real reason behind this visit is staring at me on my way out of my sister's bedroom.

Truth? I wanted an excuse to see Dani.

Her eyes drop to the floor as soon as she sees me. I met this girl for sixty seconds two weeks ago, and she's all I can think about. Fuck, I've had dreams about her. I never obsess over girls, so I don't know why I can't get her off my mind.

I'm not sure why she avoided me at Ryan's, but I'm pissed now thinking about everything she overheard. If she disliked me before, she must think I'm a real douche now.

All I know is that when Natasha kissed me in front of Dani, I swear Dani looked at me like I was cheating on her. Here's the crazy thing—I'd be lying if I said it didn't feel like that for me too.

I rub my forehead, deciding that Clem probably doesn't want me here when she returns. I look at Dani and point at the box on the coffee table. "Don't let her throw that away. She wants that shit. She just doesn't know it yet."

And before she says anything—because God, I don't want to hear what she has to say—I walk out.

CHAPTER FOURTEEN

- Dani -

Brady Shepherd is twenty-five, and he's getting his master's in painting, not what I expect from someone who looks like he was born on a Harley.

He sits across from me in the cozy coffee shop, ignoring the food in front of him. "So business, huh?" He finally gets to the question that perplexes anyone who knows me.

I nod. "Marketing."

"Hmm." Brady's eyes travel over my messy ponytail and paint-splattered t-shirt. "I guess I figured with those hot pink streaks in your hair you had to be an art major. And didn't you draw your tat?"

"Yeah."

Under his snug black t-shirt, dark tattoos snake down both muscular arms. He's the opposite of Jax. Black hair and pale skin emphasize his intense green eyes and square jaw. His broad chest tapers into jeans, which lead down to scuffed-up combat boots.

Jax has a preppier vibe with that messy blondish hair and tan that highlights his sky-blue eyes. While he's muscular and cut, he's leaner than Brady. It's probably all that soccer. His sister says he's going to go pro and that scouts come to each of his games.

All evening I do this, draw distinctions between these two guys, which is completely counterproductive to my plan to move on. It's ridiculous to still feel so hung up on this ghost of a relationship I wasn't even in.

I've relived that reunion at Ryan's in agonizing detail—the blank look in Jax's eyes as I stood there like a dumbass, his frown when I apparently blocked the touchdown on the flatscreen behind me, the horrid realization that the gorgeous model meant something to him as she snaked her tongue into his mouth. And let's not forget all the photos of him online with freaking gorgeous women.

Yes, I went home and spent an inordinate amount of time stalking him after Travis showed me that website. But seeing it with my own eyes is what I needed, and I swore off feeling anything for him, preoccupying myself with school and work.

But overhearing him and his sister argue last week has me conflicted, especially since Clem gave me a copy of her book. Now that I know her, I see how the whole story is autobiographical, just with different names.

All the gory details are in there. How she and her brother grew up with Daren, how he was her first love, how her best friend who claimed to hate Daren slept with him, and how all their friends knew and lied about it.

And I really can't get over how Jax and Clem's parents don't seem to give a shit about either of them. They're both so talented. My mother would be through the roof if I could write like Clem, and Jax is this totally amazing athlete. I guess it goes to show that money can't buy you love.

No wonder Jenna is protective of Clem. Reading that book makes me want to throw my arms around Clem in a giant hug. Not that she'd let me. She's been betrayed by so many people, and it turns my stomach that I betrayed her too.

Of course, I didn't mean to lie about hooking up with

her brother, but I'm mortified about the whole thing. How do I tell her? Clem looks at the girls he dates like they have the plague, and she and I are just starting to become friends. If I tell her, she'll hate me for lying. Shit. I wouldn't blame her.

I wish knowing how Jax lied to protect Daren made me hate him, but it doesn't. Instead, I see the kid who was neglected by his filthy rich parents. In her book, Clem doesn't make her brother out to be the bad guy. She thinks he's selfish and self-absorbed, but she loves him because he's her only family.

Even though Clem acts tough, it's starting to make sense why, and seeing how much Jax loves his sister makes it harder to tune him out of my head. I hate knowing so much about him, like how he and his sister spent their Christmases alone in their big house, opening gifts the housekeeper got them, or that no one ever threw them birthday parties because their parents were too busy.

But just because Jax has been through a lot of shit doesn't change my mind. I need to stay away from him. I obviously care too much, and I don't want to set myself up for heartbreak, and that boy has disaster written all over him like the *S.S. Titanic*.

Struggling to focus on the guy in front of me, I force myself to smile. Brady must think I'm a total dullard, sitting here like a piece of lint.

I don't know what I expect from hanging out with Brady. Butterflies? Nerves? Hell, I'd settle for lust. But sitting across from him at the coffee shop isn't making my heart race the way being near Jax does, which sucks because Brady seems like a great guy, and he's definitely easy on the eyes. I'd have to be blind to miss the stares he gets from every girl who walks by.

"So why not art school?" he asks, breaking into my thoughts.

I tear at an empty sugar packet, ignoring his question. "Can I ask you something?" I look up and squirm a little under his intense stare. "What am I supposed to do with an art degree? You're all set because you do tattoos, but everyone—my mom especially—thinks that I should major in art, but I haven't figured out how that pays the bills."

"So you're doing something safe?"

I don't like how he says that, like he's challenging me to take chances. That's easy for him to say when it's not his future.

He must sense the tension in my body, and he reaches over and places his hand on mine. "Hey, I don't mean any offense by that. I get it. I just regret taking that same route when I was in my undergrad program, that's all."

I pull back my hand, uncomfortable that he's touching me. "Why? What was your major?"

"Pre-law."

Brady smiles warily, like the memory of his undergrad experience cost him more than money, and in that moment, I see myself, the fatigue of trying to become someone who isn't quite me.

"It's exhausting, isn't it?" I ask. "No matter how hard I work or how hard I try, it's never enough. I swear my profs at the business school have made a pact to make me miserable. And yet, when I'm in the art department, things work, people like my stuff, and the world makes sense."

"So switch majors."

I blow out a big breath. "It's not that easy. As much as I'm loving the graphic design class my boss helped me take, I'd have to flip my schedule upside down for the next year and a half to come close to getting enough credits. And take summer school."

"And that's a problem?"

"Yeah. I need to get home." My eyes drop to my coffee mug. "My mom's been sick. I'd like to spend more time with her. She's in remission right now, but I can't shake the feeling we don't have a lot of time left together."

My eyes well up with tears, and I blink furiously.

"Hey, I'm sorry." He scoots out of his side of the booth and sits next to me, dropping his big arm across my shoulders and hugging me to him. "I didn't mean to bring this up." He rubs my back, and I'm surprised how good it feels to let him comfort me.

I shake my head, using my palm to wipe away an errant tear. "No, it's not your fault. I'm not used to talking about it."

"Then let's not talk about it." He squeezes me one more time, slides out of his chair and holds out his hand. "Come on. Let's go for a walk."

The evening air is crisp, and we stroll through Harvard Square, stopping to check out street musicians and vendors. We talk about classes and profs we've had in common. I keep hoping to feel a spark, some chemistry, but it never comes. I start to tell myself that sexual attraction isn't the only thing that matters, but the words I utter next stop me cold.

"This is nice."

He must sense it in my voice. Disappointment flickers behind his eyes as he realizes what I'm saying, what I didn't actually intend to voice out loud. I wonder if he hates that word as much as I do.

He gives me long look as he weighs my words. Then he surprises me and laughs. "I'm going to pretend that you're not trying to give me the kiss of death here."

I start to protest because that seems like the polite thing to do, but he holds up his hand. "I'd be lying if I said I don't want to see you again because you're a cool girl." He bites his lip for a moment. "Your friend Travis mentioned you were getting over some guy, so I just want to declare my intentions to be your friend. And if we evolve into more down the road, great. If not, I can live with it."

I'm not used to guys being so direct. Maybe it's because he's older. I like his confidence, his willingness to go out on a limb. But that doesn't obscure my first order of business, which is to kill Travis.

"Thanks for being so understanding. I've had a bad streak of luck with relationships this year, and I'm feeling a little burned. Trust me when I say this has everything to do with me and not you. Honestly, if you had asked me out this summer when I got my ink, I'd have been all over you."

He smirks, and I laugh at how forward I sound. A second later he groans and runs his hands through his dark hair. "I'm kicking myself for not asking you out when we met. I thought about it."

I would have said yes, and I wonder if dating him before I met Jax would have made a difference.

By the end of our date, I have to admit Brady is great. Maybe we could be more than friends down the road. We decide to hang out next week and maybe grab a movie, and I'm beginning to feel a little more optimistic about life when he drops me off at my brownstone.

When I get home, Clem accosts me at the door. "What are you doing tomorrow morning?"

I take off my jacket and drop my bag by the couch. I shrug. "Some homework. Nothing major. Why?"

"Would you mind doing me a huge favor?" She almost looks embarrassed, and I wonder if she needs more help with her book. I hooked her up with a friend who did her website, and I created some book covers, but I think she's pretty married to her old one. But I like Clem, and I want us to be friends, especially now that I know all the shit she's been through.

"Sure. Whatever you need."

"Would you mind coming with Jenna and me to BC to see my brother's game?"

My heart sinks, and the polite smile I had on my face a minute ago freezes. She sees my expression and nods.

"I know it sounds lame, but Jax is a great player, and I'll totally spring for lunch. I used to go to all of his games, but I haven't been to any this fall, and I've kind of blown him off since we had that argument last week."

She looks away as her mouth twists into a frown, and I feel bad that I'm not being supportive. I guess I can do this for Clem.

I try to smile again. "Sounds like fun. Count me in."

CHAPTER FIFTEEN

- Jax -

When I see my sister in the stands, I jog over, but I almost stumble when I realize who she brought. Dani is wearing the letter X across her snug-fitting shirt.

I turn back to my sister. "Shit. You went all out. You haven't done the t-shirts since high school."

After our "heart-to-heart" last week, I was sure Clem wanted to murder me in my sleep, so I was more than surprised when she called a few days ago and asked for tickets to my game. She told me she wanted to move forward, that she wanted me in her life. I can't even express what that meant to me.

Clem reaches over to give me a hug. "It's my way of making up for missing so many games this season."

The girls are wearing the letters that spell my name, but I'm only drawn to one. "X marks the spot." I don't intend to say those words out loud, but I do.

My sister's eyes follow mine, and I realize she sees me staring at Dani, who is talking quietly with Jenna.

Clem nudges me. "No, Jax."

I get the message. Off limits. I want to tell my sister that I know, that I remember what happened the last time, but I don't.

But damn it, Dani looks good. Fresh-faced, wide-eyed, laughing with her friend.

I half listen to my sister talk about my game, and as I'm about to head back to the field, she punches me lightly. "Go kick some ass, Apple Jacks."

I smile and then look up into the stands. I don't know why I look. Nothing ever changes. My mother never comes. You'd think it wouldn't bother me anymore, but it does. This is the game I play. I pretend to still be her son, return her calls, see her when she beckons, and the bills get paid. Yeah, there's a lot of love. Part of me doesn't understand why my sister couldn't do the same thing—do things my mother's way—but the other part respects the shit out of her for cutting the cords.

As I run back, I swear I can feel Dani's eyes on me. Either that or I'm turning into a fucking nutcase. She wouldn't even look at me when I was standing two feet away, so I don't know why she'd be staring now.

One thing is for sure, though. Having Dani in the stands makes me play like my life depends on it. I score two goals, including the game winner. My coach is pleased as a fucking peach when I walk up to the bench.

"Son, good game. I liked the fire I saw in you." He pats me on the back and leans toward me like he wants to impart some kind of parental advice. "You're an amazing athlete and my best forward, but you've been missing that spark. You had it today. Keep it up. Don't let anything distract you."

The way he says that gets under my skin. I want to tell him that I'm not the screwup he thinks I am, but it's not worth it. But he's right that something's been missing. I don't know if it's because my sister and I have cleared the air or the fact that her roommate came, but today I cared, and I haven't cared about anything in a long time.

My roommate Nick joins me on the walk back to the locker room. "I forgot how hot your sister is."

I turn to him, and in all seriousness, want to threaten every bone in his body. "She's off limits, dickhead."

He smirks and punches me in the arm. "I know. But how about her friends? Damn, they're gorgeous, especially that one with the pink in her hair. You know how I love those BU girls."

That doesn't make me feel any better.

I shoot him a dirty look. I know he's just jerking my chain, but I'm still pissed about it. My sunny disposition takes another nosedive later that day when Daren stops by my condo.

"I need to talk to her," he says gruffly.

I don't need to ask who. I know he saw my sister in the stands today.

"Do you really want to do this?" He just got engaged to my sister's former best friend, and now he wants to talk to Clementine? "I think she has a boyfriend now. Some guy named Gavin."

"Yeah, I met him. He looked like he wanted to punch me."

My head jerks toward Daren. "When did this happen?"

"At your game during half time." He smirks. "He didn't look excited when I hugged her. Either time."

I bark out a laugh. "You've got balls, brother. I should deck you for him."

"Yeah, but you won't. I don't want to make the moves on her. I've put her through enough shit. But I need to apologize. I never manned up to her and said what needed to be said, and when I saw her today, that all came crashing back to me." He wipes his hands on his jeans. "Jax, I miss her. She was always there for me, and I fucked up, royally. But I know you two haven't been the same since I screwed up. That's not fair to you guys."

I walk toward the window and pull back the curtain.

"What are you doing, Jax?"

My head turns up toward the sky. "Checking to see if pigs are flying since it looks like you got your head out of your ass." I duck because I know what's coming. The pillow whizzes past my head, and I laugh. "You're losing your touch, Heisman."

CHAPTER SIXTEEN

- Dani -

As I finish putting out the snacks on our coffee table, I decide I have to ask.

"Do you think she's ready for this?"

Jenna gets a mischievous smile on her face and winks. "Too bad if she's not. Clem's been holed up for weeks, and it's time to live a little." Then she leans closer to me. "This is why she loves me. I push her. Trust me. She needs pushing."

"You know her better than I do, but if she knocks you over the head with a dildo, I'm out of here."

Jenna laughs. "She's going to have a great time. Besides, Gavin will thank us for keeping his girl fully stocked."

I can admit that Clem might need a little pick-me-up, but I'm not sure this is the way to go about it. The coffee table is littered in neon-colored phallic objects. The vendor has spread out an assortment of toys that looks like candy-flavored sin. I'm pretty sure Clem is going to have a heart attack when she sees this.

The last several weeks have been a whirlwind of bizarro drama.

Clem's dirtbag professor who stalked her a few years ago was at it again. Fortunately, the asshole is behind bars now. She's even worked out things with Daren, who looks at her like she walks on water. It's funny to see Clem with her little entourage of hot guys. Between

Gavin, Daren and Jax, she's the envy of every girl on campus, not that she's the kind of person to care about things like that.

Of course, this means I see Jax constantly. Now that he and his sister have worked through their issues, I swear he's always over here hanging out.

We continue to have painfully awkward conversations that generally end with me ducking into my room. It would be so much easier if I could disconnect from my attraction to him, but my body wants him the way a diabetic lusts for fudge. I swear his pheromones must be super charged because if he's in the room, my follicles stand on end like he's magnetized.

I know Clem appreciates that she's close with her brother again, but it makes it pretty damn hard to forget about him.

It's sweet to watch them together. They're always giving each other shit, but they never push too far. It makes me ache to see my mom.

I'm lost in thoughts about Chicago when a gasp makes me turn my head.

"What the fuck is this?" The horror on Clem's face makes me laugh.

"You're early!" Jenna pulls her through the front door. "We're having a sex toy party. Girls only of course. And Travis." She winks at me. "People are getting here in about twenty minutes." Jenna turns Clem toward her bedroom and sends her off to change with a pat on the ass.

"You can get her to do anything," I muse. "You're the Clementine whisperer."

Jenna snorts as she reaches for her phone. "I have to get her in the right frame of mind. Time for a few rounds of Out-Skank."

Out-Skank is Jenna's sexting game. The winner usually gets a free dinner or a drink the next time we go out. I'm guessing tonight's winner will get something from the coffee table of sin.

She shows me the text she sends Clem: *"I want to rub your nub, baby."*

A minute later, I hear laughter coming from Clem's room. She writes back: *"I want to waggle your man meat."*

Jenna and I giggle, and she hands me her phone to respond. I write, *"Waggle me in your hot muff and tell me some slut smut."*

We erupt in laughter, and Clem walks out ready to join the party. For the first time since I met her this fall, she's all smiles and laughter. Wow. Clementine actually giggles. I didn't know she was capable of making that sound.

When the party gets started, I can't help but blush when Denise, the sex toy consultant, demonstrates how to use the various instruments. One rotates, another vibrates and whirrs, the purple one strokes one spot and the pink one gyrates the other. For the life of me, I had no clue that women had so many erogenous zones to manipulate.

I pick up a small jar of Nipple Nibbler balm.

"That's one of my biggest sellers," Denise says, pointing to the item in my hand. "It plumps the nipple and makes it tingle with a lovely warming agent. It tastes like cinnamon and doubles as a fabulous lip gloss that makes your lips look fuller."

Jenna practically knocks me over reaching for it. "I want one! Ryan is going to love this. Does it come in a jumbo container?"

All the girls laugh. Jenna and Ryan's sex life is legendary. I've accidentally walked in on them twice. Both times I was pretty sure their positions were threatening the laws of gravity.

Travis leans over Jenna and grabs the container and twists open the lid so he can take a whiff.

"Hmm. Yummy." He cocks an eyebrow. "So, uh, can this stuff nibble other stuff? Like, if it ends up on my junk, it won't hurt my Balzac or anything, right?" Leave it to Travis to refer to his man parts by referencing a French author.

I have to hand it to Denise. She doesn't blush at his question, instead kneeling in front of Travis to assure him that this is an all-purpose balm.

Fortunately, the orders are done privately in one of the bedrooms. I decide to splurge on a purple vibrator and a pink rabbit thingy that stimulates the nubbin. In the gift bag, I also get a complimentary Nipple Nibbler balm and a little ring made of this green stretchy plastic that reminds me of a giant gummy bear.

When I'm done ordering, I walk back into the living room and grab a seat next to Jenna. I pull out the green ring and lean over to her, whispering, "What's this for?"

"Omigod! How cute! A cock ring. What a great stocking stuffer!"

I look at Clem. She looks at me. And while we both turn deep shades of crimson, everyone laughs.

CHAPTER SEVENTEEN

- Jax -

Ryan and I are sprawled out on my couch playing *Grand Theft Auto*.

"So did Jenna throw you to the dogs tonight?" I screech the convertible through a busy intersection, avoiding a near-collision.

"No." Ryan snickers, and I turn my head long enough to see the wicked grin on his face. "She and Dani are throwing a sex toy party."

The controller slips out of my hand, clattering on the floor.

He shakes his eyebrows at me. "It's like a tupperware party but with vibrators and shit."

The thought of Dani and sex toys makes my dick hard. Okay, this might have something to do with the fact that I've been damn near celibate all semester with a few minor exceptions, but the last time I tried hooking up with a girl, I accidentally called her Danielle, and she threw her shoe at me. I'm tired of being with other girls and thinking about her. Dani barely acknowledges my existence, but here I sit with a raging hard-on for her.

I've never pined over a girl. I need to get my shit together.

My hand dips to grab the controller, and Ryan laughs. "Apparently, Jenna wanted to cheer up your sister."

Uh, yeah, the boner is gone. "Shut the fuck up, asshole."

"She's been through a lot."

I shoot him a dirty look. No one needs to tell me that.

He says, "Jenna is on a crusade to cheer up Clem. She was thinking we could all go rock climbing this weekend. You wanna come?"

"Yeah. Count me in, but no more talk about sex toys."

Ryan slaps me on the arm in agreement and resumes the game.

By Saturday afternoon, the temperature has dropped. I froze my balls off this morning during our game, but we won.

I probably shouldn't be rock climbing. My coach would have a fit if I got injured, but the promise of seeing Dani is all the encouragement I need. When I pull up to the park, I immediately spot my friends and jog over to the climbing wall. I sign the little "I won't sue you if I die" waiver and leave my ID with the attendant.

Jenna, Ryan, Clem and her boyfriend Gavin are huddled next to the wall as they wait for their turn to climb. I hug my sister, making a point to scruff her hair.

"Hey, loser." She grabs my arm. "Did you win this morning?"

"Of course."

"Sorry I had to work. I wanted to see you play."

A lot of people might say things like this, but she means it. I can't count how many of my games Clem has attended over the years.

I give Jenna a hug and then shoot the shit with the guys.

The roar of a motorcycle behind us gets my attention, and I turn to see Dani hop off the back of the bike. The guy she's with is pretty built, and he looks older, maybe mid-twenties.

I'm pissed, but I tell myself that she can do whatever

she wants. She's not mine, and I have no reason to be jealous.

"Hey, guys," Jenna chirps, her perkiness getting on my nerves.

"Hi." Dani walks up with that guy. Her nose is red from the cold, and her cheeks are pink. Goddamn it. She's beautiful. When she sees me, she smiles, but there's something sad in her eyes that digs into me. "This is Brady." She turns to him. "I think you've met Jenna and Clem, but this is Jenna's boyfriend Ryan, and this is Clem's brother Jax."

I don't know why, but hearing her say my name does weird things to my chest. Brady nods, and I nod back.

"How did your econ presentation go?" she asks me, her eyes peering out beneath long lashes.

I can't believe she remembers that. I mentioned it last weekend when I was hanging with Clem and Gavin.

"I survived. Barely." It wasn't my best work, but I eked it out.

There's that smile again, and for a second I forget that we're with all of our friends. Her date moves closer to her like he's staking his claim, and she turns her attention to him.

We all stand around for a while, and I try to keep my back to them to avoid feeling like a jealous lunatic, but after a while, I can't resist. Brady has Dani curled up into his side like he's trying to keep her warm. My first reaction is to rip his head off his body. They're joking around, talking quietly, and the next thing I know, she's stepping away laughing.

"If I fall, it's your fault," she tells him. Dani tucks her sweatshirt into her jeans, re-ties her ponytail, does a handstand and starts walking around upside down. After a minute, she flips onto her feet, and we all clap. She laughs, and the light in her eyes threatens to kick me on my ass.

"What else can you do?" Jenna asks.

Dani shrugs. "Almost any gymnastics move, really. I can still flip and do all the mat routines. It's the bar that always did me in. I have a hard time finding my balance up there. I guess I get scared easily." Her eyes catch mine before they dart away.

"That was amazing, hot stuff," Brady tells her, pulling her into a hug. She rolls her eyes and hugs him back. Her phone buzzes, and she pulls it out of her back pocket.

"That's Travis. Can we stop by his place on our way back?" she asks Brady as she stares at the screen.

"Sure. He still owes me from that poker game."

"I can't believe you hustled him." She shoves him playfully, and he laughs. They're clearly close, but he hasn't kissed her, so I'm not sure they're official. Something about that gives me a glimmer of hope, which is stupid because I shouldn't be trying to put the moves on my sister's roommate.

Ryan bumps me with his elbow. "She's a sweetheart." He says it under his breath so I'm the only one who hears. When I don't say anything, he murmurs, "They just started going out a few weeks ago. I don't think they're serious." I nod like I don't care, but he won't drop it. "Jenna says she's super loyal and has become a good friend to your sister."

That right there is what I need to remember. That I shouldn't mess with my sister's friend. Clem's been through enough bullshit. The last thing she needs is for me to break her roommate's heart.

As Ryan moves up to strap into his climbing gear, my eyes drift back to Dani. She's standing a few feet away, and when she points another glance in my direction, gravity shifts beneath my feet.

"You okay, man?" Gavin asks. He stands there studying me, and I mask whatever emotion just threatened to choke me.

"Yeah. I'm fine. Thinking about all the shit I need to do before school is out on Wednesday for Thanksgiving."

He nods, and his eyes drift toward my sister who is staring at him with a lovesick grin plastered on her face. It's weird to see her with a boyfriend.

Even though she and Daren dated most of their senior year of high school, I never saw them get mushy. I never knew if they felt weird around me or if that's how they were. Seeing her with Gavin, though, I can tell he's different somehow. Just… more.

"Do you mind that I'm stealing Clementine for Thanksgiving?" he asks quietly as we watch Jenna scale the wall.

"Not at all. I'm going skiing in Maine, so I'm glad she'll be with you." It's kind of a relief that he's looking out for her. Someone needs to. My parents sure as hell don't.

I'm still pissed at my dad. I had just talked Clem into meeting with him for coffee when he texts about a "European acquisitions SNAFU" he has to "untangle." I could fucking punch him in the nutsack for bailing on her. But when I broke the news to Clem this morning, she didn't sound surprised.

I turn to face Gavin. "So… meeting the family?" I'm not surprised he's taking this step, but I'd be lying if I said I wasn't nervous about the whole thing. I don't want my sister to have to deal with anymore disappointment.

Gavin takes a deep breath, the weight of what I'm really asking evident in the sudden tension in his face. "I love her. I want her to meet the people who are the most important to me."

I cough, uneasy for some reason. I lean toward him. "That's nice and all, but if you break her heart, I'll beat your ass."

He laughs and nods like he's on board with my plan. "No worries, man. She's it for me."

Part of me, the suspicious part, wants to run a background and credit check on the guy, but that sounds too much like my mother, a thought that chills me. The other part of me, the sane part, knows he worships my sister.

He'd fucking better.

Dani's voice catches my attention as she talks to that guy Brady.

"I don't know." She looks up at him shyly. "I've never done anything like that before."

Brady nods. "Travis says you can put it on your list, whatever that is." He tosses his arm around her, and my gut hurts.

She covers her face. "He told you about that?"

Now I'm curious.

"It's art, Dani. Relax. But you don't have to be naked if you don't want."

That really fucking gets my attention.

Jenna is rappelling down the wall and yells, "Who's getting naked?"

Dani pushes Brady's arm off her shoulder and yells back, "No one. No one is getting naked." She realizes we're all staring, and she sighs. "Travis wants me to model for some nudes he has to do for class, but we're talking *Playboy* nudity, not *Hustler* nudity."

"There's nothing wrong with *Hustler* nudity," Ryan says under his breath, making me bristle.

"I bet you'd look beautiful, Dani." Jenna wiggles out of her climbing gear and beelines it to her roommate. "Brady, are you doing nudes too, handsome?" Jenna looks over to Ryan and winks. He laughs like he doesn't care. I don't get those two. They never seem jealous. Must be nice.

Brady grins back, and that sick feeling in my stomach returns. "Travis wants to contrast my tattoos with Dani's bare skin. She has that one tat I did on her back, but she'd still make a great canvas."

I get several things from this conversation.

One, he inked Dani's tattoo. I saw it the other day when she ran out to do the laundry and was wearing an off-the-shoulder shirt. I think it's some kind of star.

Two, I'm guessing to contrast Brady's tats with her skin, they're going to have to be close or touching. Naked. Judging from his expression, he'd like this.

And three, I definitely want to beat his ass.

Just as I'm thinking I should talk to her, get her attention away from this guy, someone yells my name.

"Jax! Oh my God!" A curvy blonde bounds toward me and throws her arms around my neck like she hasn't seen me in years. I turn my head just in time so she ends up kissing my cheek instead of my mouth.

As she starts to pull away a little, I'm well aware that my friends are watching this with interest. Except Dani, who has her back to me. But Brady is watching.

"Hi, doll," I say uneasily. That's right. Doll. Because I can't remember her name.

"It's been too long, Jax. What, since spring break, right?" The girl's arms are still wrapped around my neck.

"Yeah, I guess." She's pretty in a been-there-done-that sort of way.

A brunette calls out to the blonde, "Jasmine! There

you are…" A smile creeps on this other girl's face. "Wow. Jax."

Shit. This can't be good.

But it gets worse when the second girl strolls over and places her lips on mine despite the fact that her friend Jasmine is wrapped around my body.

Then it dawns on me. *Cancun.*

Last spring, the soccer team and a few BC soccer groupies headed down for a tropical getaway. *Jasmine and Judi. They annoyed the fuck out of me by saying "J-squared" all night like they were some elusive mathematical equation.*

"Jax, you naughty boy, you got away without giving us your number," one quips.

Yeah, just the way I like it.

I'm about to blow them off when I catch Brady and Dani out of the corner of my eye. He has his arms around her and is whispering in her ear. She nods slowly, glances at me, and burrows herself back into him before he kisses the top of her head.

Jealousy eats through me like a worm. So what do I do? Embrace my inner asshole.

Reaching around so one chick is tucked under each of my arms, I gear up to put on a show. "My apologies, girls. Nick told me he had your numbers. What are you doing over Thanksgiving? The guys and I are going skiing. Wanna come?"

Jasmine purrs into my ear, "Yes, I want to *come.*"

Someone snorts behind us, and when I look up, I see Clementine shooting daggers at the girls before she sticks her finger in her throat to pretend like she's puking.

I laugh, but it lacks enthusiasm.

After we exchange numbers and the J-squared duo leaves, my sister grabs my arm. "What is wrong with you? You're going to catch something from those girls. Did someone drop you on your head as an infant?"

"You can't blame a guy when that falls into his lap."

Clem shakes her head at me. "Why can't you date a nice girl? Perhaps someone who doesn't announce wanting a three-way like she's ringing a dinner bell?"

That's easy. My eyes connect with Dani, who's strapping into her gear and getting ready to climb. "Nice girls have the good sense to stay away from me."

CHAPTER EIGHTEEN

- Dani -

This afternoon did not go as planned. Jax wasn't supposed to come climbing.

"You okay?" Brady's gruff voice has an unexpected softness I'd never expect from a guy like him.

"Yeah. This whole thing is stupid." I toss my bag on my bed.

"Why don't you tell him?"

I close the door behind Brady, not wanting my roommates to hear this conversation.

Yes, I told him my whole sob story last weekend over a bottle of tequila. I'm not sure what sucks more, that Jax doesn't remember we hooked up or that Brady is so great about my stupid feelings for Jax.

Damn it. I wish I hadn't read Clementine's book. I didn't want to know that he built his sister a tree house when they were twelve. Jax had been trying to cheer her up because their parents were leaving for a month-long vacation—without them. I didn't want to know about his childhood, that he stayed up with her all night when she had a hundred and three degree fever or that he gave his sister his lunch whenever she forgot hers.

Brady clears his throat, snapping me out of my thoughts. "Tell him. Get this over and see how he feels."

I sigh. "That makes sense on one level. Except I can't handle the humiliation of telling him what happened, especially after all this time. Besides, he left me at the club that night and headed straight into the arms of another woman. A ridiculously gorgeous woman." I drop my head into my hands as I sit on the edge of my bed. "And honestly, the thought that Clem might look at me the way she looked at those girls today makes me ill."

The bed shifts as he sits next to me, and I blather on. "Plus, she had this horrible experience with her best friend in high school who slept with her boyfriend, and everyone lied to her about it. She hates liars. And that's me. I'm a liar."

"This isn't the same thing, Dani. She'll understand."

"Maybe. But what's the point if Jax is banging girls two at a time?"

Brady's lips form a straight line. I take one look at him and groan. "I suck. I'm sorry. I'm going to shut up now. Let's talk about break. What are you and your family doing?"

That seems to relax him a little. "We're headed to New York to visit my aunt. Your flight takes off on Wednesday evening, right?"

I nod, realizing I should get my act together if I have any intention of going home in a few days.

"How's your mom doing?" he asks.

"Okay, but she sounds tired. And she never got the camera on her laptop fixed, so we can't Skype. I really miss her, and I'm worried she's not getting enough rest." I shake my head. "I'm sure I'm making it worse in my head because I can't see her. She's probably fine, living it up on homemade cookies and crockpot dishes."

When Brady leaves, I hunker down and try to get some homework done, but I keep replaying the afternoon in my head.

The whole thing is on an endless loop. Busty girls in Jax's face. How he's probably had sex with both of them.

At the same time. And obviously plans to do it again.

Ugh. #ShootMeNow

Once I finally stop thinking about Jax, I still end up tossing and turning, worrying about an art project that won't affect my G.P.A. and wondering why I'm not more concerned about my marketing class, which does affect my G.P.A.

I get up around one in the morning, grateful that Jenna is staying with Ryan, and flip on my bedside lamp. My hand digs around in my bag, and I pull out my journal to work on a graphic design project. The topic is wealth and money, and we can explore any opinion about it as long as we convey the message with a dominant image and use two different fonts.

My journal is filled with sketches, some in black ink and others in watercolor marker. I've decided to explore how money corrupts, taints what might be otherwise innocent. I draw dollar signs and other images associated with wealth until I can't keep my eyes open.

On Monday when I show Professor Zin my sketches, he's delighted and points out his three favorite, which I have to perfect for my formal submission after break. He starts to walk away after reviewing my work, but stops and leans down to me.

"I know you're only a junior, but I might have a full-time job here for you at some point. Let's keep this between us for now. I'll be able to tell you more in December when I get my budget for the new fiscal year."

"Wow, Zin. That would be amazing. Thank you for considering me, sir."

He chuckles and fixes his tie. He's such a grandpa. "I want to call you my star student, Dani Hart, except I've never had you for class. Maybe we can change that too for second semester. Check out the course listing in my office after your shift and let me know what you might want to take."

I'm beaming all the way home despite the B I get on my marketing assignment. So I had difficulty feigning enthusiasm for marketing dog food. Sue me.

Wednesday morning comes too fast, and my roommates scurry around our suite, packing and preparing for the long weekend.

Clem gets to the door with her bag in hand and looks like she might vomit. "Holy shit. I can't believe I'm going to meet Gavin's family. What if they hate me?" This would be comical except she actually gets panic attacks every once in a while.

"Not possible," Jenna says.

I chime in. "Gavin adores you. His family will too. Just relax and have fun."

"Shit." Clem rubs her forehead. "I feel like I'm forgetting something." She stands in the hallway and checks to make sure she has her wallet and cell phone before she shrugs. "Whatever it is can wait, I guess. Wish me luck, girls."

Jenna and I hug Clem before she leaves. Jenna is the next to go. She and Ryan are taking off to see his family in Pennsylvania.

Unfortunately, I still have several hours before my flight, but I get ready anyway and call Travis to chat before he leaves for Cape Cod.

"What are you wearing?" Travis asks, using his sex voice.

"Pasties and a thong."

He laughs, and I brush my hands over my favorite pair of faded jeans that fit just right.

"Dani, you could meet the perfect man on your flight. Romances always happen on airplanes. Aren't you glad you beautified this weekend?"

"You mean, am I glad that I had my privates glazed and de-furred by a German woman I swear was a Nazi in a former life? I don't know that any man is worth the effort. Besides, I thought we were still operating under the assumption that Brady is the right guy, and once I get Jax out of my system, I'll come to my senses."

Travis sighs, and I can almost see him shaking his head. "I love Brady, I do, but if you're not feeling any chemistry after hanging out with him for the last month, he might not be the one."

"Don't say that. He's perfect for me. He's artistic, sweet, funny, thoughtful. I have a list here somewhere."

"You and your lists. Look, that's how you ended up with Reid. You thought he was the right kind of guy, and you dated him despite the lack of connection."

"Ugh, you're depressing me." My phone clicks with an incoming call. "I gotta go. Clem's calling me. Be safe on your drive, and I'll call you when I land in Chicago."

"All right, sweets. Miss me."

"Miss me more."

I switch over to Clem. "Hey, what's up? Trouble in paradise already?"

She ignores my question. "I need a *huge* favor, Dani."

"Okay," I say slowly.

"Remember when I said I had forgotten something?"

"Yeah."

"I just figured it out as Gavin and I are caught in gridlock traffic." I wave my hand at her as though she can see me urging her to spit it out already. "I have my brother's driver's license. He forgot it when we went climbing last weekend, so I grabbed it, and it's sitting on my desk. I know you said your flight isn't for several hours, right?" She doesn't wait for me to answer. "Could you possibly drop it off to him?"

"Sorry, Dani," Gavin calls out in the background. "It's probably my fault she forgot. I've been distracting her this week. A lot."

I hear a smack, and he laughs before mumbling, "What? You're the one who bought all those toys."

She muffles the phone, and I can't help but laugh at the two of them. I clear my throat. "I'm going to pretend I didn't hear you discussing vibrators. Clem, I don't have to get to Logan until 6:30, but I don't know how I'll be able to make it to Chestnut Hill and back in time."

"Don't worry. I'll have Jax give you a ride to the airport." God, a car ride with Jax. I start biting my lip, anxious about seeing him. "Dani, I'll text him now. I'm sure he'll give you a lift. He has to. My idiot brother has been driving around town for the last several days without his ID, but he's going to Maine, and I don't want him to leave without it."

Although the last thing I want to do is spend time with Jax, I'd feel terrible if he got in trouble for not having his license.

I take a deep breath. "I'll head out now, but it'll probably take me forty-five minutes on the T." The Boston subway system is pretty decent, but BC is a hike.

"No, I'll call for a cab. That way you don't have to drag your luggage all over the city. There's cash in my top dresser drawer. Take fifty and get lunch afterward."

"Are you sure?"

"Yes, you're doing me a huge favor. The least I can do is pay for the cab. I'll call for one now and text you with the info in a few minutes. Dani, I totally owe you."

I shake my head. "No, Clem, you don't."

CHAPTER NINETEEN

- Jax -

"Why the hell did you invite them?" I grip the steering wheel as Nick frowns at me from the passenger seat.

"I was under the impression that you had already invited the girls to go skiing with us," he says with more sarcasm than necessary.

I grab my phone and check the time. Dani is late. Blowing out a breath, I grumble, "Newsflash, genius. I didn't mean it." I had ignored their calls and thought I was out of the woods.

I sit with the engine idling for ten minutes debating whether we should grab lunch now while we wait.

"Hey, if you don't want to wedge yourself between two gorgeous women and their unnaturally large breasts, that's fine by me. They're not too discriminating if I recall correctly, so..."

He lets his comment hang in the air as he waits for me to lay claim to them. Which I don't.

Shifting my car into first, I pull into the street as my phone rings. *J-squared.* Shoot me the fuck now. Maybe I should call this off before I find myself having to avoid them on the slopes.

I'm putting the phone to my ear and about to shift into second when Nick yells and throws his fist into my chest.

My heart is caught somewhere in my throat when Dani steps off the curb. Right in front of my car.

* * *

My whole life flashes before my eyes as I slam on the breaks, but my BMW slides on the damp road and barrels toward her. Dani watches as though frozen, her hair gusting in the wind. Her eyes close at the last minute when she makes contact with my car, her hand slamming onto my hood with a loud thud before she disappears on the other side.

"Dude, you hit her," Nick says, stating the obvious.

I leap out of my seat and race around the car to find Dani on the ground, her luggage a few feet behind her. Her hair splays out beneath her like she's floating in water. I fall on my knees next to her and brush a few strands out of her face.

Although I'm grateful I don't see any blood, that doesn't make me feel any better. She could still have internal injuries.

"Dani, can you hear me? Dani?"

She moans, and at the sound of her voice, my heart begins beating again.

"Jesus, man." Nick stands next to me, offering nothing but ongoing one-liners.

Somehow I manage to find my phone.

"911, what's your emergency?"

Speaking is difficult, but I manage to croak, "I hit a girl with my car. Hurry up, she needs an ambulance."

I toss the phone to Nick to finish the conversation, and I turn to Dani. My thumb wipes away a tear that's sliding down her cheek. Even though she's unconscious, I'm struck by her beauty. Her smooth skin. Her perfect lips. The way her eyelashes barely touch her cheek. I'm overwhelmed the way a kid is the first time he realizes that space is somehow infinite and expanding.

Yeah, scared shitless.

A brief image of Dani dancing behind a cage flickers behind my eyes for some reason, and I fight the urge to cradle her in my arms.

"Why did you hit me? I wasn't that late." Her voice is soft, barely a whisper.

My breath catches in my chest and then I find myself laughing. "Fuck. Dani, I'm sorry, sweetheart. I'm so sorry."

"The cab dropped me off on the wrong street…"

Her eyes flutter open, and one glance at her has me aching in ways I didn't think possible anymore. Something taps my wrist a minute before I realize it's her hand.

"You're going to need this," she says, wincing.

I look down as she unwraps her fingers to reveal my driver's license. My heart pounds out a frenzied beat as I realize I'd be totally screwed right now without it.

A siren finally cuts through the sound of blood roaring in my ears. Nick bumps me hard with his knee. "Coach is going to have your ass, man. He'll probably kick you off the team for this."

I grunt at him, irritated that he's probably right, but that's not what's important right now. Heavy doors slam to my right as a cop runs up to us.

"Sir, step away from the woman."

I swallow. God, I'm in deep shit.

Dani tugs on my hand. "No, don't leave me, Jax." Tears well up in her eyes and spill down her pale cheeks.

The policeman kneels down to take a closer look at her.

She closes her eyes briefly before she says, "Jax is my friend. I want him here." She struggles to say every word.

With a surprised look on his face, the cop stares at me

long and hard before he turns back to her. At least he doesn't ask me to move. He feels for her pulse, asks a few questions about her injuries, and then, satisfied she looks stable, takes out a notepad. "Ma'am, can you answer a few questions about what happened?"

She shouldn't have to deal with this. "I hit her. It was my fault. I was driving and—"

"It wasn't his fault." Dani pulls on my hand again until I look at her. Her face is wet, and her eyelids are heavy. Her eyes shift back to the cop. "I was, uh, on the phone, and I didn't look for traffic when I crossed the street. I was coming to see him. Jax is my friend."

No, I was the one on the phone. The truth is hammering in my chest until I feel like I'm suffocating, and I look to Dani to tell her she doesn't have to do this, but when my eyes meet hers, she shakes her head slightly.

The ambulance finally arrives, and an EMT races up to us and checks her vitals.

I stand there, answering the cop's questions while the paramedic rips up the leg of her jeans to reveal a huge bruise along her knee and thigh. Jesus Christ. I could have killed this girl.

"Shouldn't I know your name before you start ripping off my clothes?" she asks, making the paramedic grin. He's a young guy, maybe in his mid-twenties.

I feel myself scowling at him.

The policeman takes another emergency call and prepares to leave. Satisfied that I didn't intentionally try to run her over, he says I didn't break any traffic signs and doesn't even give me a citation.

Fuck, I owe this girl.

I watch the cruiser pull away. Nick lets out a sigh.

I'm starting to think everything will be okay, that Dani is alive and things could have been so much worse because I'm clearly a total dumbass, but that feeling of relief is short-lived as Dani starts crying when the paramedics load her in the ambulance.

"Can I go with her?" My voice is thick with emotion.

The guy shakes his head. "Family only, sir. I'm sorry."

I don't know where the words come from, but they're out my mouth before I can stop. "She's my girlfriend. I can't let her go alone."

Finally, he shrugs. "If it's okay with her, it's okay with me." He mumbles something to her and then turns to me. "Come on."

I toss my keys to Nick. "Here, grab her stuff and meet us at the hospital."

CHAPTER TWENTY

- Dani -

Someone is stroking my head gently.

I'm cold. Freezing. And my mouth is dry. I want to reach down to pull up a blanket except when I do more than breathe, every muscle in my body cries out.

My chest radiates with fear. Why does everything hurt so much?

Opening my eyes, I stare at the face that's been haunting me for the past two and a half months.

"Am I dreaming?" I swallow and wince at the pain in my throat.

Jax smiles weakly. "I wish you were, Dani."

The rhythmic beat of machines pulsing draws my attention. *I'm in the hospital.* The memory of what happened comes flooding back to me.

Jax pulls away and runs his hands through his shaggy dark blond hair, leaving it sticking up at odd angles. I close my eyes, eager to shut out his magnetic presence.

He sighs, letting the air whoosh from his lips. "I am so sorry. For all of this. Shit, I almost had a heart attack when I realized what happened. And seeing you on the pavement like that. Fuck."

Despite my exhaustion, I struggle to look at him. The usual don't-give-a-damn glint in his eyes is gone, replaced with worry.

I lick my dry lips, but I don't have enough moisture in my mouth to accomplish anything.

"Here." Jax gets up and pours me a cup of water out of a pink plastic pitcher. He hands it to me, and I try to smile in appreciation. I can't drink it yet because my whole body aches, and it takes me moment to catch my breath.

Finally, I take a sip. I've never tasted anything so good before.

"Can I ask you something?" he asks. His blue eyes crinkle in the corners. His lips are tight.

I nod slowly and then let my head rest on the pillow, too tired to do more than convalesce. A silence yawns between us.

Finally, he asks, "Why did you tell the cops this was your fault? I know you saw me on the phone."

Because I have a huge-ass crush on you? Because I want to have your babies? Because I haven't stopped thinking about you since we met?

I stare at him, realizing that while those sentiments are true, they're probably not why I did it.

"I heard you and your friend talking."

"My roommate Nick?"

"I guess." I take another sip of water. "I heard what he said about you getting in trouble with your coach, and I didn't want to be the reason you got kicked off the team."

Jax frowns and looks at me like I've sprouted an extra head. "Seriously?"

"Yeah." I laugh a little, but it hurts, and I groan. "Don't make me laugh." I take a couple of deep breaths until the pain subsides. He's sitting so close I can smell his gorgeous cologne, which is crisp and clean. "Your sister always talks about how you're supposed to go pro and how you have scouts at all your games. She's really proud of you."

He scoffs, and it's funny to see doubt on his beautiful face.

"Anyway, I didn't want to screw that up for you."

The silence between us is thick. Jax tilts his head up and stares at the ceiling for at least a minute. "Well, shit."

I'm taken aback by his intensity. "Don't think so hard about this. Let's just chalk it off to the fact that I hit my head, okay?"

His mouth pulls up into a crooked grin. "I might fucking love you right now."

My eyes widen, and I'm sure I'd be blushing right if my circulation was working properly. "If love nearly gets me killed by your Beemer, I'd hate to see what hate gets me."

He barks out a laugh that makes me jerk back, and I smile once the pain of that sudden movement subsides.

I start to look around the room, and when I see the clock, my heart sinks. "Oh my God. I can't believe it's so late. Where's my phone?"

"The nurse put all of your stuff in a bag. Hold on." Reaching over me, he grabs a plastic sack that says "patient" and hands it to me.

I slowly root around in the bag until I find my phone. I have messages and texts from my mom, Travis and Brady.

Jax tells me he's going to track down some dinner for us. I don't bother listening to the messages. I just dial home. My mom picks up on the second ring.

"Danielle, shouldn't you be on a plane right now?"

Tears prick my eyes. "Mom, don't freak, but something happened. I'm okay, but…" My voice trails off as I fight to not cry.

"Tell me everything. I won't be mad. You're on the phone and alive. That's all that matters." Her voice is cool and calm. I love this about my mother. In a crisis, she's amazing.

"I kind of got hit by a car, but I'm okay," I say over her gasp.

Twenty minutes later, when Jax walks in, I'm a mess.

"Shit, Dani. What's wrong? Are you in pain?"

I'm crying into my hands, every sob transporting pain throughout my body. I keep my face covered. "I promised my mom I'd be home for Thanksgiving, but I missed my flight, and everything is sold out." The last few words sound more like hiccups. "She was really sick last year. She had cancer. And I haven't seen her since this summer. And…"

The bed sags as Jax sits on the edge and leans over to hug me, making me cry harder. "I'm sorry, babe. This is my fault."

I cry into him until the tears run out. I cry until my heart can't take it any longer. Tilting my head back so I can wipe off my face, I see how wet his shirt is.

"You're going to drown if I don't stop crying." A shudder runs through me.

"Come here. Don't apologize." He wraps his arms around me again, and he smells so good, so fresh and sexy. He's warm and comforting, and for a minute, I forget about my flight home.

I snuggle into him, relishing his muscular chest and how nice it is to be pressed up against him again.

And then it hits me. *I'm snuggling with Jax Avery.*

My heart starts beating furiously, and an alarm goes off next to me. Jax pulls back, and we look at each other. A second later, an older nurse scurries in and presses a button, making that horrible sound stop.

"Honey, you all right?" She shoos Jax off the bed before she pulls back the neck of my gown to check the leads that are taped all over my chest, and then she gives me a once over, surveying me for signs of distress. "I'm Charlotte, and I'll be your nurse tonight." She checks the heart monitor and turns to me. "You need to stay calm. I don't know what has you all riled up," she says, looking to Jax, "but you can't get so excited."

"Sorry. I was upset about not being able to go home for the holidays." That sounds so much better than "I was so excited Jax had his hands on me."

She pats me on the hand and gives me a sympathetic smile. "Of course. Well, at least you have your cute boyfriend to keep you company." I start to tell her we're not together, but she cuts me off to talk to him. "You're a lucky guy. Danielle is gorgeous. And what a smile! You two make an adorable couple!"

My mouth falls open, and I stutter, trying to find words to clarify my relationship to Jax, but the smirk on his face stops me, as do his next words.

"She is gorgeous."

The alarm goes off again, my heart rate racing. The nurse laughs, and my face heats up. "I should have known you were the reason." She clucks at Jax as she walks around my bed and turns off the alarm. "I'll be back in half an hour to give you your pain meds. Until then, no more alarms." She points at Jax, who holds up his hands like he's innocent. His charm works, and my nurse grins and walks out.

Jax's attention shifts back to me, and I look down. God, that was embarrassing.

Picking up my phone, I scroll through my texts, ignoring Jax's stare. It takes me a few minutes to focus on anything besides how much I miss his warmth in this cold room.

But when I read Brady's text from this afternoon, the

reality of where he and I are headed comes crashing back to me.

"I've met someone."

I groan. Those three words fill me with such doubt.

The rest of his text is worse. "*I wanted to let you know. To see if you felt any differently about us.*"

Am I doing the wrong thing in letting Brady go? I'm sitting here enjoying Jax's attention, but just because he's flirty and sweet doesn't mean he likes me. Brady *actually* likes me, and he *actually* wants me to be his girlfriend.

Jax taps me on the arm. "Your heart rate is spiking again. I don't want Charlotte coming back and busting my balls." When I dare a glance at him, his beautiful blue eyes look concerned. He nods toward my phone. "Message from your boyfriend?" He sits forward in his chair and rests his elbows on his knees.

"Oh, Brady? No. He's not my boyfriend. Not really." I rub my face. "Or not anymore. I don't know."

"Is it because of you or him? The reason why you're not together."

I bury my attention in my lap. "Uh, because of me."

He doesn't say anything for a while. "So you broke up with him?"

Shaking my head slowly, I say, "No, I didn't break up with him. You have to be together to break up."

Jax seems to think about this for a minute. "But he wanted more?"

"Yes. But I didn't feel right about it."

"What do you mean?"

My lips purse as I think of how to explain. "Brady knew I didn't feel that way about him—I was honest from the beginning—but he still wanted to give it a shot even though I've been trying to get over someone else." I don't look up. I can't. I'm afraid Jax will see straight through me. But it feels good to get this off my chest in some small way. "Anyway, I think he gave up because he texted that he met someone, and I was about to write him back when you decided to add some excitement to my afternoon and run me over."

Jax doesn't laugh. "What are you gonna tell him?"

I rub the side of my head where a swollen lump throbs. "To go out with her. That I want him to be happy."

"But you don't sound excited about it."

My shoulders slump. "In my heart it feels like the right thing to do—to let him go—but I'm upset with myself for not moving on, for not being able to try things out with Brady, because he's been a great friend despite my hang-ups, and I know he cares about me." I sigh, my fingers fidgeting with the strip of medical tape that binds the IV to my wrist. "But if he found someone, I don't want to be the reason he can't be with her."

"Even if it makes you unhappy?"

When I look up at him, I'm struck by how we can have this conversation even though there's so much between us that Jax doesn't even know exists. But maybe we can be friends. Maybe this is what I should have wanted with him all along. And I guess friendship starts with honesty.

"Do I want Brady—who's become a great friend and is totally gorgeous—worshipping at my feet because I can have him there? Because having his attention would be good for my ego? That sounds pretty shitty to me. I may suck at relationships, but at the very least, I can be a decent person, a decent friend."

"Is he that guy I met? The one with all the tattoos?"

I nod, thinking about how Brady consoled me while those two girls threw themselves all over Jax.

"He seemed really into you."

Another sigh escapes me. "I know."

I only wish Brady were the one I wanted.

CHAPTER TWENTY-ONE

- Jax -

She's so fucking cute. I know I shouldn't be staring at her while she sleeps, but my chair is two inches from her bed, so I blame the layout of the hospital furniture.

Dani's hair is pulled into a tangled ponytail. The pink streaks make her seem like some ethereal creature rather than a girl. I don't get how she can look so stunning when my two-ton vehicle plowed into her a few hours ago.

A hand grabs my shoulder, and I flinch. Turning around, I see Nick. "Jesus, you scared me."

"Sorry, man." He has the good sense to whisper so he doesn't wake Dani. Nick grabs another chair and sits next to me. His eyebrows are knitted tight on his forehead. "You're so lucky that girl said this was her fault."

"She has a name, dickhead."

He rolls his eyes. "Well, I told Coach *Dani's* version of what happened, and I think you're going to be okay."

"Who gives a shit about that? I almost killed her."

He looks at me like I'm a whack job. "Yeah, I caught that. I was there, remember? Don't be an idiot and say you don't care this situation almost got your sorry ass kicked off the soccer team your senior year, right before the championship game."

I don't say anything. It's pointless to argue with Nick. He eats, sleeps and drinks soccer twenty-four hours a day, seven days a week. He doesn't get why I don't care about it anymore. But if I'm being honest, I haven't cared about anything in a long time. Sure, I'll have great games—I push the fuck out of myself—but it's all muscle memory, like my body is propelling itself toward this goal because it has nothing else.

"Shit, dude, you could have been arrested," he says.

Okay, that would have sucked.

Nick runs his hand over the stubble on his chin. "Can we go now? I brought her stuff."

The reaction in my gut is immediate. "I can't leave her."

His expression evolves from shock to frustration. "What about the trip? The guys have already left."

I shrug. "So go. No one is stopping you."

"But you paid for it."

As if I care. "No worries. Enjoy."

Nick shakes his head at me like I'm some screwup. We sit there for a minute, and I watch the IV drip into Dani's arm. He motions toward the bed. "Is she going to be okay?"

"Yeah. Nothing is broken. Just a lot of bruising and swelling. Maybe a strained tendon in her knee, and you know that hurts like a bitch. They wanna keep her tonight to make sure the swelling doesn't get any worse, but it looks like she can go home tomorrow."

"Okay, so why don't you join us once they release her?"

I stare at him like he's a dumbass. "She lives in a four-story walk-up. All of her roommates have gone home for Thanksgiving, and Dani's from Chicago. I can't ditch her."

He raises his hands, his question evident.

"I thought I'd bring her back to our place for a few days until my sister gets back from her trip."

At that, his eyebrow tilts up.

I huff out a frustrated breath. "Get that fucking look off your face, Nick. She's a friend. I. Ran. Her. Over. I don't think looking out for her for a couple of days is that outrageous."

But this is the strangest part… I get the feeling she'd do the same for me.

* * *

Dani talks in her sleep. It's more of a mumble, but it's endearing nonetheless. At one point she opens her eyes, and when she sees me, a huge smile breaks on her face. "I've missed you, Jax. I wish you'd remember." Her eyelashes flutter shut, and she whispers, "You're so pretty."

I chuckle as she snuggles back into her covers. Later, she tells me something about visiting with the Cookie Monster. Yeah, the nurse gave her some serious drugs before bedtime.

In the morning, I wake up half hunched over her bed. I try not to groan as I sit up because I know the sore muscles in my back are nothing compared to what Dani is going through.

That's when I realize I've been sleeping close to her injured leg. My head jerks to look at her. She's already awake.

"Shit, Dani. I didn't mean to collapse on your bed like that. Did I hurt you?"

"I'm okay." She smiles as her eyes pass over me. "You have a waffle pattern on your cheek from my blanket."

My fingers reach up to find criss-cross indentations on my skin. I grin. "Adds to my charm, no?"

She rolls her eyes at me and laughs.

"How long have you been awake?" I ask as I stretch to try to regain some circulation in my extremities.

"Half an hour maybe."

The door swings open behind me and a new nurse shuffles in.

"Happy Thanksgiving, Danielle. I'm Carol."

Dani returns the greeting, but she suddenly looks sad. God, it sucks she's stuck here. I wish I could get her home.

Carol checks her vitals and rushes in and out of the room a few times. Finally, she returns with a clipboard.

"I have some good news. The doctor is pleased with your recovery so far, and since you had a great night and responded well to the meds, you get to go home today." She pauses to frown. "You must be a pretty healthy girl to begin with. Are you an athlete? My guess is you're a runner."

Dani shakes her head slowly. "I used to be a gymnast, but it's been a while."

"Well, you're in great shape, so I bet you'll be up and about in no time. That knee of yours might hurt for a little while, but at least you can recover at home. Do you have anyone who can help you? You'll need a hand to get around."

"I, uh—"

"Yeah, she's staying with me. I'll take care of her."

Carol's face squishes around her eyes as she smiles broadly. I turn to look at Dani and notice her mouth is hanging open.

"Jax, I—"

"You're staying with me over break until your roommates get back."

"Wonderful," Carol says, turning back to Dani. "I need to show you how to put on your brace and clean up your cuts." She shuffles around and brings over some supplies and shows me how to apply the different meds. It's hard to watch Dani flinch in pain as the brace gets strapped on, but she's a trooper and never complains.

The nurse taps her pen on Dani's leg. "Only use this brace if you're moving around for the first few days. It's better to keep it off to maintain circulation. So while you're kicking back on the couch eating some Thanksgiving leftovers tonight, just brace your leg with pillows. Once the swelling goes down, you can keep the brace on longer. And don't forget that you'll need to see the doctor in a week."

Carol turns to me while she clicks her pen. "All right, son, if you're taking care of her this week, you can get started by getting her dressed while I finish her paperwork."

Dani's eyes widen as she stares at me. Guess we're letting this boyfriend charade go on a little longer. Fine by me.

The nurse leaves, and I walk over to Dani's luggage.

"Jax, you really don't have to do this. I know I can't make it up all those stairs at my place, but I can stay at a hotel for a few—"

"No way." I place her bag on the edge of her bed. "Don't argue with me."

She nibbles her lower lip. "Don't you have a trip to go on or something? I thought, I thought you were going with those girls."

I stop moving, frustrated with myself for being such a royal dick last weekend and trying to make her jealous. Turning toward her, I wait until her eyes meet mine. "The trip isn't important, and neither are those girls. In fact, I was in the middle of canceling plans with them when our accident happened." I run my hand through my hair. "Trust me when I say that this is the least I can do after you saved my ass yesterday." I unzip her bag. "Okay, what do you need? Maybe sweats and a t-shirt? That's a big brace, so I don't think you'll want jeans. You can clean up when we get back to my condo. I have a huge tub, and you can take a long bath."

She grabs my hand. "Thank you. You're… so sweet."

My chest somehow constricts and expands at the same time. I laugh. "Yeah, well, we'll just let that be our little secret."

I help scoot her to the edge of the bed. She winces and groans a few times, but we take it slowly until her toes hit the floor.

"I take it you like pink, huh?"

She giggles, the sound somehow making me feel lighter. "How can you tell?"

"Hmm." I stare down at her feet, which are remarkably pretty. "Hot pink toenails, pink tips in your hair… and that room of yours looks like a bottle of Pepto-Bismol exploded."

She's wrapped in my arms as I get her to balance against the bed, but she pulls back to look at me.

"When have you seen my room?"

"I've only seen it from the living room, but the color is hard to miss." I just like giving her a hard time. Her room is actually covered in art with graffiti-like pieces everywhere. She's fucking cool as shit.

I reach down to help her pull up a pair of sweatpants under her gown before I grab a t-shirt. "The Cure?" The fabric is soft, like it's been worn a million times.

"Don't you dare give me shit about The Cure."

She looks so serious that I laugh, making her smile. "All right, Dandelion, why don't I turn you so that you're facing the bed? You can brace yourself with your uninjured leg, and that way we can drop your gown and pull on your shirt without me getting an eyeful. Not that I mind, but I'm trying to be a good guy, which, as you know, is not my forté."

She gets a playful look on her face and nods. I reposition her to face away from me and she shrugs, letting the gown fall. At first, all I can do is stare at that beautiful tattoo, but as my eyes travel across her bare skin, I freeze.

"Jesus." My hand reaches out to touch her before I even realize what I'm doing. "I'm so fucking sorry."

Angry purple and black bruises cover her shoulder, back and hip, disappearing under the fabric of her sweats. Her head tilts slowly.

Dani's voice is soft, reassuring. "Jax… I bruise easily. I'm okay. I might be little, but I'm pretty tough." She swallows. "Now help me get dressed before I flash an orderly."

I don't know how she does this, tries to make me feel better when this was my fault. I clear my throat, needing a minute.

"Trust me, it would make his day," I say, trying to get my shit together.

She laughs, and I relax a little, enough to admire her lean frame.

I hold the shirt above her head and help her maneuver it on. When she's dressed, I turn her back to face me and pull her hair out from the collar of her shirt.

She may have just been hit by a car, but fuck, she's gorgeous. Her face is free from makeup, and she's got that banging girl-next-door thing going on that has me wishing she weren't my sister's roommate.

I start to pull away when she grabs my t-shirt and pulls me to her until her head rests on my chest. My arms automatically go around her, and my nose buries in her hair. She smells like apples, like spring, like possibility. This seems so familiar that I practically choke on the feeling of déjà vu.

Dani whispers, "Thank you," and I'm struggling to say something when the door swings open, and Carol waltzes back in.

"Aw. Aren't you two so cute?"

We pull away from each other. I look at Dani and grin, enjoying the pink staining her cheeks.

Yeah, she should definitely stay with me.

CHAPTER TWENTY-TWO

- Dani -

He called me Dandelion. I don't know why that nickname melted my heart, but I turned to mush the moment the word left his mouth. No one has called me that since I was a kid.

As Jax wheels me down the hall, a giant blue fuzzball gets my attention. "Look, Cookie Monster! I swear I saw him walking around last night."

Jax looks down the hall toward the children's ward and watches the life-sized character for a minute before turning back to me with the strangest expression on his face. I'm about to ask him what's wrong when his phone rings. After glancing at the caller ID, he groans.

The second he picks up, I hear an angry female voice yelling. At first, my heart sinks as I wonder if this is one of his girlfriends calling to complain about his change of plans. Several minutes later, he releases my wheelchair and leans against a pillar.

"Clem, I told you it was an accident." He covers the phone and whispers, "She says she's going to kick my ass for running over one of her friends."

I wave for him to hand over the call. She's still yelling when I put the phone to my ear. "Clem? They're giving me some really good drugs here, so don't yell at your brother. If I ever wanted a pill addiction, I'm well on my way."

She growls into the phone, "I am fucking killing

Jackson the next time I see him. I ask you to do us a favor, and this is how he repays you?"

"He's been taking good care of me, so don't be too hard on him." I try to keep my voice casual. Jax starts to wheel me down the hall as I brace myself for bumps.

"Good. Make him your bitch." Clem has a way with words.

I snort. "I don't know about that…" I laugh despite the fact that every turn sends little shockwaves of pain through my body as we head toward the parking garage.

After a brief silence, she sighs. "Dani, do you want me to come home? Gavin would totally understand if—"

"No. Definitely not. Go have fun with your amazing boyfriend and his family. I will not be the reason you come back." After a quick turn where I find myself gripping the armrest, I ask, "How's it going over there?"

Clem doesn't usually confide these sorts of details to me. I've gotten to know her because she'll vent to our other roommates, and I happen to be around when they hang out, so I'm surprised when she answers my question.

She lowers her voice just above a whisper. "It's fine, but I'm not used to all this getting-to-know-you shit. It makes me uncomfortable. Gavin is so outgoing and great with meeting people, and as we both know, I'm not. It makes me feel like I'm defective."

She always looks so put-together that you'd never know she struggles with anything.

"Clem, I realize I only met you three months ago, but when you let your guard down, it's hard not to love you. Let his family see the real you. Don't be afraid about their judgment. Otherwise, it'll be hard to relax. I find tequila works wonders. Or apple martinis."

"Or morphine," Jax says from behind me. I'm

wondering what that means, but I can't swivel my head around to look at him because my back is too stiff.

Clem sighs into my ear. "Thanks, Dani. Here you're the one mauled by a car, and you're giving me the pep talk."

"If you need to get in a better mood, we could go a few rounds of Out-Skank."

She blows out a breath. "Don't get me started with that game. The last thing I need is for the words 'cock monster' or 'cunt muffin' to come up in a text message while I'm having dinner with Gavin's family."

I break out laughing, which makes me catch my breath until the pain subsides. When I get off the phone, Jax is quiet as he wheels me through the long, white corridors of the hospital.

"You okay back there?" I call out.

"Yeah. Just thinking about how you're friends with my sister." Something about the tone of his voice is off. He sounds distant.

"Why do you sound funny?" I might as well really say what's on my mind.

I think the drugs the doctor gave me have lowered my inhibitions a little because I just want to be myself. I feel stupid for being so uptight around Jax these last few months.

That's what I realized yesterday as I was crashing into the pavement a few inches from the tires of Jax's BMW. My mom is right. Life is too short to have regrets. When I talk to her this weekend, I need to tell her that I understand.

Jax ignores my question so he can get the car, which Nick dropped off yesterday. He pulls up in front of me and opens the passenger door. I try to get out of the wheelchair but fail miserably.

"Don't try to do that alone. Here." He reaches over around my shoulders. "Are my hands okay here? I don't want to press anything that'll hurt."

"This works," I say, our faces inches apart.

He nods, his eyes passing over my face. I'm sure I look like hell, but I'm done being weird about him.

"If my morning breath kills you, at least we're already at a hospital."

He snickers before he scoops me up and helps me maneuver into his car. Once he's in the driver's seat, he turns to me with a grin. "First order of business. Food. Massive, massive amounts of food."

"Isn't everything closed? It's Thanksgiving."

"I've already done a little research and called in an order. I hope you're hungry." He pauses. "You're not a vegetarian or vegan or anything weird, are you?"

Chuckling, I answer, "Hell, no. Bring the meat."

He laughs. "Great. Because I can't stand girls who eat a leaf and call it a meal."

"That makes two of us. Besides, do I look like a girl who eats that way?"

Jax starts to say something but stops himself. I nudge his elbow with mine. "Come on. Don't be weird. Say what's on your mind."

The corner of his mouth tilts up while he looks for traffic. "I was gonna say you look perfect, but I didn't want it to go to your head."

Warm fuzzies build in my chest, and I remind myself that he's just being nice.

And you know what? I've decided that's okay too. There's nothing wrong with being nice. I've hated that description for so long, but I'm done apologizing for who I am.

#OwnIt

CHAPTER TWENTY-THREE

- Jax -

"You want some smashed potatoes?" Dani asks.

Her leg is propped up on the couch, and like the gentleman I'm trying to be, I've even given her full command of the remote control. An array of Thanksgiving food is spread out on the coffee table—everything from turkey and stuffing to green bean casserole and pie.

"Did you just say *smashed* potatoes?"

She grins, light beaming in her eyes. "Maybe." The little giggle that escapes her mouth is so fucking adorable, I could kiss her. "That's what my mom and I always call them." I feign disappointment, which makes her smile widen even more. "Come on. You know you want to call them smashed potatoes. Give in to the Force."

"Are you making a veiled *Star Wars* reference?"

"Of course."

"So that means you're not a Trekkie?"

"No way. *Star Trek* is for geeks. *Star Wars* is for cool people."

I've never seen her this way. Relaxed and funny. Usually, she's quiet around me. Careful, even.

Rubbing the scruff on my chin, I ask, "How intense are those drugs you're taking right now?"

She laughs, grabbing the remote control and flipping through the channels. "I'll be honest. They're pretty good. I can see how addictions form. A little something to take the edge off, and bam! I'm a meth-head with bad teeth and a dealer named Jerry. Ooh! You have hardcore sports channels. Okay, do you want to watch some Pac 10 featuring USC and Arizona or should we go pro with the Bears and Cowboys? I'm thinking pro because Daren's game is on Saturday, and I want to save my college ball enthusiasm for BC. And then we definitely have to catch the Bulls tonight at eight."

She turns to me, and the sight of this gorgeous girl on my couch asking me which game I want to watch on Thanksgiving practically gives me a semi.

"You like sports?" I ask.

"Yes. Actually, no." Her eyes widen dramatically. "I *love* sports. Like, an all-consuming passion kind of love."

All I can do is stare. "Who are you again?" Not only am I fucking thrilled I'm not stuck here watching *The Notebook* or some other crappy-assed romance, this girl actually wants to watch a game.

She laughs like this is not a big deal. "Thanksgiving means three things." She holds up her hand to count. "Vast quantities of carbs, snoozing and sports. In no particular order." She takes a deep breath and lets her head sink into my leather couch. "I don't know… Almost dying has a way of putting things in perspective." Her eyes shift toward me. "Who knows? Maybe I'll even thank you some day for trying to kill me."

Dipping her fork into a pile of stuffing, she brings the plate closer to her mouth so she doesn't have to lean over to shovel it in. I'm not used to seeing girls eat in front of me, and the fact that she seems so excited about the meal makes me grin.

Pointing at me, she says, "I want to hear about all the trouble you and Daren got into as kids. Your sister told me a story or two. Like, did you guys really cover her bed in worms when you were ten?"

I shake my head. This girl is cracking me up. "Did Clem bother to tell you that she started the war of worms?"

"War of worms?" She raises a suspicious eyebrow at me before she scoops up a mouthful of macaroni and cheese, moaning about how good it is. I find myself forgetting about my story as her mouth wraps around the fork.

Focus, asshole.

Scrubbing my face, I try to gather my thoughts. "Uh, there's a creek that runs behind our neighborhood, and the three of us had gone fishing, which was idiotic because there was barely two feet of water. Anyway, Clem took a handful of worms and shoved them down the back of my shirt."

"That seems ballsy."

"She may or may not have been trying to get back at me for some other brotherly prank. But the worms down the shirt meant war. And Clem likes her things the way she likes her things. She's all organized and shit, and she hated me touching her stuff. So that's when I came up with the plan that Daren helped me execute."

"So you covered her bed with worms, and when she came home, she freaked?"

I snicker. "Actually, she was *in the bed* when we covered it in worms."

Dani's eyes widen and she covers her mouth to muffle a laugh.

My laughter grows. "Yeah, payback is a bitch."

"Oooh, I definitely don't want to get on your bad side." Her eyes are playful, and I'm kind of mesmerized by the small flecks of gold that dance in her green irises.

Her phone buzzes with a series of texts, and she

reaches down to grab it. As she reads the one that popped up on the screen, her spine straightens. And then she laughs. Loudly.

"For a sec, I totally thought I was getting sexts from some random person." She snorts. Dani holds the phone to her face while she reads in a mocking tone, "Tiffany is very eager to relive last Thanksgiving. And she wants to suck on you like a lollipop." Her mouth makes a popping sound, and she giggles.

Holy shit.

She turns to me. Her eyes widen, and she stammers, "I'm so sorry. I didn't mean to read your message. Our phones are identical." She grabs the other one sitting on the coffee table and holds it next to the one in her hand to make a matching set.

Shifting in my seat, I feel like I should apologize for Tiffany, but Dani turns to me with a huge grin. "May I?" She waves my phone at me. "I want to Out-Skank her."

I swallow. "I'm sorry. What?"

Dani laughs like this isn't weird at all. "Out-Skank. It's this game all of my roommates play. We try to see who can send the dirtiest messages. Usually, there's a prize." She takes my silence to mean I'm on board.

Have I been abducted by aliens? Or is this incredibly hot girl on my couch about to sext another chick?

She holds up my cell, and I swipe my password automatically, barely taking my eyes off her. Then I watch as Dani's fingers move across the screen.

She chews on her lip. "The irony here is that I've never actually sexted with a guy, but I've gotten pretty good at this game because my roommates are all total pervs." She looks up at me. "Excluding your sister of course." Then she winks and ducks down to finish sexting Tiffany.

My head is spinning with a thousand things I want to say, but I'm lost in the way this girl takes everything in stride, the way she makes light of difficult situations, how she somehow manages to make everything okay.

"There. That will get you a hot date." She pushes send and sinks back down into the couch with a self-satisfied sigh. "Okay, Jackson, I'm thinking you need to teach me how to play poker. I'm too old to not know."

I'm still thinking about the sexting.

"Jax?" Her brow wrinkles, forming a v in her perfectly smooth skin.

"Dani, what did you write? In your message?"

She smirks like she's some kind of sex goddess and lowers her voice. "I, I mean *you*, told her that you would love to sink between her thighs and lick—"

My eyes close. I might be having an aneurysm. Blood roars in my ears, my dick, and my temples. All at once.

Dani nudges me. "Are you okay?"

Glad there's a half-eaten plate of food in my lap, I shift slowly to make room for my third leg.

"Yeah. So poker? Is that what you wanted me to teach you?"

Because Dani does not want to have sex with me. Definitely not sex. She's a good girl. A nice person. She's just messing around and having fun because she's on some serious pain medication. Teaching her how to play poker is a good distraction.

Fucking get a grip, dickhead.

"What's the sudden interest in the game?" I ask, taking a deep breath.

She rests her elbow up on the arm of the couch and waves toward me. "'Cause if I ever play strip poker, I want to win. Duh."

Yeah. My distraction technique isn't working.

CHAPTER TWENTY-FOUR

- Dani -

All the awkwardness that had built up between Jax and me over the last few months has melted in a gluttony of turkey, pro sports and painkillers. We're both slouched down on the couch, flicking bottle caps into a bowl while a post-game rundown on ESPN plays in the background.

"Favorite sports team," he says as he flips one in. It's a question, but there's no inflection in his voice because he's concentrating on sinking a cap. I'm starting to realize his intensity stems from always wanting to win. It's there, beneath his skin, like a fever. It's what must make him such a phenomenal soccer player without appearing to try.

I quirk my eyebrow at him. "Chicago."

"Yeah? Which team?"

"Teams, plural. The Bears, Bulls and Cubs—the trifecta." I flick my thumb and the cap sails wide, garnering a grin from Soccer Boy. "Don't look so damn pleased with yourself. We're playing a game that drunks attempt in dark alleys."

Jax chokes back a laugh before he asks, "What's wrong with the White Sox?"

I scoff. "You've never been to Chicago, huh?" My next attempt lands in the bowl.

He shakes his head.

"Pff." My mock disgust garners another laugh. "North Siders are Cubs fans. South Siders are Sox fans. Although

I had a neighbor once who liked the Sox, but he was an anomaly."

"So you're a Cubs fan even if that means you'll never win the World Series?"

"Winning isn't everything." I shoot him a dirty look. "It took the Red Sox almost ninety years to win one. You'd think you'd be a little more humble."

"Humility is for suckers." Chuckling, he tilts his head, his handsome face close to mine, and lowers his voice. "We should ice your knee." I can feel his breath, hot on my cheek. It smells like pumpkins and nutmeg and just a hint of cinnamon. And at this moment, I freaking love pumpkins.

Jax unfolds his long body from the couch, and I take a moment to appreciate his lean, muscular build. He looks every part the seasoned athlete. It's in the rhythm of his movement, the way his muscles look coiled tight, ready to spring. He's graceful for a man. Confident. Relaxed.

And sexy as hell.

I'm certainly enjoying having all of his attention. He's been bringing me food, reminding me to take my meds, and propping up my leg. I never would've imagined he'd be this way, so thoughtful, so gentle.

The thought crosses my mind that I should tell him what happened on his birthday. I almost feel guilty that we have this history he obviously doesn't remember. But what would I say? *We hooked up, but I never told you my name, so I can't blame you for running off with another girl?*

Yeah, not happening.

I clamp down on that idea because if I start obsessing about that night, I'll start acting weird, and we've been having such a good time together. If nothing else, we make great friends.

His movement in the kitchen draws my attention, and

I stare unnoticed. I force myself to turn away to keep from drooling. I'd hate to drool on this couch. I'm sure it costs more than my all of my Earthly possessions combined.

To say his place is decked out is an understatement. Sleek furniture, marble countertops, a fireplace, a huge flatscreen TV and every kind of game console imaginable make his place the bachelor pad of the century. I knew he was loaded, but his condo is ridiculous.

I'm surprised, but I shouldn't be. Jax is heir to the Avery throne. That's how his sister describes it. She says one day he'll be "richer than God."

But I know what Clem's been through. Her book lays it out. Their parents never gave her or Jax the time of day.

And isn't love worth more than money?

I know I'm rich in ways the Avery twins have never experienced. Because my mom would throw herself in front of an oncoming train for me.

Picking up my cell, I dial her number.

"Happy Thanksgiving, darling," she says, sounding out of breath.

"Mom, what's wrong? Why are you breathing so hard?"

She laughs. "I just ran in the door. You'll never believe how much food Susan made today."

I let her talk, comforted by hearing about the usual drama among her tight group of friends. When Jax returns with an ice pack and a bag of popcorn, I mouth "Mom" and he nods and heads back into the kitchen.

My mom asks, "How are you feeling, honey? Is your knee better?"

"The swelling has gone down a bit. Jax is making me ice it every hour for fifteen minutes, which is the schedule his trainer makes him do when he sprains an ankle. I think it's working."

She's quiet. "Sounds like he's taking good care of you."

There's more in her comment than I care to address while Jax is ten feet away. "Definitely. So listen," I say, trying to distract her from what I know she wants to ask, "I think you've been right about art. I should switch my major. I don't know why I haven't done it sooner."

Yes, I do. I didn't want to be gone from her for so long, but she's been healthy. She's in remission. She doesn't need me shadowing her like a frightened child.

I continue. "It means summer school to catch up on a few credits, but I think my professor can help me do an independent study that would help me cover more ground quickly."

There's that silence again. Panic starts to rise in me, but then she says, "Excellent. I'm so glad to hear that. What changed your mind?"

"A silver BMW." I laugh, and she simply says, "Yes."

I know she understands. Almost dying has a way of crystalizing things that should be obvious.

I look to the empty seat next to me and wonder if Jax is another one of those obvious things in my life that I should simply understand. But I tried to close myself off to him all semester, and that just made me want him more. I don't know that our time together will lead to anything more than friendship, but right now, that feels pretty good.

* * *

A few hours later, I'm ready to knock out, but I feel gross, the stale scent of the hospital clinging to my skin. I look over to Jax, who is sprawled out on the couch next to me. "Hey, would you mind if I took a shower? I can probably balance better now that I'm almost due for another painkiller."

He rubs his chin, the scruff making a scratching sound. "Sure thing. Let me help you."

"I can do it. I mean, that's what the crutches are for, right?" His dubious expression makes me snicker. "I'm a big girl. If I need help, I'll ask, okay?"

Jax stretches out before he stands up and motions for me to get up. My brace is already on my leg, and I lower it slowly and then grab his outstretched hand.

"Easy, Dandelion. After icing your knee all day, it's going to feel better than it should. Now is the time you could most easily reinjure yourself."

Ignoring his new nickname for me, I roll my eyes. "Yes, sir."

He's given me a nickname.

I let him slowly pull me up, and when I'm balanced on my good leg, he grips my waist to steady me. My nose is inches from his chest, and I can't help but think of the club and the way he pressed me to his body.

Jesus, he smells good. Clean, crisp. A faint scent of cologne and sexy boy. I've never been into how a guy smelled before, but standing here trying to sniff him covertly has me itching to get closer.

I stare at my feet, pretending to concentrate on keeping my balance as he hands me my crutches. By the time I get to the spacious bathroom, which is nestled in the back of his bedroom, he's already set my small suitcase on the vanity.

"I'll hang out in my room so I can hear you if you need anything." He smiles, and I swear it reaches into my body and makes my stomach flip flop.

On the way out, he closes the door.

God, I'm having fun with him. My leg is banged up, my body is sore as hell, and I can't remember feeling this good.

Everything about hanging out together has been so easy, but I remind myself he's doing this because he doesn't want his sister to be pissed at him. And he feels bad about hitting me with his car. Those thoughts help keep my attraction to him in check as I try to focus on how I'll clean up without killing myself.

I sit on the closed seat of the toilet and pull off my leg brace, t-shirt and bra. It takes forever, but I manage to eventually tug off my sweats and undies until all I'm wearing are my purple bruises.

Even though I'd love to soak in the tub, I don't think I'd be able to get myself in and out of it, so I decide to play it safe with a shower. I hang a thick terrycloth towel on a hook and reach in to turn on the water. Stretching out this far makes all my muscles ache, a lot, and as I flinch in pain, one of my crutches clatters to the floor. This isn't a good idea, I realize too late.

The bang on the door scares the crap out of me, and I nearly lose my grip on the corner of the shower.

Jax's voice bellows from his bedroom. "Dani, are you okay? Let me come in. I'll close my eyes. I swear."

I'm barely staying upright, my heart pounding. The door creaks open.

"I won't look," Jax calls out.

I glance at him, and he has a hand in front of his face so that he can only see the floor in front of him as he moves toward me. In two large strides, he's at my side.

"I…I lost my grip." My voice shakes, and I suddenly feel so weak.

"It's okay, babe. I gotcha." While he keeps one hand

in front of his face, his other arm goes around me. "Hang on to me."

My hand wraps around his neck, bringing my naked body closer to his. Jax tilts his head away, and I realize it's so he doesn't see me.

"I'm gonna help you into the shower, and I'll stand out here. I want you to hold on to my hand while you're in there, and if you get in trouble again, I can keep you steady."

His reassurance makes my heart slow down, and I nod.

My hand trembles as I step in. I'm holding Jax's arm in a death grip as I limp closer to the shower head. When I start to wobble, my free hand grabs onto one of the knobs, accidentally twisting it and making cold water shoot out over me. I shriek and try to keep my balance while fumbling to adjust the water.

That's when I about fall on my ass. Except Jax is there and wraps an arm around me to hold me upright while he turns up the hot water.

"Shit. I'm so sorry." I'm shaking. Exhausted. Embarrassed. I don't like needing people to do things for me. Especially in this state.

His eyes meet mine, and I'm expecting some lewd expression, but all I see is concern. "You scared me," he whispers. He has my naked body pressed against him. He's fully clothed—the only naked parts of him are his feet. His t-shirt and jeans are drenched, clinging to him and showing off his perfect physique. "Is your knee okay?"

Not able to quite find the words, I nod. His lips pull up into a relieved smile. "Okay, so let me turn you away otherwise I will ogle you shamelessly. This way I can help you wash your hair."

Nervous laughter spills from my lips, and I turn so I'm facing away from him.

He chuckles. "Do you really want to use my shampoo or do you have some girly shit in your bag you'd prefer?"

"Damn it. I totally forgot my toiletries." Frustrated that I'm being so spacey, I sigh. "Yeah, I have shampoo and conditioner, but they're in my suitcase. Don't worry about it. Just use whatever."

"If you can stand perfectly still for a minute, I can go get it."

"Jax, don't bother. It's fine. I don't care."

Ignoring me, he places both of my hands against the tile, and when he's happy I'm steady, he steps out of the shower. A few minutes later, he returns, this time shirtless.

Holy sweet baby Jesus. He's ripped. Tight, corded muscles wrap around his arms and chest, and one very drool-worthy six-pack dips down into his low-rise jeans.

He's even more sinful than I remembered.

His eyes meet mine, and I bite my lip to keep from gawking. I turn back around and hear the sound of a bottle opening. Then the scent of apples perfumes the air as he lathers it.

"This smells great, by the way." His voice is soft and so, so sexy.

I close my eyes, trying not to get turned on by the way his hands work through my long hair. His fingers are firm and massage my scalp. After several long minutes, I'm so relaxed, I moan.

Mortification spreads through me as I realize how sexual that sounded. Trying to play it off, I start babbling. "Thank you so much. I didn't realize I was so sore until I tried to do more than veg on your couch. You know…"

I yammer on all through him rinsing my hair, applying

conditioner, and rinsing again. Who knows what I said. I could have told him I was Rumpelstiltskin here to grant him three wishes.

What I do know is that maintaining a friendship with Jax when I'm buck naked is a tad difficult.

As soon as he turns off the water, he wraps the fluffy towel around me before he helps me maneuver to a small bench next to the vanity. He runs his finger gently along the lines of the tattoo on my shoulder.

"It's the North Star," I say, without him needing to ask.

"In case you get lost?"

I nod. "Something like that."

"It's beautiful." He clears his throat. "Can I get you anything else before I step out?"

I don't look at him before I shake my head. "No, I'm good." Finally, I get the guts to make eye contact. "Thank you. I'm sorry you had to get wet."

His eyebrows pull tight. "I'm cool. I'll be out there getting some clothes together so I can jump in the shower when you're done. Call me if you need anything." He smiles tightly and steps out.

Damn. There's suddenly so much tension between us. I wonder if he's pissed his bathroom is covered in water. Maybe I can wipe up some of this mess before he returns for his shower.

As though he's reading my mind, I hear him yell, "Don't you dare try to clean in there. Just get dressed."

Goodness, he can be bossy. I roll my eyes. Of course, a bossy Jax is pretty darn sexy too.

CHAPTER TWENTY-FIVE

- Jax -

Don't screw this up. Don't screw this up.

A dozen different emotions have taken residence in my body. One minute, I want to push Danielle up against the door and fuck her senseless, and the next I want to construct a ten-foot wall to protect her from the very vivid fantasies looping through my brain.

But my overriding realization is that I need to get away from her before I do something stupid like molest her.

When I step into the bathroom, I strip off my sopping wet jeans and jump into the shower where the first order of business is to deal with my rock-hard boner. Fortunately, Dani seemed so tired, I don't think she spotted my wood. It took everything in me not to rock myself against her gorgeous ass.

Yes, I saw it. No, I didn't mean to. I kept my eyes up, but a man has peripheral vision, and I happen to have excellent peripheral vision.

I was fine—keeping my eyes up and off her nakedness like I promised—until she nearly wiped out, spraying herself with cold water, and then I saw everything. All that beautiful, bare skin. The fine lines of her back and waist. *Her nipple piercings.*

Fuck me. Nipple piercings.

The strangest thing is how familiar it all seemed. Almost as though I knew they'd be there even though they're the last thing you'd expect. Sure, I've banged lots of women with all sorts of tastes, but I've never met anyone as sweet and innocent as Danielle with piercings like that.

And right now, all I want to do is take them in my mouth and tug. Hard.

With visuals like that, I'm in and out of the shower in record time. I throw on some flannel pajama bottoms and a t-shirt before I open the door.

"Dani?"

After a quick walk-through of my condo, I don't see her anywhere. But the sound of retching draws my attention to the kitchen pantry where Danielle is hunched over the trash can.

"Shit. Are you okay?" Pulling back her hair with one hand, I reach over and grab a paper towel with my other and hand it to her.

She wipes off her mouth and turns slowly to me. Tears are streaming down her face, and I decide there is nothing worse on this planet than seeing this girl cry.

"What happened?" I cradle her face in my hand and brush away the tears with my thumbs.

"I… I took my meds but I… forgot to eat something. I just wasn't hungry, and the meds made me nauseous."

Before the words are out, she jerks away and throws up again into the trash.

After a few minutes, I walk her back to my room and settle her onto my bed. I place a small wastebasket next to her on the floor and prop up a few pillows behind her back and head into the kitchen.

I call out to her, "Don't fall asleep. I'll be right back."

Dani may not feel like it right now, but she needs to eat or she'll throw up again. I come back with two bowls of my favorite cereal.

"Lucky Charms?" she asks as she peers in.

"Breakfast of champions." I glance at the clock. "Or in this case, a late dinner."

We sit in silence, and I watch her slowly eat around the marshmallows. Finally, she has a pile of color on one side of the bowl as she finishes the rest of the cereal.

"I could have gotten you something else if you didn't like this."

She smirks. "No way. I just save the best part for last." Then she scoops up a big spoonful and shoves it in her mouth. When she swallows, she gets a serious expression on her face. "Jax, you must have things to do this weekend. You don't need to babysit me. You have a life. Go do what you need to do, run errands, go on dates, whatever. Don't feel like you have to—"

"Stop. There are only two things I need to do for the next several days. One is to make sure you get better. The other is work out or I'll turn into a big fattie."

"Please! I could cut myself on your six-pack." She smiles at me from under those long dark lashes and then drops her eyes to peer into her bowl.

Ignoring her display of shyness—which is cute as hell—I say, "But I can work out from home. I have all the equipment I need in my spare bedroom. So when you get up in the morning, that's probably where I'll be."

"Okay." Dani takes another small bite and then sets down the bowl. After I help her wobble to the bathroom to brush her teeth, I set her down on the bed again.

She's still gripping my arms as she says, "I'm feeling kind of dizzy."

"It's your medicine. Your night dose is stronger. Here, lie down." I rearrange the pillows until she's comfortable. Truth be told, I don't like girls staying overnight, but seeing Danielle with her long, thick hair splayed out over my sheets has me reconsidering that.

"I feel bad taking your bed. I can crash on the couch."

"Don't be ridiculous." I duck into my closet and grab a sleeping bag and toss it on the floor. "I'd sleep on the couch, but you might get sick again, and I won't be able to hear you from the living room."

She frowns. "Tell me you're not sleeping on the floor."

"I'll be fine."

"Jax, you have a huge bed, and unless you're into groping invalids, I think I'm safe with you. C'mon."

She pats the mattress with the palm of her hand, and the one thing I know for sure is she's definitely not safe with me. Except the last thing I want to do is fuck up our friendship. I don't have friends who are girls, but in the last twenty-four hours, I've started thinking of Dani as one. So I will ignore how perfect that tank top looks on her right now—how I can see those hot-as-hell piercings and the way her sweats hang off her hips but fit snug against her ass—and be a good guy. Even if it kills me.

"Dani, I don't mind—"

"Get up here, Jax. Now."

Shit. Right now I want to tie her up and make her beg me to fuck her harder.

I laugh. "You're a feisty little thing."

"Don't I know it." Her head tilts back and her eyebrows lift as though she's challenging me to say no.

I can do this. I can sleep next to a gorgeous girl and not have sex with her, but first I need some good visuals to distract myself from the way her nipples are poking through that thin material.

Anchorman. Paul Rudd. My great-aunt Eunice and her chin hair.

Taking a deep breath, I crawl in next to Dani and

make sure to keep a comfortable distance. She sinks down into the pillows and sighs. "Thanks for taking care of me, Jax, but you're doing too good a job because I'm never going to want to leave."

My room smells like Dani and her shampoo. It reminds me of something, but I can't quite put my finger on it.

After a few minutes, her eyes close and her breathing slows.

I think she's asleep, but she mutters, "You're too sweet. And you look really good in those jeans." I grin, but before I can respond, she whacks me with her arm. "Did we eat pumpkin pie today? It's Thanksgiving, isn't it? I like turkeys. They have a waddle."

A waddle? Okay, here come her medicine-induced ramblings. I hold back the laugh that's dying to burst out of me.

She groans. "God, you looked great in the shower. And your bed is so comfortable. I bet you hear that a lot."

Aw, hell.

Then she whispers, "Lucky girls," before she knocks out.

Fuck.

Yeah, it's a long, *long* night. Dani sighs in her sleep and moans when she rolls over, little sounds that have me dying to press my body up against her. In the moonlight, her skin looks like porcelain. Against her dark hair, she looks like some kind of angel, floating on my bed with her hair covering all of my pillows. And when she whispers my name in the dark, it has me wanting her to stay long after her knee gets better.

When I wake up in the morning, her head is resting on my shoulder and her arm is wrapped around my waist.

She's nestled alongside me, her soft curves running all along my suddenly aching body.

Yeah. This friendship thing sucks.

CHAPTER TWENTY-SIX

- Dani -

The bed is empty when I get up in the morning. I can hear Jax running on the treadmill down the hall when I wobble into the kitchen. It's pretty early. Just barely 8:30.

Thinking about everything he's done for me since the accident makes me wish the last few months had been different somehow. Maybe I should've told him what happened on his birthday the first time we ran into each other at Ryan's, or maybe I shouldn't have avoided him all semester. I feel like I've wasted time hiding. From him. From me. In business school. Behind Brady.

I'm ready to just be me.

I'm not stupid enough to think Jax and I can be anything more than friends because it doesn't take a rocket scientist to see I'm not his type of girl, but I want to be a part of his life. I think about the conversation I overheard between him and his sister when he brought over that box of high school stuff. About what he's been through and the way his family neglects him. He might have tons of money and be popular and sexy, but I swear I see sadness behind his eyes—I've seen it there all fall—and part of me wants to do what I can to make it go away.

Using one crutch, I amble toward the stove and decide that all of Jax's awesomeness warrants some kind of reciprocation, and I'm guessing after a hard workout, he's going to be starving, so I decide to whip him up some breakfast. He clearly wasn't intending to be around this weekend because his cupboards are pretty bare, but I finally spot a box of pancake mix and a basket of fruit.

After settling on a stool, I set my crutch nearby as I make a big batch of my mom's favorite apple pancakes.

When Jax strolls down the hall forty-five minutes later, my decision to sit perched up high is called into question because I nearly tumble off when I see him. He's wearing a pair of running shorts, and that's it.

He's glistening, drenched in sweat, which highlights all the peaks and valleys of his perfectly sculpted body. His hair is going every which way, and he looks like some Calvin Klein model who hopped off a billboard. My memories of him half naked did not do him justice.

I close my mouth and look away.

"I, uh, made you some breakfast. If you're hungry."

Breathe. Push air through your lungs and breathe.

Clenching my thighs together, I try to ignore the sudden hammering between my legs. His steps sound behind me until I feel his body next to me.

"You made me pancakes?" He sounds so surprised, I snort.

"Yeah. It was rough. I had to actually stir."

His laughter fills the room before he plants a kiss on the top of my head. "You're perfect."

I don't get a chance to respond before he says he's going to jump in the shower and will be out in ten.

It takes me every one of those ten minutes to get a hold of myself. I'm more than glad my panties can't talk. Because they want Jax. Now.

When he comes out of his bedroom, he's wearing jeans and another t-shirt, but the water droplets on his neck remind me of what he must have looked like a moment ago in the shower. And dear God, do I want to run my hands over that body.

"I hope you like apples." I push a plate in his direction as I grab my crutch with one hand and my food with the other.

He looks down at the pancakes, curious.

"I shredded apples into the batter. If you don't like it, I can make you something else."

"I'm sure I'll love them."

We sit at the table, and his beaming smile dazes me.

As he drizzles syrup over the stack, he licks his lips. "Pancakes are my favorite food."

I watch him take a bite. As he chews, he moans. "Jesus, Dani, these are good." He shovels in another big bite. And there's another moan.

Pancakes shouldn't make me think about sex, but all this moaning makes me want to crawl up him naked.

He shovels in a few more bites and says, "How about you come over every weekend and make these for me?" His enthusiasm for something so simple makes me melt even more.

"If you ate pancakes every weekend, you'd get tired of them."

"Not a fucking chance."

I can't help the lust-filled smile on my face.

He waves toward his plate with his fork. "Besides my sister, you're the only girl to ever make me pancakes, and these are better. Hers were always a little burned, but don't tell her I said that."

There it is. He thinks of me like his sister. Probably a little sister since I'm the size of a hobbit. Trying not to let my smile falter, I nod. "It's my mom's recipe. I can't take credit."

I'm not hurt. I'm not. I'm good. We're friends. I can do this.

Grabbing my fork and knife, I slather on a little butter

and then carve a grid into my food before I pour syrup into all the nooks and crannies.

"Whatcha doing there, tiger?" he asks with a cocked eyebrow.

Ah, the disdain for my method rears its ugly head.

"I'm going to ignore your mockery and let you take a bite so you can see there's a method to my madness."

He eyes me suspiciously, like I've committed sacrilege for not simply drowning my pancakes in a river of syrup.

I spear through three perfect squares and hold it out to him. "Here. Tell me this isn't better."

He opens his mouth, and I watch the food disappear between those beautiful lips.

"Oh my God. You're right. This is amazing." Jax stares down at his stack, unsure why our food tastes different.

"Cutting the grid allows the syrup and butter to drench all of those hard-to-reach places." *The way I want you to drench all of my hard-to-reach places.*

Stop, Dani!

After closing my eyes to clear my head, I slide my plate over to him and take his half-empty one away. "I have a ton more in the kitchen. Take mine."

He looks at me like I'm an alien, and then he laughs. "You make me pancakes *and* cut my food into bite-sized pieces."

Nice, Danielle. Now he sees you as his mom. #Awesome

"Shut up and eat."

As he scarfs down three servings of pancakes, we chat about yesterday's games, transitioning seamlessly from football to basketball and then soccer. In a moment of silence, his brow furrows. "How's your knee?"

"So much better. All that ice yesterday really helped because it hardly feels swollen now. It didn't hurt that much when I got up, but I put my brace on anyway."

"That's good. We'll ice it again today." The way his eyes pass over me makes me squirm, and my eyes drop to my plate. He clears his throat. "Dani, I'm really glad you're feeling better. When I saw you on the pavement, I was so afraid your injuries were more serious."

I get it. This is Jax making sure I'm feeling better. "I'll be okay," I say, suddenly interested in my napkin.

"At the very least, I thought you had a concussion. You were so out of it."

Biting my lip, I mumble, "I hadn't eaten, so I was probably light-headed."

He looks up with a sheepish expression. "Is it terrible that I was hoping you wouldn't remember the whole ordeal?"

Laughing, I shrug. "I think it would take more than a knock on my head to forget that."

His head tilts slowly, like he's deep in thought, as he runs a finger along his hairline. "I don't know. You'd be surprised."

"You have a few memories you'd like erased?"

"Mm. Maybe one or two." His eyebrows lift. "Okay, who are we kidding? Probably a boatload." He laughs and shakes his head. "Concussions suck. I'm glad you don't have one."

"Let me guess. You got one while you were torturing your sister. She knocked you over the head with a brick for being a weenie."

His laughter rings through the apartment, and the sound carves into me the way a rainbow cuts a swath across the sky. "Ha. That would've made sense. I probably deserved a good beating from her for all the crap Daren and I pulled. No, I got one this fall, and the headaches suck. I still get them, and it's been a while."

I look at him sideways. "When did you get a concussion?" Wouldn't Clem have said something if her brother had been injured?

He laughs weakly. "My birthday."

I try to keep my jaw from dropping open. *He was with me on his birthday.* I doubt he would've been drinking at a club if it had happened earlier in the day. My heart starts to race.

"What… what happened?" Goosebumps line my skin as I wait for his answer.

He shakes his head like he's embarrassed. Maybe he got hammered that night after all. "My neighbor got locked out of her condo, and her four-year-old daughter was asleep inside. Hannah left something on the stove and was freaking out, so being the genius that I am, I scaled her balcony but slipped as I was crawling over and hit the grill with my head. Had to get four stitches, a tetanus shot and an MRI. It was a great night."

"That's a bummer." I swallow and try to wrap my head around what he just said. Trying to joke, I say, "Bet the MRI made it memorable."

"Well, that's the one reprieve I got. The whole night is a blur, but I'm told I had a great time."

#HolyShit

That's what happened! It doesn't explain why he ran off with that model, but at least I can stop making myself crazy by thinking I was too insignificant to register on this guy's radar after we hooked up.

"You did," I whisper. He looks at me, and I realize I said that out loud. "I'm sure you did. You were, what, turning twenty-one?"

"Yeah."

He didn't forget me because he got drunk. He got injured!

CHAPTER TWENTY-SEVEN

- Jax -

When the phone starts ringing, I'm so distracted by the thought that Dani made me pancakes this morning that I don't bother looking at the caller ID.

That's a mistake.

"Jackson, were you planning to tell me you struck someone with your car?" My mother's scratchy voice snaps me out of my good mood. In true Joselyn Avery fashion, she doesn't give me a chance to respond. "I'm sending my attorney over there right now."

I sigh, pressing the heel of my palm into my temple. "Over where, Mother?"

"To her apartment to get her to sign a non-disclosure. The last thing we need is for this story to end up on every gossip website. I'm closing a deal, and I don't need the bad press."

My mother keeps bitching, and I tune her out. I close my eyes, hatred seeping from every pore in my body as I curl my hand into a fist. An evil smile spreads on my lips. "That's fine because she's not at her apartment. She's here." Taking a nap. In my bed.

The gasp on my mother's end gives me some small degree of pleasure. She's always trying to ruin my life, so it's the least I can do. "What the hell is wrong with you?" she hisses. "She can sue us, especially once she gets to know you and sees all of your dirty laundry."

I don't bother telling her Dani already knows plenty

about our lives. Dani heard my sister and me arguing that day, and I'm sure she's learned all kinds of juicy details from living with Clem. I usually hate for people to learn about the shit that's gone on with my family, but for some reason, it suddenly doesn't bother me that Dani knows. "Mother, you think everyone wants to sue us."

"Don't be a fool, Jackson. When you're worth as much as we are, everyone does."

I've often wondered what made my mother this paranoid bitch. I can appreciate that running a multi-million-dollar corporation must be taxing, but she's always been this way, even before she inherited my grandfather's company. I suppose her father hating her and adoring Clem might have twisted her up, but fuck, she's the adult. Shouldn't she act like one?

Putting my mother in charge of the trust fund was the last thing my grandfather did. Then he died of a stroke. I tend to think relinquishing control of all that money to Joselyn killed him.

Something slams in the background. "Jesus, Jackson, did you fuck her?"

In a parallel universe, I have a soft-spoken mother who bakes me cookies and has the good sense to not delve into my sex life. In that world, I have healthy relationships with women because the one who birthed me is not the spawn of the devil.

In this moment, I've never hated anyone more than I hate this woman. Three more years of taking her bullshit so I can get my trust fund suddenly seems like a long damn time. But if I stop playing her game, if I tell her all of the things she deserves to hear, I'm screwing myself and my sister because even though she's cut off Clem financially, Joselyn is too selfish to know I plan to give my sister half of what I inherit.

My jaw unclenches. "No, I didn't sleep with—"

"Actually," my mother says with a spine-chilling laugh, "maybe that's better. Sweet-talk her and get her to sign. Once she sees the check, that will seal the deal. As we both know, every girl has her price."

Goddamn her. *Of course she'd bring up Giselle right now.*

"Don't waste your time, Mother. I don't think Dani will sign. She's not that kind of girl."

If she were, all she had to do was tell the cops the truth—that I was on the phone when I plowed into her with my car—and I'd be in the middle of a shit storm right now.

It's Joselyn's turn to laugh, and the sound makes my skin crawl. "After everything, I can't believe you're still so naive. I thought I taught you better than that." I laugh at the thought that my mother tried to impart anything of emotional value to me. "I hope law school teaches you a thing or two next year."

That's the bitch of it all. To play her way, I have to give up soccer. Not that my head has been in the game this fall, but it's the only dream I've ever had.

My skin is clammy when I hang up. There's only one place to work this out in my head. I go back to the treadmill.

A few hours later, Dani and I are back in the saddle, lounging in front of the TV in the living room and cueing up another movie.

"So you don't regret missing out on Black Friday shopping?" I ask incredulously.

She scoffs. "I hate Black Friday shopping."

"I thought girls lived for that shit."

She wrinkles her nose. "One, I hate crowds. Two, who needs to get up at two in the morning to save five dollars on some piece-of-crap game console that will be obsolete within the next six months? And three, if I were shopping right now, I'd be missing out on scary movies, and I love scary movies."

If making breakfast this morning didn't make me fantasize about taking her on the kitchen table, this does. She's everything I'd want in a girl—she's funny, thoughtful, doesn't hold any punches, is drop-dead gorgeous, and doesn't have a vain bone in her body. And even though I nearly killed her two days ago, she's as sweet as can be. Bonus.

Wait. When did I start thinking about what I'd want in a girl?

After watching *28 Days Later* and *Shaun of the Dead*, both movies she's seen before, I pull out all the stops.

"Have you seen *The Descent*?" I ask as I put a giant bowl of popcorn on the coffee table in front of us.

She says she hasn't, and I smile because this is straight out of my high school playbook, back when I thought I could like a girl for more than just a fun night.

The thought jars me—if anything happens here, this thing with Dani would be so much more than sex. That scares the shit out of me because Giselle was the only girl I've ever had a relationship with, and she fucked me over so royally that this is the first time I've gotten close to considering another one. And it's been nearly four years. Never mind that my sister will skewer me if this goes to hell and she has to bear the brunt of the fallout.

But before I can reconsider if watching a movie I suspect will terrify Dani is such a smart move, the room darkens as the first scene begins.

In forty-five minutes, she's moved from her side of the couch to mine. And with twenty minutes left of the film, she's practically in my lap. I have my arm around her, and her head is tucked into my chest.

"I can't look, Jax," she mumbles into my shirt. She's warm and soft against me, and fuck if she doesn't smell amazing.

"Open your eyes."

"No!"

I chuckle, and she swats me. "Don't laugh. This is really scary. I'm going to have nightmares."

"I thought you said you liked scary movies." I can't help the laughter that spills out around those words.

"Zombies aren't realistic. *This* is realistic. They're rock climbers and—"

"They're spelunkers."

"Whatever."

She opens her eyes just in time to see one of the girls in the movie get pulled down into a river of gore. After an ear-piercing shriek, Dani seems content to clutch my chest and hide, which is fine by me.

As the credits roll, the room is dark, illuminated only by the flickering light of the letters on the screen. She's clinging to me as though her life depends on it. I stroke her hair. "Dandelion? You okay?"

"Is the bloodbath over?" She peeks up at the screen and sighs. "Sorry, I'm not usually such a spaz." She wrinkles her nose. Goddamn, she's cute.

When she turns to face me, we're so close her breath fans against my skin, and my eyes dip to her lips, which are slightly parted.

I still have her in my arms, and her head tilts just slightly to the right, and mine tilts just slightly to the left.

"Dani?"

"Yeah." Her voice is sexy and soft.

"So you're really not seeing that guy Brady?"

She shakes her head slowly, her eyes never leaving mine.

"And… you're not seeing anyone else?" Because that would suck.

"No, Jax, I'm not." Her eyes dart away briefly and then shift back and pin me down. "But maybe the better question is, are *you* seeing anyone?"

"No, Danielle. I haven't really dated much all semester."

She stiffens in my arms, her breathing erratic.

When she doesn't say anything, I add, "I haven't gone out with anyone in at least a month."

In the silence that follows, I start to worry she's going to come to her senses and realize I'm not worth her time.

She leans toward me slightly. "Really?" Her voice sounds hopeful, and that spurs me on to say more.

"I know what you've probably heard from my sister, but I'm not really the man-whore she thinks I am. Anymore, at least. I know you've seen me with girls, but they haven't meant anything." I swallow, trying to say what's really on my mind. "I mean, why waste your time on someone if she's not who you really want?"

We stare at each other, and in the seconds that pass, there's an unspoken conversation about need and desire, and her eyes darken. I slowly close the distance, my lips brushing against hers. It takes a second to process that this is actually happening. That this girl I've kissed dozens of times in my dreams is here in my arms.

Scooping her up, I drape her across my lap, making sure to put down her injured leg gently.

Her tongue is tentative, flirty, dipping and stroking against mine in a way that has my heart pounding. All I can smell is the scent of her shampoo, her skin and the sweetness of popcorn on her breath. My hands roam her soft curves, and when she wiggles in my lap, my dick roars to life. Trying not to ravage her, I slow the pace, nibbling on her lip and jaw before I make a descent down her neck, which feels so familiar, I stop and grip her to me.

"Jax," she whispers.

That's all it takes. Her voice in my ear.

My mouth opens and I bite down on the smooth skin of her neck. Her head tilts back as a moan escapes her lips. Her fingers tangle in my hair, and she arches into me. This position sucks since she can't straddle me with that leg brace, so I lift her up and set her down on the couch, swinging my legs around and shifting us so we're lying down side by side.

I pause, worried that she's uncomfortable, but then her other leg wraps around my thigh, and she presses herself against me. Her hands tug my shirt up, and I rip it off. Then she struggles to pull up her shirt, but I still her.

"No, let me."

Her breath catches, and she nods and lies back. I prop my head up on my arm and stare down at her. I brush my thumb against her smooth cheek.

"You're so beautiful, Danielle." Even without makeup, I haven't been able to stop staring at her for the past two days.

Her dark hair is spread out beneath her, and she looks like my erotic fantasy come true. I even love the pink streaks that peek out from beneath the darker strands. I run my nose against her jaw as her fingers thread through my hair. I don't know what's happened between us this week, but I feel like she's infected me, like she runs through my veins.

I kiss her, slowly at first, because part of me feels like I've waited a long time for this moment, and I want to sear it into my brain.

When I deepen the kiss, her leg tightens around me,

but I can't nestle between her legs the way I want or I could injure her. I close my eyes and pause, resolving to not rush this. The last thing I want is to hurt her.

I pull away, and she stills. I look in her eyes.

"Danielle, can I touch you?" She licks her lips and nods, and my heart hammers in my chest. "Baby, do you have any idea what you do to me?"

It's not really a question, and I don't expect a response except she whispers, "I want you too, Jax."

So far, I've kept my hands in safe places—her back, her hips, her shoulders—but spurred by her words, my hand grips her perfect ass, grinding her up against my cock until we both moan.

I will not have sex with her tonight. I will not take it that far. She's not the kind of girl I fuck like that.

The words are still knocking around in my head when she tilts her hips and presses against my length again.

"Fuck, Dani."

She pulls back to run her hands over my chest and stomach, tilting her fingers just enough to scratch lightly down my skin, leaving a trail of fire.

I reach down and pull off her shirt, and the sight of her sheer lacy bra has me zeroing in on the one thing my brain hasn't stopped thinking about since that shower last night—those piercings.

I look to her first, and she nods before my hands race to unlatch the snap in front. The second it's off, her nipples tighten on her lush, perky breasts, and the small hoops glimmer in the darkness. Her hands pull my head down to her until my mouth is wrapped around her skin. My tongue flicks at the metal, and she moans.

Her breath quickens, her chest rising and falling beneath me. I'm just about to lose my mind when a loud knock on the door startles us both.

"Jax! It's Hannah. I have cookies. Open up."

Goddamn it to motherfucking hell.

Dani stills and the look on her face says it all. She thinks another girl is here to see me.

"Babe, it's just my neighbor. The one with the little girl."

I kiss her, and she relaxes against my mouth. A second later, I pull away and yell, "Hang on! I'm coming," while we scramble to put our clothes on.

Actually, I'm not *coming*. And that sucks. But Dani is here, and that makes everything right in the world.

CHAPTER TWENTY-EIGHT

- Dani -

A pint-sized princess, complete with a tiara, sparkling shoes and a pink cape, comes charging in behind her mom and attaches herself to Jax's leg. He laughs, picks her up and swings her around.

Oh my God. Jax with a kid. My insides flutter, and I have to fight to clear the images taking root in my mind: Jax with a family. With a daughter. With *our* daughter.

Shut the fuck up, Danielle!

If I could punch myself in the face right now, I would. I only met Jax three months ago. We've had two hot hookups, one of which he doesn't even remember, and I'm sitting here in crazy-land.

He points to the plate her mom is holding. "Chloe, did you make these cookies all by yourself?"

Her mom sighs and shakes her head as Chloe giggles. "Mommy helped. But I did the fwosting."

Blonde curls bob on her little head, and when she spots me, she kicks out of Jax's hold and beelines over to the couch. She looks at me sideways, appraising me. "You're pwetty. Are you Jax's gulfwend?'

My mouth drops open, and I wish she weren't so cute so I could toss her back into the hallway, but her mom comes to the rescue.

"Honey, not every girl you meet here is Jax's girlfriend," Hannah says.

Ouch.

Lest I forget about the hordes of other women milling about in his life.

She turns to me. "Sorry, she's going through this weird stage where she thinks every female is a mom or girlfriend."

Plastering on a smile, I shrug like it's no big deal. I wonder how many times this has happened—Hannah coming over while there's some random girl on Jax's couch with rumpled clothes. My heart squeezes in my chest.

While I understand what Jax told me, that he wasn't seeing anyone, I don't know if that means the same in his screw-everything-with-two-legs world as it does in mine. Does this mean he's not having sex with anyone now or that he only messes around a little?

Because I get that he doesn't do the girlfriend thing. It's not as though those sexts have stopped coming. His stupid phone lights up every couple of hours with messages from a different girl. He ignores them all, but still.

Hannah's eyes pass over me, a small smile tilting up her lips.

God, I can only imagine what I look like right now. I quickly run my hand over my head trying to smooth down the just-fucked hair. Not that we did the deed or even came close, but I know how my face looks when I'm worked up.

She lifts her daughter into her arms and turns back to me.

"Hi, I'm Hannah. I'll just introduce myself since Jax is too rude to do it himself."

I laugh softly, the kind of laugh you do when you're trying to be casual and pretend you're not dying, and Jax shrugs as he takes a huge bite out of a cookie. With a mouthful of food, he says, "Hannah, this is Dani. Dani, Hannah."

Hannah snorts. "Boys." She rolls her eyes. "I was surprised to see your cars here. I thought you were going skiing. It's all you've talked about for the last month."

Crap. I caused him to miss out on his big weekend. *Maybe… but at least he's not running around with those boobalicious girls from last weekend.*

Jax swallows his bite and motions toward me. "I hit her with my car and had to take her to the hospital. She decided not to kill me, so here we are, watching scary movies." He says it so casually that it almost sounds normal.

Hannah turns to me, gaping. Yes, apparently I'm gape-worthy.

I shake my head. "I'm his sister's roommate. Jax and I know each other. I'm not some random girl off the street he decided to mow down."

Yeah, I'm not a random girl who just took off her shirt and let him feel her up. I'm someone he knows. Someone his sister knows.

Oh, holy crap.

When he told me he got a concussion on his birthday, I was euphoric that he hadn't forgotten me because he was in some alcohol-induced haze—that it was because of some freak accident—and every emotion I had worked so hard to shut off this fall came rushing back. Then that stupid movie had me crawling up his body like a damn spider monkey.

Hannah's still staring at me. "What did he hit you with? The BMW or the Jeep?"

"BMW." He and I say it in unison, and then I turn to him and ask, "Why do you need two cars? This is Boston. There is such a thing as public transportation."

"Babe, the Jeep is for all things extracurricular." He

takes another bite, and I can't help but wonder if he's talking about activities that involve sex, nakedness and jumbo-sized breasts. My stomach sinks a little more, but then he says, "The guys and I go camping and hiking, and I need to be able to pack shit on the roof rack, but it gets terrible mileage, so I use the BMW for driving in the city."

Chloe claps her hands over her ears and stares at her mom, who gives Jax a look that tells me they've encountered this situation before.

"Sorry, Chloe," Jax says, admonishing himself for cursing. "Here, have a cookie."

Chloe takes the snack and pauses when it's halfway to her mouth. "Where's Nick? He likes my cookies too."

I almost forgot Jax has a roommate.

"Went skiing. He'll be back tomorrow."

Hannah's eyebrows lift. "Not if the weather keeps up. We're supposed to get twelve inches tonight and tomorrow. What have you been doing all day that you don't know this?"

He looks to me, smirks, and shrugs. My cheeks burn, and if I could, I would burrow my head into a deep pit of sand.

When Hannah and Chloe leave, he saunters over and smiles. "Your shirt is inside out." His grin widens. "And backwards."

I look down to see the Old Navy tag.

#OMFG

How embarrassing! I can just add that to the rapidly growing list. Who cares about the list I made in August. This one is going to make Travis lose his shit. I think I'll call it "101 Ways Dani Hart Can Die From Exposure to Jax Avery." If I'm not careful, I'm going to end up a cautionary tale with a sign around my neck like a hobo.

I collapse on the couch, too mortified to say anything.

"Hey." He sits next to me and tilts my chin up with his finger. "It's pretty damn adorable. Besides, I just want to rip your clothes off again anyway."

It only takes that one touch, and I want to stop thinking about how this could go wrong—so, so wrong—because I feel drawn to him like he's my riptide in water that's way too deep.

He clears his throat and his serious expression makes me sit up straighter. "What are you doing in two weeks? On the fourteenth?"

I shake my head. Haven't a clue.

Oh. Is he asking me out on a date? Inside I do a happy dance, but I clamp my jaw to prevent a huge grin from spreading on my face. *Play it cool, Danielle!* "Not sure. Why? What did you have in mind?" Romance? Candlelight? Sweaty sex? God, yes!

He shrugs and spreads his hands on his thighs. "You know Daren is up for the Heisman, right?"

I study his face, the way his cheekbones slope down to those perfect lips. "Sure. Everyone in the state of Massachusetts knows."

Jax smirks. "Okay, well, I was wondering if you'd like to come to a banquet with me. His parents are throwing this huge party to celebrate."

Oh. Holy. Shit.

Chill. Chill.

"Yeah, I'd love to come." I try to say it calmly, but it's rushed, like I'm out of breath.

He grins, slightly crooked, like he's almost embarrassed, and I wish I could pause my life and live in this moment. Jax Avery just asked me out, and I'm irrationally excited about it.

I lean over and kiss his cheek, and as I pull away, he

grabs my arms, keeping me close, so close that the heat from his body radiates off him, warming me.

"I could get used to you, Dandelion," he whispers, leaning down to brush his nose against mine in the kind of sweet gesture usually reserved for couples in love. Jesus. If this is part of his game, I'm lost, hook, line and sinker.

You should tell him. Tell him what happened on his birthday.

Swallowing, I take a deep breath, wanting to do the right thing.

He brushes his lips against mine before he pulls back. I'm filled with his clean scent, and all I can think about is how his lips feel like warm caramel when they're pressed against my skin.

I smile, flushing under his stare, and he starts to lean in again when my mom's ring tone, "We Can't Stop" by Miley Cyrus, blasts from my phone.

The judgment on his face makes me frown. "Shut up. I like Miley. I don't care if she enjoys licking hardware from Home Depot."

He laughs and kisses me gently.

"Hold that thought." I hold up a finger. *Damn these interruptions!*

Jax smiles and heads into the kitchen while I take the call.

"Hey, Mom. What's up?"

"Dani." She sniffles. "Do you have some time to talk?"

The somberness in her voice is all it takes for my euphoria to come to a screeching halt.

"What's wrong?"

"Oh, baby girl."

The sound of her sudden sobs jolt me.

Everything in my life stops. I don't blink. I don't take

a breath. I don't let my heart beat.

After a moment, she takes a shuddering breath. "It's not good, honey."

The last time she said that, she had cancer.

The last time she said that, she had both breasts removed.

The last time she said that, she almost died.

No.

No, no, no.

The silence that gapes between us feels like it might swallow me whole. I brace myself to hear what I already know. Tears well up in my eyes before she says the one thing I know will shatter my world.

"It's back." She cries softly into the phone. I clench my eyes shut, hoping this isn't really happening. "I wanted to tell you when you came home for Thanksgiving, but then you had that accident. I thought maybe I could wait until Christmas, but…"

She trails off, but I know what she's saying. She doesn't think there's much time.

There are no words, just a blackness that sucks me whole into the only place I've ever understood despair, and I sob into the phone.

She tells me she's known for almost three months.

My mother has known all fall and hasn't said a word.

I hiccup into the phone. "Why didn't you say something? I would've come home. There's that other treatment that one doctor thought—"

"No, honey. There's nothing left."

My world spins, forgetting its axis. Forgetting that my mom is a survivor. Forgetting that the little bit of fight I have in me comes from her strength. And now that's gone. "Don't say that. I thought you said you'd do whatever it took if it returned."

She sighs, like the weight of this has been too much. "The operation wasn't enough. It spread, and I don't want to spend my last few months in a hospital. I don't want to—"

"Stop talking like that! You're the one who's always telling me you'd beat it."

I cover my face with one hand. My other one shakes as I try to keep the phone against my ear.

There's only one thing to say now. "I'm coming home."

"No." Her response is immediate. "Finish the semester. We'll see the doctor together over the holidays and figure out what to do then. Maybe I can come out to Boston in January so you can finish out your junior year."

She's talking about the end. She's saying it's close. So close that she wants to spend her last days here with me.

"Mom, I don't want to stay. I need you. You're all I have left. Please stop talking like this. Let me come home. I bet I can get a flight out this weekend."

"Danielle, no. It was bad enough that you missed almost a month of school last year. I don't want you to have to make up another semester's worth of work just to miss a few weeks. It's not that much time."

Not that much time.

But when there's nothing left, not that much time is all that matters.

CHAPTER TWENTY-NINE

- Jax -

Halfway through assembling sandwiches, I hear the strangest sound that makes the hair on my arms stand on end.

It takes me a minute to realize what it is.

And then before I can blink, I'm in the living room, my heart hammering as I watch Dani sob into her hands.

The sound of her anguish grips me, and I kneel in front of her.

I don't know what just went down, but it wasn't good. When she was in the hospital, she told me her mom had cancer last spring, and now she's sobbing on my couch. Fuck.

Her face is in her hands. As she breathes, she trembles. I brace myself on either side of her.

"Babe, you okay?"

She doesn't move. I reach up and stroke her hair, and she starts crying again. I sit next to her and pull her into a hug. After several minutes, she pushes away, and when she looks at me, her eyes are distant.

"I'm sorry. I can't do this."

Do what? Let me hug her? Before the right response forms in my head, she says, "I'm going to take a shower."

"Do you want some help? I could—"

"No."

She doesn't look at me as she grabs her crutches and hobbles toward my room.

This whole thing makes me feel like an asshole. There are guys who always know what to say in any situation. The sky could be on fire, the Earth sucked into a vortex, and Daren would have the perfect words to calm the masses. Me? I sulk. I argue with myself about what I should do. I get pissed off and feel helpless or kick shit in my way.

So what do I do now?

I give her space. I pace in my room. I watch the clock.

Back and forth I stalk, feeling like some kind of caged animal. Finally, I sit at my desk, just outside of the bathroom, so I can hear her if she needs help. The water starts to run, and all I can think about is how she slipped and almost fell yesterday. A few minutes later, when I hear the clatter in the bathroom, I don't even think before I reach for the door.

Steam billows from the shower, and I call out, "Dani? Are you all right?"

All I hear are her muffled sobs.

I yank off my shirt as I cross the bathroom and then pull back the curtain slowly. My heart almost breaks when I see her huddled in the corner still wearing her bra and sweats, her shoulders shaking.

"Baby, I'm here. If you want me to go, tell me."

I wait and she says nothing.

That's all it takes, and I'm right behind her. I pull her into me, and she turns around, nestling against me like a little bird.

"I couldn't get my pants off," she whimpers, water pouring down around us.

"That's okay. I have a dryer." I grab her head in my hand and press her cheek to my chest. We stand there until her breathing is normal and the tears have stopped.

I kiss the top of her head. "Do you want to hold on to

me while you get your clothes off? I'll close my eyes." It'll take every goddamn muscle in my body to do that, but I will. I won't violate her trust that way.

She looks up at me for several breaths, her green eyes soft, and she sniffles. "You don't have to. Close your eyes, I mean."

Christ.

Water trickles down her bare shoulders, and through the lace of her bra, her piercings are like a beacon calling to me. Her arms, which she had tucked between us, slowly wrap around my neck and pull me closer until our bodies are flush. *Don't take advantage of her, asshole,* I yell at myself even though my dick feels like a raging beast against her taut stomach.

I have to clear my throat before I can speak. "Dandelion, we don't have to do anything you don't want. You've had a rough day and—"

Her voice is a whisper. "I want you to help me forget, Jax. Just for tonight." Her brow furrows, like she's somehow worried I won't want her for more than that.

I run my thumb over her jaw. "Babe, you know this is different for me, right?" I take a deep breath to get the balls to finish my thought, and I feel like I'm hovering over a canyon when I say the next words. "I can't explain why this means more, but it does, and I want to spend time with—"

She doesn't let me explain, her hands drawing my mouth down to hers.

My tongue gently presses against the seam of her lips, and she opens her mouth. We press together, heat and need somehow overshadowing her pain.

Our bodies are wet, slick as water rains down on us. She's not wearing her brace, so I have to be careful with her.

"Does your knee hurt?" I whisper against her mouth.

"Only if I put pressure on it, not if I move it a little." That's all I need to know before I press her back into the tile. Taking her hands, I pin her wrists above her head as I make a slow descent down her body.

Everything about this woman is perfect. Her smooth skin. Her beautiful breasts. Her tight, flat stomach. I kiss my way down her neck and lick across her clavicle. Her head drops to the side as she moans. Unsnapping her bra with one hand, I grab one lush mound in my hand and wrap my mouth over the other, yanking gently on the hoop.

"God, Jax."

The pounding of my heart increases when she says my name like I'm her last breath.

I lave her breast as she arches into me, my hand dipping to hold her hip steady. I want to lift her up, wrap her legs around my waist and pound her into the wall until she screams my name, but I know I can't be rough with her in this condition.

The bruises marring her skin have turned a darker purple in some places, a greenish yellow in others. I kiss down her hip, wishing I could make them disappear.

When I reach her sweatpants, I look up at her, releasing her hands. If she wants me to stop, I want her to feel she can say it, but when I stare at her, I don't see hesitation. Her eyes are glazed and dilated but wanting. She tangles her fingers through my hair and nods yes.

My thumbs press tighter into her skin as I pull down her pants to reveal a matching pair of black lace boy shorts. I let her sweats sag around her knees as my hands wrap around her ass and squeeze, my dick somehow hardening more. I don't remember ever wanting a girl this much, a terrifying thought that makes me close my eyes and press my head against her stomach.

She strokes my hair, as though I'm the one who needs comforting tonight, and I clutch her tighter. I say her name against her skin until I taste the water that's dripped down her body, and I long to taste more.

Looking up at her again, I watch her as she watches me strip her out of her panties. She grips my shoulders as she struggles out of her clothes, and then I'm staring at this girl who is so gloriously bare in front of me, I feel like a twelve-year-old boy who's about to come in his pants.

Because Dani waxes it all off. Fuck me.

At eye level with this amazing sight, all I can do is admire this vision before me. My cock screams at me to do something, anything, so I press my mouth against her skin, spreading her apart gently with my hands as she grips my hair. She feels so right, so good, that I almost feel shaken by some sense of déjà vu. I still as I stare up at her again, questions I can't quite word edging near the surface of my mind.

But then she gasps, "Don't stop!" and I want her to come undone around me.

I lick my lips, her sweet scent nearly derailing my ability to speak. "Do you trust me?"

She nods, her eyes telling me she's hungry for more.

Edging her over a little so she's wedged into the corner of the shower, I slowly pull her injured leg over my shoulder as I kneel in front of her.

"Does this hurt? Is your leg okay?"

A small laugh escapes her.

"Jax, only one thing hurts, and it's not my leg." A devilish smile curls her lips, and I grin back. Someone's feeling better.

I dip my tongue into her, stroking so softly that I'm

barely touching her, but it's enough that she yanks on my hair, pulling me harder toward her. I laugh against her skin, loving that I'm driving her crazy, wanting to take her right to the edge.

So that's what I do, touch everything but the spot I know she's dying to have me devour. Her breath picks up, and she's grabbing for me, one hand gripping my hair and the other scratching up my shoulder.

I can't take it any longer either, so I slide one finger into her while I finally settle my mouth on her bundle of nerves, and she screams my name, shuddering apart against me.

When she stills, I do my best to ignore my angry hard-on. This is about Dani, about making her feel better, and the last thing I want to do is take advantage of her when she's feeling vulnerable.

So I wash her body and wrap her in a towel and carry her to my bed. I go over to my dresser, and throw on a pair of boxers, trying to ignore the wood I'm still sporting before I pull out a t-shirt and toss it to Dani. It lands on her head and she laughs, yanking it off.

"Clothes? Really?" Her eyebrow arches. "I thought we were well beyond that point. Besides," she says, lowering her voice, "I'd like to reciprocate."

So much for ignoring my dick because it's like the arm of a compass pointing north. I sit next to her, my back to her. *Get it together, Avery.* When I turn around, I say it before I can change my mind. "Dani, I'm sure this is going to sound crazy, but I want to go slowly with you."

Her head tilts, confusion in her eyes.

I clear my throat. "I don't want to fuck things up and—"

"Jax, I'm not made of glass, and I won't break. Get your ass over here. Now."

Shit, I love a forceful Danielle.

She tells me to sit back on the bed, and then she rolls over onto her side, letting the towel drop open as she lowers my boxers. The sight of her breasts brushing up against my thighs has me wanting to slam into her until she comes so hard, she begs me to stop. I clench my jaw, trying to keep myself from taking over.

The metal on her piercings scratches against my skin, and I'm dying to wrap my mouth around them again. I lean up to grab her, but she stops me with her palm. "Sit still," she says, a smirk on her face.

"Yes, ma'am."

She props herself against me as she wraps her hand around my length. Her green eyes stare at me as she dips her head down into my lap where, dear God, her mouth is like a religious awakening.

Her tongue darts out and teases me until I have to squeeze my eyes shut because the sight of her wrapped around my dick nearly makes me lose it.

A few minutes later, I fall out of her mouth, and I slowly open my eyes.

She shakes her head like she's scolding me. "Watch," she purrs as she closes around me, making me hiss.

I hold out as long as I can, but she's too good. Her mouth is too wet. Too snug. Too warm.

"Babe, I'm there," I groan as I grip her hair.

The rush powers through me, seizing every muscle and joint in my body until I'm spent and gasping for breath.

As soon as I'm able to string together a coherent thought, I grab Dani and wrap myself around her. My face to her neck. My chest pressed to her side. My leg nestled between her thighs.

Her fingers thread through my hair, and her contented

sigh does something crazy to my heart. I close my eyes and breath in the sweet scent of apples and marvel at how she feels like my missing puzzle piece.

I'm not sure what I've done to deserve the blow job of my life, but when I wake up a few hours later with her body laced through mine, it pales in comparison to watching her sleep against my chest.

How have I gone so long without recognizing how much I want this woman?

CHAPTER THIRTY

- Dani -

Who was that girl who told Jax to watch her give him a blow job? Hello? That would be the alien who took over my body and turned me into a sex-craved maniac.

I have officially joined Jax's army of easily accessible girls.

When I wake up alone, the shame of what I did last night burns on my skin like hot coals.

It's not that I'm in any way opposed to the actions themselves, but damn, I'm not even dating Jax. I've never gone that far with someone I wasn't in a serious relationship with.

The girl who grew up watching old Madonna videos wants to embrace my sexual freedom and treat last night cavalierly, but the small part of me who someday wants the house, kids and white picket fence knows what I did last night is not how I'll achieve those ends.

As I stare at his side of the bed, thoughts of him naked blur behind my eyes. Everything he did, every touch, every kiss, felt so good. My skin tingles just thinking about what he did to me. And I let him know how much I enjoyed it, screaming when I came. And I'm not a screamer.

I smack my forehead before I push my face into the pillow, beyond mortified.

I could handle this morning if it hadn't felt so good to wake up in the middle of the night, warm from having

Jax's body pressed to mine. I could revel all day in the way he said my name as he nuzzled against me, half asleep. My finger traces my swollen bottom lip, memories of last night making my skin hot.

I shake my head, trying to focus.

At least he didn't accidentally say another girl's name. Thank the Lord for small favors.

A gray light filters in from the window. It's cold, and through the crack in the dark curtains, I see the snow falling. I snuggle deeper in the blankets, realizing the sheets smell like us.

A small ache starts building in my chest. When he drops me off at my place tomorrow, and all I have left of our time together are a few sore muscles and a couple of bruises, I'm going to need more than the painkillers the doctor gave me to deal with this pain.

What's worse is he's been so great, so attentive and sweet, making us meals and finding fun stuff for us to do while we're holed up here—the kind of behavior that's going to make the end that much harder. Because I realize what I have with Jax comes with an expiration date. This whole thing happened because of the car accident. It's not as though he asked me out and romanced me. He's probably feeling the need to make it up to me. Crap. I wonder if that's why he asked me to the banquet.

And then my mom called…

A humiliating thought crosses my mind. *God, I hope he didn't do last night out of pity.*

Trying to get a hold of myself, I press the heels of my hands into my eyes. Damn it. I can't even do the walk of shame properly because I'm stuck here until one of my roommates gets home tomorrow.

I take a deep breath, resolving to play this smart.

What happened here with Jax is going to get tucked into a fantasy file for future reference when I have a boyfriend who's more my speed—probably something battery-operated—while I figure out how I'm going to move back to Chicago. Because, really, there's only one person I should be thinking about right now, and it's my mother.

Before the tears in my eyes get to be more than I can handle, I force myself to focus on all the schoolwork I need to do before the winter holidays. So I get up, slowly putting weight on my leg, surprised that it doesn't hurt half as much as it did the last few days. I twisted my other knee when I was younger, and the injury kept me out of gymnastics for two months due to a stretched ligament. This is nothing compared to that injury.

If I walk slowly, I can put my full weight on it. That icing technique must have really helped. I'll have to thank Jax for the suggestion and for helping me recuperate.

I shuffle around the room as I pull on a pair of sweats and a t-shirt before I toss my hair into a messy ponytail. Reaching into my suitcase, I grab my binder and journal, stuffing them into my messenger bag so I can get some work done.

Slowly, I open the bedroom door and look down the hallway, which is dark. In the background, the treadmill hums.

Relieved that I don't have to face him yet, I limp into the kitchen where the coffee is already percolating.

This doesn't have to be weird. It doesn't. I will treat Jax the way I did before we got horizontal and pretend he hasn't seen my naked lady garden. Again.

After I pour a cup of coffee, I take a few sips and stare out the window, wondering how the storm will affect travel back to Boston. Mesmerized by the falling snow, I don't know how long I've been standing there when warm arms wrap around my waist.

"Holy shit, Jax. You scared me."

He laughs softly and kisses my neck. "You looked too good to not touch."

My head tilts back to look at him, and he nips at my skin. Judging by my rapid pulse, getting some separation from Jax is going to be harder than I thought.

Wait, this isn't how the morning-after works. He's supposed to be sullen and distant, and I'm supposed to avoid eye contact. Instead, my body responds to his, arching into him. If he pets my head right now, I think I'd meow.

He's sweaty, and the fading fragrance of his body wash and the scent of his skin has me wanting to devour him. Based on the enormous erection pressed into my back, he's feeling the same way.

"How's your knee?" he whispers into my ear, sending goosebumps all up and down my arms.

"Much better. I can walk. It's still tender, but—"

I don't finish because he spins me around, props me up on the counter, and crushes his mouth into mine. My legs automatically fall open and he nestles tightly between my thighs.

My hands run along his sweaty chest, feeling every hard muscle, and there are a lot of them. We kiss, our tongues tangling until we're both panting, and he pulls away, resting his hands on the counter and lowering his head, like he's a runner out of breath.

"Sorry, Dani. I just want you so badly." He inhales deeply. "I should stop or I'm going to fuck you on the kitchen table."

He wants me. No one has ever told me that before.

I am an ember caught in his flame, and my reaction is

visceral. I don't think. I don't hesitate. "Who says we should stop? We'll call it breakfast."

Yeah, so much for playing it smart.

He stands straight, and his eyes burn into me like nitrate, creating a firestorm that's hot enough to make me ignore all the warning bells that this isn't a good idea.

"Are you sure?" he asks, a strain in his voice.

All I can do is nod as my hands fist in his hair. We don't talk, just stare as his lips find mine.

He grips my ass and carries me to the dining table and sets me down. Now I realize how this is a better angle because he's pressing into me so perfectly, I could almost lose it now.

I reach down to grab the hem of my t-shirt, and he helps me yank it off so that we're skin to skin, and when my piercings rub against his chest, my toes curl.

Jax presses his hand against my neck as he lowers me back onto the cool surface, and his hands run the length of my torso and back up again before they settle on my breasts. He squeezes, hard, and it's just shy of hurting, but I love it so much I gasp.

With a wicked grin, he lowers his mouth and pulls on a ring with his teeth, and a low, deep moan starts in the back of my throat. When he reaches for my sweatpants, he hesitates and looks up at me, so I help him push off my clothes.

Once I am fully on display, he stops and stares, his eyes searing me. The grin on his face makes me want to cover myself, to hide, but he grabs my arms and pushes them up over my head. God, I love it when he does this, takes over.

But he doesn't move any closer. He just stares.

"Jax, you're making me self-conscious."

He growls. "I don't see why. You're fucking perfect. I

could eat you for every meal."

I expect him to crash his lips into mine, but instead, his kiss is soft, tender, making this experience a little less about lust and a little more about emotion. Not to mention a lot more confusing. Lust and sex, I get. Emotions, not so much. Because the last thing I expect from Jax is something more, and yet that's what's rolling off him. It's overwhelming and beautiful and makes me want to share every last bit of myself with him. If he weren't pressing down on top of me, I might float away from giddiness.

We kiss, long and sweet kisses that meld into each other as he caresses my body and brings me to the brink with just his hands.

"More, Jax." I hardly know what I'm saying, if I'm even speaking English, but I can't think straight. I don't know that I'd be able to breathe properly if breathing weren't an involuntary action.

He kisses me one more time. "Hold that thought."

The second his body leaves mine, I'm cold. I close my eyes, shivering, not allowing myself to think about how I look like a Thanksgiving turkey, on display like the main course.

He's back a second later. "You sure, baby?" he whispers.

I nod furiously and the tension in his face breaks into another grin.

He grabs my hand and pulls me up to sit on the edge of the table before he tears open the foil package. Placing the condom in my hand, he says, "You do it."

Um. My insides quiver. I've never been so turned on in my entire life. I've only climaxed with a guy twice and both times were with Jax.

He looks me in the eyes as he licks his lips.

My mind is hazy, a fog. The only thing I know for sure is that I am so lost in this guy, I might never see straight again.

I lower his workout shorts, and the part of him I'm getting to know so intimately greets me. My lips curl into a smile as I run my hands along his smooth skin, enjoying the groan that escapes his lips when I squeeze his hard length.

I've never enjoyed giving blow jobs before Jax. I thought it's just what you do, the way you offer an appetizer before dinner. But last night, I liked it. A lot. And part of me is itching to do it again, and I would except there's something I want to do more.

I can't explain what he does to me, how he seems to tap into this side of me I never knew existed, but I love being this carefree, this uninhibited.

Unrolling the condom, I try my best to not let my hands tremble as they travel along his impressive erection. After it's on, I grip him firmly and stroke down, and he clenches his jaw.

"Careful," he warns, "or this won't last long."

I tilt my head and smirk, loving the idea that I can make him as crazy as he's making me.

He kisses me, and his mouth is warm and hot, making me melt against the pressure of his hips nestled against mine. Reaching around, he pulls out my ponytail, and my hair falls down my shoulders.

Then he lowers me down, pulls up my knees and braces them at his side.

I brush my hair off my shoulder as he presses against me, just barely. I widen my legs, anticipation clawing in my chest.

My heart is pounding. *We're finally going to go all the way.*

But he stills, his eyes narrowing on me.

The sudden frown on his face makes me reach out and touch his cheek, and he flinches at my touch.

Okay.

"Jax, what's wrong?"

His head tilts to the side, and he looks me over, but the warmth that had been brimming over in his eyes is gone. He rubs his temple, like he's deep in thought, his gaze distant.

Trying not to freak out, I grab his forearm, and his jaw tightens.

"Jax?"

He swallows and shakes his head, finally looking at me. He opens his mouth just as the front door slams open.

Voices just a few feet away have me scrambling off the table. Holy shit. I'm buck naked.

I stumble behind Jax who yanks up his shorts.

"Jax, I brought you a gift. Two, actually. Remember Isabelle from this summer? She wants to be your snow bunny and—" Nick comes around the corner, his eyes widening when he sees us. He holds out his hands. "Shit, sorry, dude."

The sound of girls giggling behind him makes me nauseous. Nick turns around and disappears behind the partition in the entryway. I hear him mumble while I step back from Jax and limp into his bedroom a few feet away. Shutting the door behind me, I feel tears brim in my eyes.

Oh my God. What am I doing?

My hands shake as I cover my face. I nearly had sex with Clementine's brother on his kitchen table.

And Jax is acting so weird all of a sudden, like we're strangers, like we haven't spent the last several days together.

I fight to keep the tears back and take a deep breath, trying to calm the maelstrom of emotions whipping around inside my chest.

Realizing I'm still standing here naked, I reach for my suitcase and throw on a t-shirt and jeans. It takes a while to get the pants on, but I'm hoping the level of difficulty to get clothed helps them stay on longer.

I keep waiting for Jax to walk in so we can talk, but after twenty minutes, my heart sinks. I may not be the best at relationships, but I know enough to realize that him staying out there means something.

After an hour, a fucking hour, he waltzes in, still shirtless. I'm sitting in a leather recliner by the window, trying to look like I'm doing homework.

He barely glances at me as he mumbles that he's going to take a shower. Another twenty minutes later, he walks out and says he's taking Isabelle home.

And then he leaves without another glance in my direction.

No. Fucking. Way.

CHAPTER THIRTY-ONE

- Dani -

Even though I'm starving, I don't poke my head out of Jax's room until well after two in the afternoon. He's been gone for hours.

His condo is quiet, so I tiptoe into the kitchen, finding myself in almost the same position I was in this morning. Except this time I know Jax isn't going to wrap his arms around me.

Fighting the urge to cry, I grab an apple off the counter before I spread out some of my textbooks on the kitchen table.

I hate that I have to sit here at the scene of the crime, but I don't want to get ink on his bedspread. Ignoring the burn in my cheeks, I reach for my journal and pull out my watercolor markers before I begin to sketch.

Using broad strokes, I draw the first thing that comes to mind: Jax and me together, on the couch, in the shower, on the bed. A tangle of arms and legs, hands urgent and demanding. Nudes aren't my strength, but I don't know how to get the images out of my head.

Drawing until my hand hurts, I finally take a break.

I may be able to limp around, but I can't go home because I'll never make it up four flights of stairs by myself.

After Jax left, I tried calling seven motels. Everything is booked through the weekend, so unless I want to sleep on the street corner in the middle of a snowstorm, I'm stuck here. My only hope is that Travis will get back early this evening and be able to pick me up. I grab my phone, and my mood gets a little darker when my thumb reveals no new messages.

Jax left with her. We almost had sex, and he left with another woman. Again!

#Unbelievable

My face heats up and my eyes water. I don't know what happened. One minute he was calling me baby and was sweet and loving, and the next he was making for the door like his life depended on it.

Unless…

The nausea I've been fighting all afternoon burns in the back of my throat.

Did he remember his birthday? The club?

Surely that couldn't have freaked him out so much he took off like an Olympic sprinter. There were so many times this week I almost told him what happened that night, but I've been afraid it would change our dynamic. That he'd see me differently. That it would ruin the friendship we'd been building.

A door creaks open from down the hall. Padded steps echo closer.

I turn my head slowly, my heart paralyzed.

Nick stands with his hands in the pockets of his jeans looking uncomfortable. "Hey, Dani. I'm so sorry about what happened earlier." His big brown eyes are warm, and the sympathy in his expression twists something in my gut.

Grateful he's not being a jerk, I smile weakly. "It's totally okay. I'm sorry I have to crash here. I tried calling hotels but—"

"No, you don't need to leave. I'm cool. My roommate nearly made you roadkill. Putting you up for a few days is the least he can do." Nick's eyes dart around the empty apartment. "Where is he anyway?"

A cold laugh escapes me. "Your guess is as good as mine, but I'm guessing it's somewhere with Isabelle." My eyes dart down to my journal, my face burning in humiliation.

"Shit." An awkward silence spreads between us while I doodle circles in my journal. "I'm sorry about that too."

I shake my head. "Don't be. It's not like I'm not well aware of his reputation. I'm the idiot in this equation."

Nick clears his throat. "Listen, my little sister is coming over in a bit. We were going to order a pizza and catch the Celtics before the BC game. Wanna join us?"

His kindness is too much. I nod slowly. "Who are the Celtics playing?"

"The Heat."

I look up and give him a small smile. "I'm a huge Celtics fan, but I love Dwayne Wade."

He laughs. "I'm going to ignore that sacrilege and let you stay in my house."

The heaviness that bore down on me all day starts to lighten. Two hours later, Nick, his sister Sammy, and I are all yelling at the TV.

"Can you fucking believe that call?" Nick mumbles over a mouth full of food.

"Okay, don't be a hater," I say, pausing to look him in the eye, "but Wade was fouled on the way to the basket. I don't think it should have been a technical, though."

"Good because I was about to kick you out of my living room."

I laugh and reach for my soda.

Nick grabs the bowl of *queso*. "This is the best damn dip I've ever had."

Grinning, I hand him the bag of chips. "It's an easy

recipe. I'll write it down for you so you can make it any time."

He nods as he continues to stuff his face.

Sammy nudges me.

"I like you."

"Thanks." I nudge her back. She looks older than eighteen with thick, chestnut-colored hair and beautiful brown eyes like her brother.

She stares at me. "You're not like one of Jax's typical girls."

Trying not to choke on my soda, I laugh. "I'm sure there's a compliment in there somewhere because I've seen the girls Jax dates, and they're all gorgeous."

"They're all bitches. And dumb. He's an asshole for leaving you."

My eyes widen.

She shrugs. "My brother told me what happened."

"Gee, thanks, Nick. I didn't need to be humiliated any more today or anything."

He grumbles as he chows down, and I get that he doesn't want to talk about it. Trying to change the subject, I pick the first thing that comes to mind.

"How was your ski trip?"

Setting the bowl on the coffee table, he turns to me. "It was killer. I have great video of it." He pulls out his phone, connecting wirelessly to his Apple TV. A moment later, the screen is filled with a GoPro video, making it seem as if I'm living the experience firsthand.

"Wow. This is amazing footage."

Nick races down the slope, and when he turns his head, the camera shows several guys behind him. I'm guessing they're all soccer players too like Jax.

"This is nothing," he says. "Wait until you see the night video." He cues it up, and I'm completely riveted.

"I had no idea this kind of technology existed to do night footage like this."

"Jax jerry-rigged it himself. He attached a camera with night vision on the helmet."

The footage is exhilarating, putting me front and center on the slopes. "So you can't buy this, the camera and helmet combo?"

Nick shakes his head. "You have to buy them separately and mount the camera."

Excitement tingles in my chest, a dozen ideas exploding in my head. "Can I see it, the helmet?"

"Sure." He jumps up and a minute later, he returns with a black ski helmet, which he places in my lap.

My fingers run along the edges of the metal attachment. "But this camera is so small. I thought GoPro cameras were larger."

"They are. This is a prototype by a different company."

"This is a great product." I can imagine a dozen different applications. I'd love to take footage like this, but the idea of having to mount a camera myself or—even once I got it attached—having some huge piece of metal attached on my head is such a turnoff. But this, this has so many possibilities.

I'm still turning over ideas when a knock comes at the door. Before Nick gets off the couch, several guys saunter in. One says, "It's time to order more pizza, man."

Nick laughs and introduces me to his friends who are all on the soccer team. They break out a case of beer, and then we're all back to the Celtics game. Guys are shouting, and it's loud, and I'm having a great time. We argue about calls and plays. Popcorn gets thrown at me because I groan when Wade misses a shot. We talk trash, and by the end of the game, I'm feeling right at home.

Sammy and I chat the whole time, and she giggles in my ear about how she has a crush on one of the boys. We swap numbers so we can grab lunch together later in the week.

Finally, when the BC-Syracuse game starts, Nick turns to one of his friends and quietly asks, "Have you seen Avery around campus today?" His eyes dart to me, and I look away.

"Yeah, I saw him with that hot-ass blonde at that diner he likes a little while ago. Looks like our man is back in the saddle. What the fuck was up with that dry spell?" The friend laughs, and I feel sick.

And so very stupid.

Jax is such a prick. I don't know what I've been thinking, who I've been kidding, but those rumors about him don't do him justice. I'm not sure why I ignored four days of sexts on his phone from every girl in the Tri-State area. I need to get my head examined.

A text buzzes on my phone. It's Travis. *"I'm downstairs."*

#ThankFuckingGod

I write back that he should come up, and I scramble up to get my stuff together. Sammy comes into Jax's bedroom while I throw all my shit in my bag.

"Dani, this sucks."

"Yeah, it does. But whatever. I'm not his problem anymore. You can tell him that."

She grabs my arm. "I still want to hang out this week." I nod, too frazzled to think beyond the next few hours.

When I reach the front door, Travis is standing there talking to Nick.

"There's my girl." Seeing my best friend makes all the emotion I've held back burst to surface, and when he pulls me into a giant hug, I start to cry. It's been too much. The car accident, my mom, Jax leaving. I just want to hide against Travis's chest until this horrible week ends.

"Hey, hey, it's okay." Travis strokes my head, and I shudder against him.

"Just get me out of here." I wipe my face with my arm and turn to Nick and his sister. "Thanks for everything, guys. I really appreciate the hospitality."

Sammy and Nick both give me a hug, sympathy or maybe pity swimming in their eyes, making me feel worse. They've been awesome today, but I feel like some science experiment gone wrong.

Travis picks up my stuff with one arm and uses the other one to help me hobble down the stairs. When we're in his car, I start crying again.

"I hate him," I whisper as an SUV pulls up, and two scantily clad girls run into the building I just left.

Travis grips the steering wheel until his knuckles turn white. "I am going to kick his ass from here to Christmas the next time I see him."

"So not worth it." Shivering, I reach to over to turn up the heat.

The snow isn't as bad as I thought it would be. The streets are already plowed, and tall snow banks line the sidewalk.

"Can I stay with you for a few days?"

Travis reaches over and pulls me to his chest. "You already know the answer."

CHAPTER THIRTY-TWO

- Jax -

The funny thing is that no one needs to tell me I'm an asshole. I'm in touch with that. The fact that I left Dani to hang out with Isabelle, a girl who can barely go two sentences without talking about her hair or makeup, crystalizes everything wrong in my life. It's fucking diet food and saccharin and light beer when a man only wants something real. But I'm finding that being real is a fleeting pastime for most, an afterthought.

Even now, hours later, Dani's lie burns in my stomach. Why didn't she tell me we hooked up on my birthday? Why has she pretended all semester? Pretended this week?

Only one other girl has lied to me like that.

Giselle. And she wrecked me.

I've never been so glad to be cockblocked in my entire life. I mean, yeah, I could have fucked Danielle and that would have been that, but something about our time together tells me it would have meant so much more. And that scares the ever-living shit out of me. Especially if she's been lying to me this whole time.

I can't deny she always felt familiar, each interaction wrapping me in the sense of déjà vu. And when I finally remembered, when I realized who she was, it was both euphoric and a knife to my gut. Like Adam in the Garden of Eden wishing he could just… forget.

It was the way she flipped her hair over her shoulder,

the way she turned her head slightly and lifted her chin to look at me through hooded eyes. And I knew.

When I remembered, at first I was flooded with lust—I want her, I still do—but then reality crashed into me, reminding me why I don't do relationships. Reminding me why I don't go there. Because girls lie. And they rip your fucking heart out and laugh while they do it.

Thank God Nick walked in.

The greater irony is that now he looks pissed. At me. But he doesn't say anything when I walk in. The guys are all sitting around eating pizza and watching Daren's game. Damn, I can't believe I almost forgot about it. When Sammy sees me, she gives me the finger. Nice.

"It's great to see you too, Sammy."

"Fuck you, Jax."

Okay then. I walk into my room, bracing myself for the fallout from this morning, but the room is dark and still. Dani is gone and so is her stuff.

Shit.

When I reach the living room, Nick barely looks up from the game. "She left already. A while ago."

"She was crying," Sammy says, glaring at me.

Something in my chest cracks, but I grit my teeth. "You don't know what happened. Stay out of this."

Sammy laughs coolly. "What I do know is that you're a bigger dumbass than I thought. You wouldn't know a great girl if she kicked you in the balls. Which she should do, by the way. I can't believe you ditched her to hook up with one of your skanks."

The rest of my teammates sit with their eyes glued to the TV, dutifully ignoring the fact that a teenager is bitching me out.

"I didn't hook up with Isabelle." Not even close. I barely let her hug me. And the whole time I was with her

I obsessed over Dani. Warning myself not to get attached. Kicking myself for leaving. Wanting to explain why my head is so fucked up.

Sammy shakes her head at me. "That's not what it looked like, Jax."

Reaching into my pocket for my phone, I head into the kitchen for some privacy while I call Dani. Voice mail. I try again with the same result, so I hang up.

She lied. I don't know why, but she did. And what did I do? Dick her over. Honestly, in the moment, I panicked. My feelings for her already felt out of control, and like a total douchebag, I ditched her.

Running my hands through my hair, I look around, and all I see is Dani, cooking for me, laughing at me when I make a dumb joke, snuggling against me when she's afraid.

Damn it. I should have just asked her what happened, asked her to explain. But I'm not wired that way. I don't do heart-to-hearts when it comes to shit like this. Not anymore. I learned that lesson a long time ago. Because if you don't get close to the fire, you never get a chance to get burned.

Which is why I spent the day with Isabelle. Helping her shovel her drive, taking her to lunch, listening to her yammer on about bullshit. She's safe. I'm not going to lose my head to that girl. She'd be a great lay, a fun time, and then I could cut and run without a second thought.

But Dani isn't like that.

Dani makes me remember wanting a relationship. Because I loved spending time with her. And I'm not even talking about the naked parts, although that was all pretty spectacular too. But just hanging out. Talking about school. Shooting the shit about sports. The fuck of it all is that I felt like myself around her. Like when I was around her, I wasn't some soccer player or rich kid. I didn't feel like I had to play a part for her.

She made me forget why I can't let myself trust women.

My eyes fall on a black leather book on the kitchen table. Dani's journal. I had seen her doodling in that over the last few days. She said it was her art book.

I open it slowly, feeling like I shouldn't be prying, but I want to get another angle into this girl.

Flipping slowly, I ignore the writing, only letting myself look at the drawings. Color jumps off every page with bold strokes, delicate blends and artful contrasts. She's so fucking talented. What's she doing wasting her time with business? Clearly, she's an artist.

But then I see the money signs, literally, scrawled on more than a dozen pages. Dollar signs and money in different colors and sizes fill page after page.

Every girl has her price. My mother's words make me want to chuck this book through the window. Was this all some big ploy for cash?

Of course, it's at this moment that I remember her friend at the club accusing her of stealing her necklace.

Just when I think I'm done, that maybe Dani has had some fucked-up motive all this time, I see the nudes, and my hands shake. The two of us. Together. Entwined.

She must have done them this morning. They're beautiful and stark. Emotional. The crack in my chest spreads a little more.

Grabbing my keys and her journal, I head for my car. I need to find Danielle. At the very least, I need to hear her out.

After starting the engine, I tune my radio to the BC game before I pull onto the street. It takes me an hour and a half to make the otherwise half-hour drive to her place. Braving rush-hour traffic after a snowstorm is nothing I'd attempt to do under normal circumstances, but I need to talk to her.

Just my luck. No one is home, and my sister won't be back until tomorrow night, so I can't even ask her to help me.

Clementine is going to freak the fuck out when she finds out what happened. That's a headache I don't need.

My phone buzzes with a text. I grab it, hoping it's Dani, but it's my coach.

"Practice tomorrow. I hope you guys have been staying on top of your workouts. Text me tonight to check in."

He's been texting the guys every evening over the Thanksgiving Break. He says he wants to keep us focused. I can't say I blame him. Because right now, focus is one thing I do not have.

* * *

After practice on Sunday, I try calling Dani again with the same result, so I text. *"I'm so sorry. Let me explain."*

Her response: *"No need. I'm fine. Take care."*

I figure she'd be pissed. Curse me out. Tell me I'm a dick. But this? The cool blowoff? The "you don't mean shit to me, so I'm fine" approach hurts like a motherfucker. *Is this how all those girls feel when I don't call them back?*

Goddamn it.

I call again and get her voice mail.

Even though I plan to run over to her place tomorrow, I'm slammed with class, practice and the homework I've blown off for a week. Finally, on Wednesday, I trek back to BU. I don't know if I'm more worried about how Dani will react or my sister, but when

Clem opens the door, she smiles widely and gives me a hug.

When she doesn't give me a piece of her mind, I breathe a little more easily. My eyes dart around her apartment, but it's quiet. We shoot the shit for a few minutes, and I make sure to ask how Clem's trip home with Gavin went. She's all mush and gush about their relationship even though she's trying to seem nonchalant, but I can tell she's batshit crazy about him.

I clear my throat. "So, uh, how's Dani? Is her leg better?"

Clem frowns. "I think it is. I don't really know. I haven't seen her around, but I haven't been home much." Her eyes narrow on me, and her frown deepens. "Why? What happened?"

Ignoring the question I know she's really asking, I go for the obvious. "Oh, you know, just wondering how the girl I hit with my car is doing." I shrug my hands into my coat pockets and try to change the subject. "You and Gavin doing winter break together too?"

She can't help talking about her boyfriend and thankfully shifts gears. But Clem's easygoing attitude is gone by the end of the week.

I'm walking to class when I get my sister's text. *"What the fuck happened between you and Dani? She hasn't been home all week. Jenna saw her and said she looks like shit. Did you fuck her over?"*

I'm about to ditch class and speed over to BU and find Danielle if I have to scour each dorm room on campus when my phone rings. I start to pick up, thinking it's Clementine. But it's not my sister.

It's my mother.

Joselyn laughs in my ear. And the only thing she says is, "I told you so."

CHAPTER THIRTY-THREE

- Dani -

All week I debate answering Jax's calls. His text said he wanted to explain. Explain what? That my boobs aren't big enough? That my hair isn't bleached the right shade? That my IQ doesn't match my shoe size? Because I'm sure the girl he ran off with had that in spades.

What a fucking prick.

My anger rages like a black and destructive storm until I think about my mom, and then it feels like my chest might collapse on itself.

How do you live when you know the one person you love more than life itself will die? How do you go on? How do you do the routine shit like go to school and do laundry and concentrate on homework when your mom's very existence sits like an hourglass running out of sand?

Sometimes it's too much, and I can't breath. Some days I go through the motions like an automaton, one step in front of the other, until whatever stupid task is accomplished. Like today.

I sit in class as my professor drones on.

When the lecture ends, I don't have a clue what he said or what I could have written on three sheets of notebook paper. Because the class might be discussing analytics and responsive design and viral content, but I only hear four words: Your mother is dying.

When the lecture is over, I pack my bag and wander into the hall.

"Ms. Hart?"

I turn to find a man in an expensive suite walking briskly toward me.

He says my name again, and I nod. The man extends his hand toward an alcove off to the side, ushering me out of the path of oncoming students.

"Ms. Hart, I'm Phillip Berringer, Jackson Avery's attorney."

I tilt my head. Did I hear that right? Jax's attorney? I try to swallow only to realize I can't. *Why did he send his attorney?*

He hands me an envelope. "I understand you were involved in a car accident. Mr. Avery said he'd like for you to sign this. He hopes this check covers the inconvenience of what happened last week."

I open my mouth, but no sound comes out. Again, my lips part, and I feel like a fish washed up on land, gasping for breath.

Finally, my lungs fill. "Jax… Jax sent you?"

The man nods, motioning for me to open the envelope I'm gripping. A piece of rectangular paper flutters to the ground when I unfold the contract, and I stare at it, wondering what kind of price Jax put on our friendship.

The man picks up the check and hands it to me.

I stare at the numbers before my eyes shift to the nondisclosure agreement. I don't have to read the words to know what this means. Jax wants me to keep my mouth shut about the accident, and he hopes he can seal the deal with cold, hard cash.

Blinking several times, I fight the tears forming in my eyes.

#FuckingAsshole

- Jax -

"I told you," my mother snorts into the phone.

"What, Mother? What did you tell me?" I roll my eyes. The text from my sister minutes ago has me headed for my car.

"When will you learn?"

"I'm late for an appointment, so if you want to say something, spit it out." I reach for my keys when I spot my car on the other side of the street.

"When will you learn that every girl has her price?" I stop in the middle of the crosswalk, but before I can say anything, Joselyn drops the bomb. "That girl took the deal. And she was cheap. The dent in your grille will cost more to repair."

My hand trembles as I hold my phone. I close my eyes.

Tell me this isn't happening again.

A horn honk gets me out of my catatonic state, and I make it to the sidewalk before I look down at my cell, the sound of my mother's voice warbling through it.

Rubbing my eyes with the heels of my hand, I press until white dots appear. And then I pitch my phone at a nearby tree and watch it shatter.

CHAPTER THIRTY-FOUR

- Dani -

Sleeping next to Travis is getting old. He hogs the bed, and despite his insistence that he doesn't snore, he does. Loudly. After two weeks of bumping around each other in his single occupancy dorm room, I'm sure he's ready to get rid of me too.

"I'm going home today," I tell him over breakfast.

His eyebrows shoot up. "No shit. Really?"

"I've taken up enough of that prime real estate," I say, nodding toward his bed. "Besides, I need to talk to Clem. It's overdue. I can't hide out the rest of my life."

"Sweets, you can stay here as long as you want. You know that, right?"

I reach over and hug him. "I appreciate that, but I need to be a big girl." Resting my forehead on his chest, I try not to think about what I'll do when I don't have him by my side. When I'm in Chicago and he's here.

He keeps his arms wrapped around me. As though reading my thoughts, he asks, "Have you decided what you're going to do next semester?"

"I guess I'm going home. I contacted Northwestern about transferring, but there are, like, a thousand kids ahead of me. But I don't think I have a choice, right?"

He runs his hand over my head. "No, honey. I guess you don't." He sighs. "Maybe you should wait and see. Don't make any decisions until you can talk to your mom."

I nod to appease him, but I think we both know what's going to happen.

We sit in silence as the tears stream down my face. We do this a lot lately. Travis has gotten good at just letting me break down. Today I cry because my mom has cancer. Because I'm going to have to leave my best friend. Because it looks like I'll have to drop out of school for a while even though I can't bring myself to make it official.

And underneath it all, I cry about Jax. That I miss him as much as I do when I'm barely an afterthought to him.

After wiping my face with the sleeve of my hoodie, I glance at the time. "I have an errand to run today before work, so I'd better get going."

Travis grabs his now soggy cereal and swirls his spoon in the bowl. "BC won the championship game last night," he says quietly.

Nodding, I let out a weak laugh. "I know. Jax scored two goals." I bite the inside of my cheek to keep myself from crying again.

Travis's eyes harden. "I still can't believe that fucker sent you a contract."

"Nothing says love like non-disclosure." My composure dissolves as my eyes fill with tears again. "Rich people, huh?"

Travis pulls me back to him.

He called me an inconvenience, like I was an unplanned oil change or a cavity that needed filling. I thought seeing Jax traipse off with another girl hurt, but this about knocked my heart out of my body.

As I trudge down Bay State Road several hours later, I try to soak in this street I love so much. Everything is bathed in white. Snow perches along every window ledge and cobblestone, and twinkle lights peek out from a few windows, announcing that it's almost Christmas. In the fading light of evening, it's so breathtaking, it's almost painful, reminding me of the postcard I kept on my pin board at home when I was a senior in high school, the one that made me want to move halfway across the country.

My brownstone is the fourth one on the left, and from the narrow street below I can see my room, shades drawn and dark. Just seeing it makes my heart speed up.

I can do this.

I'm glad I waited this long to return because I think I'm all cried out. I'll tell Clem what happened, apologize, and be done with it. All I can do is hope she'll understand. Even if she doesn't, I probably won't be here next semester anyway, so she can live with it for another week while we take our finals, and then I'll be out of her hair.

When I reach my building, the limo pulling up makes me do a double-take, and I freeze mid-step when I realize why it's here. Crap, the banquet.

Daren Sloan, Mr. Football himself, jumps out, and before I get a chance to feel awkward, he yanks me into a big hug.

"Congrats, Daren," I say into his tuxedo, barely still standing upright after he nearly pulled me off my feet.

"Thanks, Dani." He holds me out in front of him as he scans my new look. "I love the red. It suits you." I took the pink out of my hair last week and dyed large swaths of red for a photoshoot.

I force myself to smile. "Great game against Syracuse."

He beams that prime-time smile. "Thanks." He motions toward my place. "Could you tell the girls we're down here?"

I nod and my eyes drop to my feet.

From inside, Gavin and Ryan tell me hi, and I'm about to return their greeting when I hear a giggle and then a breathy, "Jax." I turn slightly and, through the open limo door, see a long, tanned leg through the slit of a glittery white dress.

My mouth unhinges, and I try to hold in a gasp.

He's here. With another girl.

#UnFuckingBelievable

You'd think the check and confidentiality agreement would've been enough for my stupid little heart to go stone cold for Jax Avery. I want to smack myself in the head for being in knots over this guy for the last couple of weeks. I should move on. He clearly has. *Because I obviously missed the memo the last two times he left me for other women.*

I roll my eyes. *So predictable.* I turn and run up to my building.

I'm heading in as Clem and Jenna are heading out, and they both look stunning.

"Holy shit, Dani. Where have you been?" Jenna asks as she hugs me. When she releases me, I lean over and hug Clem.

"Just hanging out with Travis." She knows this. I've texted her every couple of days to let her know I'm alive. "You two look drop-dead gorgeous," I say in my perkiest voice even though I'm still dying a slow death from what happened in the limo.

Clem grabs my arm. "We miss you. Glad to see my brother left you in one piece."

My brow furrows. "Oh, the car accident." An empty laughter falls from my lips as I paste a fake smile on my face. "Yeah, I'm okay." Barely.

We agree to do lunch the next day to catch up, and

then I watch them disappear down the stairs. When I'm back in my room, I collapse on my bed, too tired to pack my room or study. I need some rest if I plan to have that talk with Clem tomorrow.

One more week. That's all I have left here. Ignoring my compulsion to cry, I reach for some blank paper and start to draw.

Getting ditched on his kitchen table wasn't humiliating enough? You had to go and leave your art journal at his place?

Who knows what Jax thought when he went through it. At least, I imagine he went through it. Unless he simply threw it away. He tossed me to the curb. Why wouldn't he just ditch some book?

I shake my head, not letting myself go down another Jax Avery spiral. This is it. Just a few more days. When I leave Boston, I won't have anything to remind me of him.

Except feeding him pancakes.

And how he laughs when he thinks I'm being a goof.

And the way he feels against my bare skin in the shower.

Ugh! The pen in my hand immediately starts drawing thick, dark lines, and inside a cage, the edges of a butterfly start to take shape. Why I placed a butterfly inside a cage is beyond me, but that's the beauty of art. I don't have to understand it, just express it.

Which is why my business classes mess with my head. When I'm asked to explain why I think a particular image works for a marketing campaign, I can talk in art terms, about the shades of color or the weight of fonts, not business terms that dissect the beauty from anything aesthetic, the way a scalpel dissects a frog.

Before that call from my mom, I was ready to make the leap, to switch majors, but now, knowing I really will be alone soon, I have to finish my business degree, even if it's not here at BU. Because I'll only have myself to rely on.

Even though I tuck myself away in my favorite flannel sheets and down comforter and I'm so tired my eye sockets hurt, sleep is elusive.

Why couldn't Jax have been an asshole the whole time I stayed with him? Why did he have to pretend he cared if he didn't?

Clem and Jenna come home late, and I wonder what the night was like. Maybe it's better that I didn't go. It looks like I'm moving for good, and it would be just that much harder to leave someone like Jax anyway.

At least that's what I tell myself.

* * *

The next morning is quiet, and I sit on the couch drinking coffee, trying to commit this apartment to memory. A rumpled cashmere blanket hangs off the edge of our couch. A dozen Pizza Hut napkins rest on our micro-fridge. Several pairs of boots sit in a neat pile by the door.

I'll miss this place.

Reaching for my bag, I pull out a manila folder and leaf through the eight-by-ten photos Brady dropped off to me at work yesterday. Despite how uncomfortable I felt taking them, I have to admit they're beautifully shot, and although there was ample opportunity for awkwardness, he made me relax. He treated me with respect. He was a gentleman.

Inwardly, I groan. Why couldn't I like Brady?

The door to Clem's door swings open, shaking me from my lament, and she trots out wearing her winter running clothes.

I drop the photos on the table and pick up my coffee mug. "Morning. Did you have fun last night?"

She heads towards the couch and sits next to me. Her lips pull into a half smile. "Yeah, last night was great." A pensive expression crosses her face. "It would have been better if you were there, though."

I shrug. "I don't know Daren that well."

Her elbow bumps mine. She's silent, and I look up at her. Clem's eyes are wide and assessing. "You know what I mean."

I swallow the lump in my throat. My eyes fall to my lap. "I wanted to tell you, but I've been a bit of a mess."

"I kind of wondered if something had happened between you and my brother when you didn't come home," she says softly as she hugs me. It's too much, and I lose it. Deep sobs spill from me, and she lets me cry on her shoulder. After a few minutes, I pull away.

I whisper, "It goes farther back than Thanksgiving, which is part of the problem." I wipe my face. "I need to tell you how it began."

After taking a deep breath, I start at the beginning, how I had that stupid list that included getting a tattoo and a one-night stand, how I met Jax at the club, and how I had no idea who he was until I officially met him a week later at Ryan's.

Ignoring the way my face burns, I let it all out. "I'm so sorry for lying to you, but I felt ashamed. I heard how you talked about the girls Jax hooked up with, and I hated that you'd see me as one of them."

Clem grabs my arm. "Dani, I would never think that about you. Yeah, I wanted to warn you about my brother, but that was mostly to protect you." She grimaces. "Okay, there's one other reason I don't want him sleeping with my friends." The expression on her face makes my stomach tighten. "He slept with my roommate freshman year, and she flipped out when she realized it was just a one-time thing. Then she made my life hell until I moved out second semester."

Yeah, that sucks. "I would never do that," I say as I pick imaginary lint off my pajama bottoms.

She laughs. "Yeah, I know." After a minute, her eyebrows pull tight. "So what happened over Thanksgiving? Was he an ass?"

My eyes shift down. "How much do you want to know?"

"On a scale of one to ten, ten being he ran off with another girl right after you two hooked up, where would you place my brother?"

I groan and cover my face, not wanting her to see me when I confess what happened. "I'd say a nine point nine nine."

She huffs. "I am going to kick his ass."

My hands drop into my lap. "No, don't. I knew what I was getting myself into, and he honestly did take really good care of me up until he took off with that blonde."

Her eyes narrow into slits. "What the fuck is wrong with my brother? I am seriously going to nuke that boy off the planet."

Assuring her that's not necessary takes a while. Eventually, we sprawl out on the floor with a couple of bowls of cereal.

As I scoop up a bite, I sigh. "I was trying really hard to stay away from him, if it means anything."

She frowns. "Shit, I begged you to go over to his place before break. If I hadn't, you wouldn't have missed your flight home. I'm so sorry."

"It's okay. I'm headed to Chicago at the end of the week, so it's fine." Shifting the contents of my bowl around, I fight the burning in my eyes. "I might have to stay home second semester. Maybe permanently."

"What?" Her eyes bulge before her spoon drops into her bowl with a clatter.

"My mom's sick. She's… dying." Wet drops slide down my cheeks. "Her cancer is back. She doesn't have very long."

"Oh, Dani." Clem slams her cereal down on the coffee table and hugs me again as she mumbles in my ear, "I can't believe you're going through all of this with Jax dicking you around."

I laugh through my tears. "You have a way with words."

She lets go of me and raises an eyebrow. "You're not the first person to tell me that." She picks up her bowl, and I grab my empty coffee mug, too exhausted to refill it. Bumping me with her shoulder, she adds, "If it's any consolation, last night my brother looked as miserable as you do." My head jerks up as she says with an evil smile, "Of course, I'd say he deserves it."

I don't put too much stock in that. He could've been miserable because his date was a ditz or didn't reveal enough cleavage.

Clem and I hang out all morning, and she eventually kicks off her running shoes. We're contemplating lunch when I realize I haven't explained everything.

"Clem, I hope you're not mad, but there's one more thing…"

CHAPTER THIRTY-FIVE

- Jax -

The last final of the semester is always the biggest bitch. Stretching out my hand that cramps from gripping a pen for the last two hours only reminds me how much I'm going to hate law school. As I head toward the parking lot, my phone sounds with an incoming text. I pull it out of my pocket to see a message from my sister.

"Have I told you lately that you're a total dumbass?"

She doesn't give me time to respond before she buzzes in with the next one. *"Just wanted to show you what you're missing. Think about this long and hard."*

I'm guessing this has something to do with Dani. I've been avoiding talking to Clem about what happened over Thanksgiving. Even though we went to Daren's banquet in a big group, I managed to stick my date Trina between my sister and me for most of the evening, which did the trick. Clem might've seemed polite on the outside, but I knew she was ticking off all the reasons she didn't like that girl in her head.

Seeing Dani the night of Daren's banquet almost did me in. With the red in her hair, I couldn't miss her, even through the dark tinted windows of the limo. I hated the look of disgust on her face when she realized I was with a date, but as much as I miss her, as much as I fight myself every damn day to not call her, I can't forget what she did. I can't forget that she took that money from my mother, who kindly faxed me a copy of the non-disclosure so I could see it with my own eyes.

My thumb hovers over the attachment that I'm tempted to delete. Surely Dani didn't tell Clem about accepting the check, something my sister would hate her for even more rabidly than me.

I click on it anyway, and the moment I do, I wish I hadn't.

The burgundy hair is the first thing to get my attention. All the color is stripped from the photo except for that hair and those perfectly plump ruby lips. Gone are the playful streaks of pink. Gone is the smile and lightness in her eyes. Gone is the touch of sweetness that reminded me of a kitten.

In fact, Dani's expression is haunting as she stares back into the lens. She looks a little too thin, her cheekbones too sharp, her expression too pointed. But Jesus, she's gorgeous. My heart knocks in my chest, reminding me that we were so close to having something real. Until we imploded.

The second thing I notice is all of her creamy white skin. The crest of her breasts. The elegant lines of her neck.

But the third thing, the one that feels like a kick to my balls, is the fact that Brady's tattooed arm is tightly wrapped around her naked torso, hiding those piercings, as he presses his bare chest to her back and looks over her shoulder. They look like a couple.

Is that what my sister is trying to tell me? That Dani is with Brady now?

I shouldn't be jealous. I've forced myself to go on a few dates since Dani left. Each one felt worse than the one before because I can't seem to move on. I've been out with gorgeous women, but their touch makes me cringe. And each night, when I close my eyes, there is only one girl who invades my dreams.

I keep telling myself it's better that I know who Dani really is now before I'm in too deep. I'd rather know that beneath that sweet exterior is a gold-digger.

Fuck it to hell. I hate when my mother is right.

CHAPTER THIRTY-SIX

- Dani -

I used to love airports. The frenzied way people scurried to their gates and the excitement of what lay beyond the steel-tipped wings of the planes made me buzz with anticipation.

But now, staring down at my boots caked with the salt and silt of a winterized Boston, all I feel is dread that what the future holds are days without my mother.

As I run my thumbnail along the styrofoam of my Dunkin' Donuts coffee, making small indentations, all I can think about are the goodbyes I've said this week. Most were casual because I didn't want to talk about my mom, but having to hug Travis one last time nearly broke me in two.

"I'll come out over spring break," he mumbled into my hair last night as he hugged me once more. "I bet Zinzer will give you your job back in the fall when you come back." Nodding, I tried to smile even though I couldn't say whether I'll ever return to Boston. It feels tainted now.

I packed most of the stuff in my room, and Jenna said she'd ship it to me when I decided what to do, but she wouldn't let me touch my bed. She said she had a feeling I'd be back, and she wanted me to know it was waiting for me in case I could return.

I'd held back the tears all week until that point, but before I knew what was happening, the waterworks began. Jenna and I had been glued at the hip ever since she walked in on my heart-to-heart with Clem, who filled her in on what went down with Jax. They both showered me with TLC from that moment until the cab came to pick me up this morning.

I can't believe I thought Clem would hate me for being with her brother. She couldn't have been more kind or compassionate. She even told me that if she had been in my shoes, she probably wouldn't have told him what happened on his birthday either.

An announcement blares. "American Airlines flight 243 to Chicago O'Hare is now boarding at gate twelve."

I have one more thing to do before I board my flight.

Opening the e-reader on my phone, I click on Clementine's book. My finger hesitates for a moment before it flicks to the left and deletes the file. I know my roommate would understand.

Goodbye, Jax.

* * *

I should be happy to be going home because it's been so long since I've been back, but when I take in the Windy City as the plane descends on the runway, I feel even more crestfallen. The snow along every sidewalk and street corner has hardened in the frigid air, and a gray soot blankets the ice, dimming any brightness.

Like the city is already mourning my loss, I think bitterly.

No, I can't let myself be a basket case. I have to be strong. Mom needs me to keep my shit together.

At least for now.

I pull my luggage behind me as I scan the arrival loading zone, looking for my mom's beat-up Toyota Corolla.

I expect to see her wearing some silly holiday sweater with ornaments hanging off an obnoxious fringe. I love those stupid sweaters.

"Danielle!" Someone calls my name from the open window of a minivan.

I don't immediately recognize the woman, mostly because I'm not expecting my mom's neighbor to be here. Mom has never sent anyone to get me.

Walking slowly to the van, I peer in, hoping to see Mom in the passenger seat, but it's empty, except for Susan, her long-time best friend who lives next door.

"Hi," I say cheerfully so I don't start bawling.

I'm twenty. You'd think I'd be okay with someone other than my mother picking me up from the airport. But deep down, I know this can't be good.

Susan runs around and gives me a hug before she helps me load my luggage. We chitchat as we drive out to the suburbs, and the longer she waits to explain why my mom's not here, the more I'm filled with dread.

Finally, I can't take it anymore. "It's that bad, huh?" I ask as I stare out the window.

She's silent, and I turn to look her in the eye.

"Yeah, sweetie, it is." Susan's hands grip the steering wheel. "Because you know she loves picking you up from the airport."

Thinking back to all the phone conversations I had with my mom over the last few months, I'm suddenly able to pinpoint when she realized she was sick.

"My mom's laptop camera never stopped working."

"She didn't want you to worry, honey. Beth thought she had more time, that she could fight it, and she tried one more medicine, but it made her sicker. You know how proud she is of you going to school in Boston. She figured you'd just come rushing home, and she wanted you to finish your degree." Susan sniffles. "She tells me all the time that she was never as brave as you when she was your age."

Hot tears stream down my face as the city rushes by my window. I would never call myself brave. Two weeks of avoiding my roommate attests to that fact, but I don't bother to defend myself because the boulder-sized knot in my throat prevents me from saying anything.

When we pull up to my house, I wipe the wetness from my face. If I've ever needed to be brave, now's the time.

CHAPTER THIRTY-SEVEN

- Jax -

The older man approaching me in front of my apartment building has a strange expression on his face.

"Jax Avery?" he asks as he looks down at a piece of paper.

"Who wants to know?" God, I sound like a dick. Happy fucking holidays.

"Maxwell Smith. I'm the director at the Boys & Girls club of Roxbury."

He extends his hand to me, and after eyeing him warily for a minute, I extend mine. It's Christmas Eve, and I've never been in a worse mood.

"What's up?" I have forty-five minutes before I need to get on the road. I'm meeting a few friends in New York for winter break, and after the last few weeks, I could use the distraction of getting out of Boston.

"Sir, I just wanted to thank you." Hearing him call me sir makes this interaction even odder.

I laugh, but it lacks any conviction. "I'm sorry. What are we talking about?"

The man pats me on the shoulder. "The donation. I wanted to thank you for the donation." What the hell drug is this dude on? "We are able to keep our doors open for the next year because of you, and your assistant expressly stated that we needed to maintain the soccer program, which we will of course. In fact, I was wondering if you'd like to do a couple of small camps with the kids. They'd be thrilled to see a real soccer star, and—"

"My assistant?" I'm seriously so lost. I scrub my face with my hand. "Honestly, this is strange."

He chuckles. "It was very strange indeed. It's not every day someone donates that kind of money and then turns around and waits to catch a bus."

"Okay, back up. I'm confused."

He grins sheepishly. "Please forgive me for tracking you down. I know the young lady said you wanted to remain anonymous, but I had to thank you in person, and your name was on the check. This money is going to help so many children who would otherwise be relegated to spending time on the streets, getting in trouble."

"What young lady?" Even as the words leave my mouth, I know what he's going to say. Time stills as I wait for the answer that will elate and kill me in equal measure.

"Pretty girl. Red hair. She didn't tell me her name, just stipulated that the soccer program had to be developed."

Dani.

My heart sinks as I put the pieces of the puzzle together.

What have I done? I accused her of one of the worst forms of betrayal without ever asking her to her face, and she goes and does this? She basically signed away all of her rights in that non-disclosure agreement and then gave away the money. To a cause she knew I'd love.

Goddamn it. I'm a fucking idiot.

I don't remember the rest of our conversation. I barely remember how I get into my apartment. When I knock on Ryan's door an hour later, I can hear voices talking cheerfully, and the pit in my stomach grows. I know my sister is here, glued to her boyfriend Gavin, and even though I suspect the odds are slim that Dani is still around, I need to talk to her.

Jenna opens the door, her usual easy grin sliding into a forced smile.

"Merry Christmas, Jax." She pauses and looks away as she opens the door a little wider. "Come in."

Behind her, Ryan and Gavin sit at a card table as Clem stalks toward me.

I guess by the expression on my face she knows why I'm here because she points her finger at me and says, "You're too late, Einstein. She already left for Chicago." Clem shakes her head. "And she's probably not coming back."

"What? Why?"

"Her mother is dying." Clem looks at me like I'm an ass. "She has family obligations and some pretty heavy shit on her shoulders, not to mention you jerked her around like she was trash. But, yeah, she packed all of her stuff before she left. Jenna is waiting to hear what things are like back home before she calls UPS."

Dani is leaving. Possibly for good. Fuck.

The friendly banter that floated from this room when I got here is replaced with a thick, suffocating silence.

"If it's any consolation," Clem says, her eyes narrowing, "I think you were the icing on the cake. Jesus, Jax, this girl has enough going on. Did you really have to fuck with her?"

Ignoring the uncomfortable atmosphere, I ask, "She told you I'm the reason she's not returning to school?"

"She didn't have to. She avoided coming home for two weeks. She stayed with Travis the whole time because she was embarrassed about what happened between you two. Thanks for fucking up my roommate, by the way. Couldn't you have picked one of your slutty dates to entertain you that weekend? Did you have to screw with Dani? She's a nice girl."

That's what I can't explain—that I tried to stay away from her, and the longer I tried, the closer we got as friends and the more I liked her.

"You don't know the whole story, Clementine," I tell her gruffly.

Clem's eyebrow tilts up. "Enlighten me."

"She lied to me. She knew me this whole time, since my birthday, and—"

"And she didn't fall and worship at your feet after you left her high and dry at the club without saying goodbye?"

Well, when Clem says it like that…

My sister pins me with a glare. "Did you realize there's a photo of you online the night of your birthday leaving Cages with that model?"

Shit.

Clem doesn't wait for me to respond. "The same girl who, coincidentally, stuck her tongue down your throat at Ryan's? You really expected Dani to interrupt that when you couldn't remember her name because you had a goddamn concussion?"

Okay, I guess Dani told her more than I thought. But there's one thing I'm sure she didn't disclose that convoluted everything.

Her arm waves in front of me, cutting me off. "Don't even start about the money."

I still, my body going rigid. "You've known?" I feel the pulse in my temple. "For how long?" Now I'm pissed. My own goddamn sister knew Dani didn't keep that check, and she didn't tell me.

"Since the day after Daren's banquet. She told me everything and apologized." Clem shakes her head.

"Aside from what I'm guessing was the pure humiliation of hooking up with some guy who didn't remember her, she was afraid I'd judge her or be pissed that you two got together." Her lips tighten. "That's my fault because I don't have anything nice to say about the typical women you date, but I certainly don't include her in that group. So I assured her my cautionary words about you had everything to do with you being a slut and not about me thinking she wasn't good enough for my brother, dim-witted though he may be."

Emotions churn in my stomach like grinding gears. "So you knew that she donated thirty grand to the Boys & Girls Club?"

"Yup." Clem's nonchalance has me one step away from strangling her.

"Why the fuck didn't you tell me?"

"Because if you really thought she was into you for the money, then you don't know her, and you certainly don't deserve her." Just in case I'm not listening, Clem pokes me in the chest. "Let me be clear. You haven't convinced me otherwise."

I run my hands through my hair, exasperated. "I jumped to conclusions. I admit that. But I've been burned by a girl like this before, and it just cut too close to home." Giselle decimated me with one lie, and then she took the money and ran. "Clem, I think you understand what that feels like."

For years after her breakup with Daren, my sister was a mess. Didn't date anyone until she met Gavin earlier this semester.

My eyes slide to him, and he stares back, his expression telling me I need to chill out.

I take a deep breath, willing myself to back off the ledge.

Clem's shoulders relax marginally, and she's quiet a long minute. Finally, she nods.

"I'm listening."

CHAPTER THIRTY-EIGHT

- Dani -

The white house sits nestled in a blanket of snow, but the walkway is clear. Never in my life have those steps been harder to make. I thank Susan for the ride and force myself forward, my eyes trained on the slight figure sitting on the couch near the large front window.

"Mom?" I call out in the entryway after letting myself in.

"In here," a weak voice says.

After I close the door behind me, I pause. The air is cold, not quite as frigid as outside, but cold enough that I can see my breath. It should smell like cinnamon and sage, my mother's favorite spices. Instead, antiseptic and bleach scent the air.

I drop the handle to my luggage, turn up the thermostat in the hallway, and head toward the living room where I stare at the person in front of me, not quite recognizing my mother.

"Hi, darling." She waves me closer.

She's a rail. Thin and pale. Like she hasn't left the house or eaten properly in months. She's swimming in a bright red sweater that features Rudolph, whose nose blinks on and off like a broken stop light.

"Like it?" She points down at her chest, and I try to ignore her bony fingers.

"Yeah." I have to clear my throat. "It's great, Mom." I sit next to her and wrap my arms around her narrow shoulders. Tears sting my eyes and the back of my throat as she pats my shoulder.

"Hey, kiddo. I've missed you." She kisses the top of my head, and I almost lose it.

I will not break down. I will not break down.

Biting my cheek until it hurts, I focus on that pain instead of my dying parent. When we break apart, the look of love in her eyes threatens to shatter me. Where will I ever find that kind of love again? Once my mother is gone, I'll be alone.

"None of that!" she chides. "No crying before Christmas. That's some kind of sacrilege. Susan left a few meals in the fridge for us. Why don't you pick one out and pop it in the oven for dinner."

I bring the food to her when it's ready so she doesn't have to expend the energy to get up. She smiles, tipping her fork toward me. "I love your red hair. It's beautiful. It's bold. It's perfect."

In the blur of coming home, I had forgotten she hadn't seen it.

I return the smile and push the food around on my plate.

"So," she says, breaking the silence, "I'm considering getting a small apartment in Boston. What do you think?"

Staring into my bowl of noodles like I might be able to find the right words somewhere in the Alfredo sauce, I nod and force another smile.

"Sounds great, Mom." The lie slips off my tongue. But I'll play along through Christmas. Maybe even through the New Year. After that, I won't be able to hide my plans to come home.

She talks animatedly while I eat the casserole, but I know what she's doing—pretending this isn't as bad as it is—but it's hard to ignore how she picks at her food and clenches her jaw like she's trying not to throw up.

Our discussion about Boston reminds me of how I'd always ask for a pony when I was a kid, and she would describe where we'd go to buy one and the stall where we'd keep him, the kind of apples he'd like and the little sounds he'd make when we'd pet him. We could talk about my horse for hours even though I knew we could never afford one. The talk was what mattered, the possibility, the hope. I see the same look in her eyes now. She just wants hope. A reason to live.

After I put our dishes away and settle back on the couch with two mugs of hot chocolate, my mom reaches for a manila folder and hands it to me. I open it and stare, not sure what I'm looking at.

"Those are all of my accounts. Our accounts. I had your name put on everything—the deed to the house, my bank account, my IRAs. Oh, and that stock you suggested has performed really well this month. I'm glad that school is teaching you something." She reaches for my hand, her cold skin a reminder of what's to come. "I left you off my credit cards, though." She chuckles. "I figured you could do without those balances."

"We don't have to do this right now." The numbness inside me grows, like roots pushing up through a sidewalk.

"Yes, honey, we do." Her eyes, deep pools of green with flecks of amber, look dim.

Her words ricochet inside of me until I can barely breathe. I curl up, dropping my head into her lap and cry, for all the time we won't spend together, the memories we won't have, the laughter we can't share. She strokes my hair softly, her gentle touch making me sob harder. She's dying, her last breaths are numbered, and I'm the one crying. I'm suddenly furious that I let myself get distracted all semester by some guy when my mom's been here dealing with this by herself.

When the tears stop and all I can do is whimper into her flannel pajama bottoms, I sit up.

She clears her throat and whispers, "Do you have friends you can go to… afterward? I need to know you're not alone."

"I have Travis." I wipe my face with sleeve of my sweater. "I had some pretty great roommates this semester too."

"Anyone else?" she asks hopefully. "A boy?"

I stiffen, not sure what to tell her. I want to make her feel better, for her to know I'll be okay, but the aftershocks of what happened with Jax are too fresh.

"No." My eyes shift to my lap. "Not really." She lifts my chin, forcing me to look at her, so I add, "There was someone, but it didn't work out."

Her eyebrows furrow. "What happened?"

A thousand things run through my mind. Jax is a total player. I lied to him by not telling him what happened on his birthday. He ran off with a blonde and left me in his room naked.

I finally go with, "It's complicated."

Her mouth twists, and she gives me a knowing look. "Was it the boy who hit you with his car?"

My mouth falls open. "Seriously, how do you do that?" I never gave her any indication I liked Jax.

She laughs. "Ah, I nailed it." With a little wink, she pats me on the hand. "I thought you sounded a little too happy after getting knocked on your ass by a BMW."

I groan, embarrassed.

"Okay, so tell me about him. I want all the details." She watches me over the lip of her mug as she takes a sip of her hot chocolate.

"How about *some* of the details?" I ask, feeling my face flush.

Her grin widens. "It's juicy. I can tell!" She wiggles a little in her seat like I just dropped the best bit of gossip in her lap.

I'm not used to talking to my mom like she's a girlfriend. Sure, she's always been supportive, but deep down I'm kind of a shy person when it comes to talking about my love life, especially with my mother.

"Spill it. I've been cooped up all fall. I need something good. Let's start with the basics. How cute is he?"

I drop my head into my hands and groan again. "He's definitely *not* cute. So not cute. He's hot. Like off-the-charts hot. Like out-of-my-league hot." The word volcanic comes to mind.

She tsks me like I've been bad. "Have you looked in the mirror lately? You are gorgeous, my girl. A guy would have to be a total dumbass not to see that."

I laugh and shake my head. It's still weird that she curses.

"Well, he *is* an ass, so there's that." I start to tell her how we met, leaving out my goal that night of a one-night stand. I change the "he went down on me at the club" to "we kissed." Scrubbing the rest of the story to give it a parent-worthy PG-rating, I finally get to the end, that after hanging out the entire Thanksgiving break "snuggling," he bolted with another girl.

"Hmm," she says. "Well, I'm surprised 'snuggling' got you to turn that shade of red, but I'll let it go for now." She nudges me with her elbow, and I fight the fire that's taken residence in my face. "It sounds like you weren't super honest with him, and I'm surprised you left without a fight, especially since it seems like you were pining over him all semester."

I gasp. "I was not pining."

She snickers at me. "Here's the thing, Dani. You said his family is estranged, that he comes from a very wealthy background. Those kind of people aren't exactly known for their love and affection for their children."

My lips twist as her words seep in. Having lived with Clementine for the last several months was eye-opening. Her parents have all but disowned her, which sucks because she's amazing. I can't imagine what it's been like for her brother.

And then my mom really surprises me. "I think you should give him another chance."

"What?" This is the last thing I expect my mom to say. "Why should I do that? He's a total man-whore, Mother. I can't believe you'd want me with someone like that."

"Someone who waited on you hand and foot while you recovered from your injuries?" she asks, all judgmental.

"Ugh. Fuck. Why do you have to remind me?" Realizing I dropped an f-bomb, I apologize.

She laughs. "It's okay. But if you're going to say it, really mean it. It's better that way." She elbows me again. "So I'm guessing the sex was good?"

"Holy shit." I cover both of my eyes like she's blinded me. "I can't believe you just asked me that." Who is this person and what has she done with my parent, the one who used to block the TV from my view when people kissed?

She continues as though she did not just ask me about screwing.

"Sexual compatibility is very important in a relationship. I wish someone would've told me that when I was younger. I probably wouldn't have married your father. I mean, a penis should be good for something."

I might die now.

She adds, "Of course, I'd go through it again just to have you, but our sex life was about as exciting as grouting a tub."

Okay, my parents did not have good sexy times. Duly noted. That must explain the divorce. But I probably could have done without that bit of information. I scratch my head, wondering if this conversation is going to land me in therapy some day.

Eventually, my horror begins to subside, and we move on to other things. I even get the nerve to show her my tattoo, which she loves.

By 7:30, I can tell she's exhausted. I help her use the restroom before I tuck her into bed.

I'm just about to walk away when she grabs her chest and winces.

"Mom? Are you okay? What do you need?"

She points to the closet. I think she's going to direct me to a stash of meds or painkillers or even a bag of pot, but she has me grab a wrapped gift.

"Why don't we do this in the morning?" I hand it to her, worried that I'm wearing her out.

"No. I want to give it to you now."

I swallow hard, afraid to speak, knowing that we're running out of time. When I can breathe again, I tell her I need to grab her gift, and I use those few minutes to collect myself.

She laughs when she opens my present and reads it out loud. "I paid for my kid to go to Boston University, and all I got was this lousy t-shirt." She looks at me and grins. "I fucking love it!"

I shake my head at her and chuckle at her profanity.

But my laughter fades the moment she pulls off her

sweater and I see her skeletal frame. Slowly tugging on the t-shirt, she mumbles something about how the school should give these away considering how expensive the tuition is.

By the time she settles back on the pillows, she's out of breath but pushes on to talk. Grabbing my wrist, she says, "Promise me you'll graduate. There's enough money. I took out a decent life insurance when your father left, and it's all yours."

She rattles off more mandates, like I should sell the house because there's still a big balance on the mortgage; I should trade in her car and get something new; I might want to move somewhere warmer eventually. I can tell she's running through a checklist in her mind, the kind you make just before going on a trip. *Take out the trash, unplug the coffee maker, lock all the doors.*

She grips my hand again. "Danielle, don't be afraid to fall in love. It's scary as hell, but it's worth it."

The tears drip down my face so when she eventually motions to open the gift in front of me, it takes my eyes a few moments to focus.

It's hard to unwrap something you know is probably the last gift a loved one will ever give you. The paper is beautiful, and my shaking fingers struggle to open it without tearing the pattern, but with each tear, the fabric of my life unravels just a little more.

The gold locket glimmers in my hand.

It snaps open. Inside is a picture of my mom and me, cheek to cheek, grinning like lunatics before I left for Boston my freshman year.

"One side for all my love that you'll always carry with you. The other side is for that special man who knows a good thing when he sees it."

The empty side feels like such a huge void, and my

chest clenches at the reminder that Jax is no longer in my life.

Nodding, I smile, wanting her to see only my gratitude. She doesn't need to see my heartache.

She helps me put on the delicate chain, and as it dangles down my collarbone, she puts her frail hand across the gold heart and sighs.

"Danielle, you're the best thing that ever happened to me. I'm so proud of you. Never forget that." And for the first time today, tears stream down her cheeks. "I'm sorry we don't have more time." She scrunches her eyes. "Goddamn it. I never showed you how to change a tire."

I laugh at the absurdity of my mom even knowing how to change a tire, much less wanting to show me how to do it. We hug, and I hold her close, grateful for every minute we have together.

By the time I close her door, I'm somehow sure that tonight is one of the best and worst nights of my life.

Before I go to bed, I text Jenna four words: *Please send my stuff.*

CHAPTER THIRTY-NINE

- Jax -

If I knock any harder, Travis might call the cops, but I have to do something. I couldn't sleep after I got the text from my sister telling me Dani isn't coming back, and after some major creeper-type behavior on Google, I tracked down her best friend at his house in the 'burbs.

The door finally swings open, and one very pissed-off and disheveled-looking Travis answers the door. "I should kick your ass. Waking me at the asscrack of dawn on Christmas isn't even at the top of my list why I should smash that pretty face of yours."

I hold my hands up, trying to make peace. "She's planning to stay in Chicago."

He rubs his eyes with the palms of his hands. "Shit." He rubs his face again. "Yeah, I knew that was a strong possibility." He shoots me another dirty look. "You didn't exactly help the situation any, asshole."

"I want to make it up to her. I need to make it up to her. But to do that, I need your help."

"Explain why the fuck I should help you on Christmas when you've only been a shithead?"

"Because you care about Dani, and you know she's going through a lot right now. And I can help her if she'll let me."

An older female voice yells from the hallway behind Travis. "Who's there, son?"

"No one, Mom. Just an asshole."

"*Mijo*, that's not nice. Tell your friend to come in. I'm making coffee." Pots and pans clatter. "Ask him if he wants some breakfast."

I smile at Travis, breaking out the charm. "Your mom sounds lovely." My smile broadens as his eyes narrow.

"God, you're a good-looking fucker." He sighs. "Fine. Come in. But this doesn't mean I'm helping you."

CHAPTER FORTY

- Jax -

My eyes are bleary and bloodshot. Chugging another Red Bull, I ignore the way my hand shakes from the caffeine. I don't like how it reminds me of all-nighters and partying, but it does the trick and keeps me awake. Nauseous, but awake.

I toss the empty can in the back seat and listen to it rattle around with the others.

The skies are dark even though it's ten in the morning. Salt and snow and dirt grind beneath my tires as I drive through the semi-deserted streets of Chicago.

I laugh to myself when I think about how pissed my mother is going to be when she finds out what I'm doing. Not that she's the reason I've just driven a thousand miles, but telling her to fuck off is a definite perk.

I could barely contain my anger when I realized what she did, making it seem as though I was the one who wanted Dani to sign that fucking contract. No wonder Dani ignored all the texts I've sent her in the last two days. The girl probably wants to punch me in the throat. Hell, I want to punch myself in the throat.

God, I miss her.

I don't bother looking in the rearview mirror before I switch lanes, which gets me several honks from the car behind me a second before a fist socks me in the arm.

"Don't kill us before we get there, dickwad," Travis grumbles from the passenger seat. "Remind me again why we're not flying? Why aren't you traveling my ass first-class?"

"We've been over this already. One, it's Christmas. Or it was," I say, looking at the date display on my phone. "Two, that snowstorm disrupted service in the Midwest, backing up flights. And three, the earliest one didn't leave until tomorrow."

He grunts at me, not bothering to reply.

It bothers me that Travis still thinks I'm a lower lifeform. I've told him everything, bared my soul to him, and he rolls his eyes at me like I'm the biggest douchebag he's ever seen. Maybe I am. I guess I can't fault him. I did some seriously stupid shit when it came to Dani, but I'm here to make it right.

Now that I know who she is, who she really is, I can't let go. I'm an idiot for not seeing it sooner, for not realizing that she was probably just as afraid of what was happening between us as I was, and the second there was a reason to doubt her, I ran like hell. Fucking pussy.

As we drive through her neighborhood, Travis turns in his seat. He looks me over like he's debating something. "When you ditched Dani at the club on your birthday, she was pretty crushed, and when you showed up at Ryan's with another girl and didn't remember her, she tried to brush it off, but I know she was hurt." Then he tilts his head toward me to underscore what he's about to say. "But when you left her over Thanksgiving, she was devastated." I don't need him telling me that was a dick move—I know it was—but the guilt residing in my chest tells me I deserve every minute of his tirade, so I sit here and take it.

Travis isn't a huge guy. He's tall and has kind of a lanky build, but with the tension radiating off him, I'm sure he could do some damage if prompted. He points at me. "I'm only going to tell you this once. If you hurt her again, I will make sure that pretty face of yours meets with my fist."

I smile grimly at him. "If you think I'm here to make her miserable, why did you come?"

"Because she hasn't texted or called me back since she got home." He grabs his phone and scrolls through the screen. "We've never gone this long without talking." His eyes flick toward me. "I'm worried about her. Even when you landed her in the hospital, she texted me right away. She hasn't responded to her roommates either."

My jaw tightens, and I drive faster, my back tires sliding as we curve around a bend. Spotting my destination, a pristine but small white two-story at the end of the block, has me exhaling in relief.

The curtains at the front of the house are pulled back, and Dani's red hair immediately catches my eye. She sits near the window, still, like she's frozen, even though a half dozen people move around in her living room. I'm still not quite used to the red streaks in her hair, but she's impossible to miss.

"Maybe they're having a holiday party," Travis says as an older couple walks up to the house with an armload of tupperware.

"Yeah." But even as I say that, I think it's odd there are so many people in Dani's living room, but she sits there alone like she's in her own little sphere.

Glancing in the rearview mirror, I groan. "Fuck, I look like shit."

Travis smirks. "Didn't want to go there, but since you're pointing it out…" He lets the sentence fade, and I try to ignore the way that gets under my skin.

Maybe I shouldn't have come straight here after driving all night, but I can't let this go on any longer. I can't let her think I wanted her to sign that contract. Jesus, it makes it seem like… like I used her, like I made a move on her because I wanted something.

"Now don't fuck this up." Travis zips up his jacket and gives me a mocking grin. "And let me do the talking. She likes me."

"Thanks, fuckwad. Good to know," I mumble as I stretch out my legs for the first time in hours.

My stomach is in knots when Travis knocks on the front door. An older-looking blonde woman opens the door. Is that Dani's mom?

"You must be Dani's friends," she says, relief in her face when Travis nods. "Thank goodness. I haven't been able to get her to eat anything in days, and I really don't think Jack Daniels qualifies as food."

I look at Travis who frowns.

The woman ushers us in and takes our coats. Turning to the living room on the right, Travis heads straight to her and drops down on the couch like he owns the place. Dani's eyes barely leave the small flatscreen TV. She brings a tumbler of amber liquid to her mouth and takes a big gulp. I wanted to give her time to talk to Travis first, but seeing her pale and thin and obviously drunk has me stalking across the living room. I sit next to her, and she barely seems to register that either of us is here.

The people who had been milling around take the hint and shuffle off to another room.

"Dani, sweets, are you okay?" Travis asks, petting her hair.

She laughs, but it's cold and lifeless. "Wow. I did not realize I drank that much." Her words slur. She stares into her drink. "I must be really fucked up if I'm imagining you and Jax." Her eyes well with tears. "If I'm trying to make myself feel better, why the hell would I imagine him? Hey, hot guy who looks like Jax, want to fuck me over too?" There's that lifeless laugh again, and it guts me.

"Dani," I say slowly, "we're really here. I wanted to apologize." She blinks at me. "I texted you and called on Christmas, but you didn't pick up."

Her head turns toward me, tears streaming down her face, but she doesn't look surprised to see me.

"She would have liked you," Dani says. Blowing out a big breath, she laughs. "I tried telling her you broke my heart, and she seemed to think that was okay, that it was part of living." She rolls her eyes before she takes another swig of her drink. "Fuck, that sounds stupid."

I want to pull her onto my lap and hold her, but Travis wraps his arm around her shoulders and she goes willingly, snuggling up to him. He shoots me a worried look, and I feel totally helpless. I don't know what has her so despondent. I know our relationship is fucked up right now, but my sister said Dani had finished the semester strong and was in decent spirits before she left for home.

Getting up, I decide to find her mom. She might have some choice words for me, but I'm done fucking around. I can handle whatever she sends my way.

The living room leads to a small dining room. Turning, I find everyone in the kitchen. I see the woman who opened the door for us.

Lowering my voice, I extend my hand. "Hi, I'm Jax." She smiles at me, her eyes warm and welcoming. I clear my throat. "It's good to meet you, Mrs. Hart."

Her face pales, and everyone stills around us. She blinks several times, and it takes her a few moments before she looks at me again.

"I'm so sorry." She shakes her head. "I'm not Beth.

I'm her neighbor Susan."

I start to apologize and ask for Dani's mom when Susan places her hand on my arm. She leans toward me, her eyes watery, and quietly says, "Beth passed two days ago."

Beth passed. Passed where?

When I look around, everyone averts their eyes. That's when I realize most of them are wearing dark colors.

Understanding grips me like a vice.

Dani's mother died.

CHAPTER FORTY-ONE

- Dani -

My head is throbbing a frenzied beat against my skull. Groaning, I roll over, and a voice in the darkness tells me to drink some water. A strong arm loops around my waist and sits me up, and a cold glass of water is placed in my hand.

I take small sips, my stomach turning inside out with each bit of liquid that goes down.

"I don't think she has anything left in her stomach to throw up, so that's good," someone says.

The shadows cast against the wall make me think about how much I hate being alone. A warm hand pushes the hair off my forehead when I lie back.

"You're not alone, baby. You're not alone," a voice, soft and reassuring, whispers in my ear as though reading my mind.

My eyelids flutter closed as the room spins and spins and spins.

* * *

Hours later, the harsh morning light makes me wish for death. I grab my pillow and stuff my head underneath it.

"Can she breathe like that?" a male voice asks.

Another guy says, "Close the curtain. It's bothering her."

That voice. It teases me with the kind of familiarity

that sends a flood of sadness sweeping through me.

My eyes crack open, but from this angle, all I see is my comforter and a patch of the floor.

"What do I look like? Your maid?"

Recognition jars me. *Travis.* Someone grunts and shuffles across the floor and then the offending light dims through the crack in my pillow cave.

My ears perk up. I thought it was all a dream.

"We need to get her to eat something." Jax. That's Jax. Holy shit.

Nausea rises up the back of my throat, and I bolt upright, scattering pillows across my small room. My eyes narrow on him as I struggle to not throw up by pressing my hand across my mouth.

Jax and Travis are sitting on my purple love seat across from my bed. Their clothes are wrinkled, and both are sporting dark circles under their eyes.

When I can talk, when I'm sure my stomach contents won't come spewing up, I pin Jax with my glare and say the first thing that comes to mind.

"What the fuck are you doing here?"

On any other day, I might have had a different reaction to seeing him—I can't deny that I've missed him—but right now, all I can think is that he has a knack for leaving me and taking little slivers of my heart with him. And right now, with my mom gone, I have nothing left. Nothing.

Jax's eyes widen for a split second before he nods and looks down. When he looks up again, I see the remorse in his face.

"I fucked up, Dani. I want to explain." He runs his hands through his hair and closes his eyes.

I fight the urge to comfort him and shrink back into my bed. Travis sits next to me, and I let him hug me for a second before I push him away.

"I might throw up, and I'm saving it all for him," I say, motioning toward Jax. "So don't get too close."

My best friend nods, scooting back a little. Jax shoots him a strange look, like he's confused that Travis is on my side. Which is weird. So weird.

Unless...

I turn to Travis, afraid of what I need to ask. "Did you come here with... *him*?" I can't help the hurt that tinges my voice or the tentativeness of my words.

He shrugs and gives me a sheepish smile. I bite my cheek to keep from crying. Because if anyone knows what I went through over the last three weeks, it's him. My eyes burn.

"In that case, fuck both of you."

The shock spreads on Travis's face when he realizes I'm not kidding, and then I jump out of bed, ignoring the way the floor shifts beneath me like I'm rocking on a boat out at sea. I stumble into my bathroom and slam the door behind me, flinching from the throbbing pain in my head.

Having Travis get all chummy with Jax when he should be taking my side hurts. For a fleeting instant, I see my former friend and roommate Ashley hooking up with Reid, and my stomach turns. Ashley and Reid, Jax and nameless blondes. Travis taking Jax's side. Different people in different situations, but they all feel like betrayal.

At least this time I didn't stand there silent.

When the water in the shower pelts my back, I let myself fall apart. I hate that I don't have any control of my emotions, but everything in me feels raw and ripped open after losing my mom.

Lost. I feel so lost, and I cry until it seems like the

oxygen has been pulled from my lungs and the water runs cold.

After dragging myself out, I wrap a towel around my chest and tuck it so it holds. Using my elbow to wipe off the condensation, I stare at the girl in the mirror. A sad laugh escapes my lips. I look like crap, and I don't have the energy to do anything about it. I let my hair sit tangled on my shoulders and ignore the way I shiver in the cold.

I don't bother to look at either Travis or Jax when I walk back into my bedroom and grab a change of clothes.

One of them starts to talk, and I cut him off. "Get out," I say, a few seconds before I toss the towel on the bed.

As I'm pulling a thermal, long-sleeved t-shirt over my head, footsteps pad away and the door closes. I'm too angry to care if they see me naked. Life is too short to give a shit about stuff like that.

* * *

Several hours later, I wake up with the dried tracks of tears on my cheeks, so I splash some water on my face and decide to brave a trip downstairs.

Stilling every few steps to see if I can hear anyone talking, I lean forward and listen.

Maybe they left.

For some reason, that doesn't make me feel any better. When I get to the first floor, I hear the hum of the TV. I peek around the corner and find Travis sprawled on the couch.

I watch him flip through the channels. He rubs his eyes, and I realize how tired he looks. He came all this way only to have me yell at him. I feel a twinge of guilt.

For the last three years, he's been nothing but loyal.

"Hey," I say from across the room. "I'm sorry for yelling at you. I don't know what got into me. I—"

"Shut up. You don't owe me an apology." He pats the space next to him, and I scurry to him. The second my butt hits the couch, he yanks me into a tight hug. I don't have the heart to tell him the pressure of his arms around me makes me want to hurl.

His arms relax, and I stay pressed to his chest. He whispers that he's sorry about my mom, and I nod, not able to form words.

After several minutes, Travis squeezes me. "How's your head?"

"Hurts like a motherfucker."

He lets out a laugh that makes my temples throb harder. I grab my head, and he tells me he has something that will help my headache. He gets up, trots to the kitchen and returns with a tumbler of dark liquid. "Here, drink this."

I eye it suspiciously and then give him a pointed stare.

"Don't look at me like that. Drink it. Jax says it's the best thing for hangovers."

Hearing Jax's name makes me stiffen, and I drop my eyes. "Did he leave?"

Travis chuckles like I'm cracking a joke. "That man just drove over a thousand miles to see you. He ran down to the grocery store to get some coffee. He was going through withdrawals after drinking a dozen Red Bulls in the last few days."

I'm surprised by the relief I feel knowing that Jax is still here. Surprised but scared.

Travis puts the tumbler in my hand and motions for me to drink. I start to bring it to my lips when he stops me. "Jax says not to smell it. Just chug it."

The idea of chugging anything makes me more nauseous, but I'm desperate to make this hangover go away, so I take a deep breath and down half before I can't stand it any longer.

"Oh my God. That's disgusting." My face contorts.

Travis points at my expression and laughs. "Where's a camera when you need one?"

I smack him in the arm, chiding him for finding any humor in this. After another ten minutes, I'm able to finish the horrible concoction, and I lean back into the couch and close my eyes.

A silence settles over us as I struggle to figure out what I want to say. Finally, I turn to him. "How did you know my mom died?"

"I didn't. Your boyfriend dragged me here."

I roll my eyes at the boyfriend remark.

He grabs my arm. "Sweets, I'm so sorry about your mom. I wish I could've been here." He tucks me against him again, and I close my eyes and try hard to breathe through the rising panic that she's gone.

Once I'm calm, I clear my throat. "I know I freaked out earlier, but it means a lot to me that you're here. I still don't get why you guys came, though."

"Girl, you don't listen to your voice mail, do you?"

I shrug. "I don't know where my phone is. Kinda lost track of it after Christmas Eve."

"Everyone's been trying to reach you since you got to Chicago. But Jax is the one who insisted we come. By the time I realized you hadn't written me back, Jax was pounding on my door and dragging my ass out of bed on Christmas morning." Travis tucks a loose strand of hair behind my ear. "Jax found out about that donation you made, and he realized he's had his head up his ass. He feels like shit."

"I never expected to see him again." The reality of that statement twists something inside me.

Travis sighs. "I think he really cares about you. In fact, I think he lo—"

Footsteps on the front porch halt our conversation as Jax walks in carrying an armload of groceries. "Fucking hell, it's cold. I thought Boston was cold, but it's nothing like the Midwest." He sees me and smiles. "You people are crazy for living here."

His voice makes my heart want to leap out of my chest, and I school my expression because I should be mad at him. Livid. But seeing that stupid grin on his face and the way his nose is red from the sub-zero temperatures outside makes me want to wrap him up in a blanket and spoon-feed him tomato soup.

Shit. What is wrong with me?

"I hate you for making me that terrible drink," I say, motioning toward my empty glass.

He laughs, his eyes passing over me like he hasn't seen me in years instead of a few weeks. He clears his throat and looks into the bag he's carrying.

"I got us some coffee because you only have organic tea here, and I don't know what to do with that. And I got us lunch."

"Any Red Bull in there?" Travis asks wryly.

Jax groans. "Dude, I think I might throw up the next time I even look at a can of that shit."

I glance down, feeling bad for going off on him earlier today. I can't totally wrap my head around the fact that he drove here.

"Thanks for coming," I say softly, a thousand things running through my head.

"Yeah, no problem." Jax shifts in the doorway. "I'm so sorry you lost your mom, Dani. I wish there was something I could do."

I nod as a heavy silence settles over the room. Travis gets up and holds out his hand to Jax. "Keys."

Jax frowns. "You know, I'm gonna have your ass if you crash my Escalade."

"When did you get an Escalade?" I ask. The man already has a Jeep and a BMW that probably costs more than Rhode Island. Does he really need a third car?

He shrugs. "I've always had it. I just didn't have it parked at my condo."

I stiffen, remembering that money is at the root of what went wrong between us. Well, that and a long pair of legs attached to a life-sized Barbie.

I get up and scoot past the guys, reminding myself not to be an idiot. Jax probably just wants to assuage his guilt for being such a prick. Then he can go back to living in his little world of easy-access skanks.

I pour myself a glass of water in the kitchen as Jax asks Travis where he's going. Travis scoffs, and I can almost see him rolling his eyes behind me. "Dad, I already told you. I'm catching up with a hot piece of ass I hooked up with last year."

I turn and shoot Travis a look, pleading for him not to leave, and he shakes his head. What the hell?

"Text me the address," Jax says gruffly.

"Good lord, you're a pain in the ass." Travis digs his phone out of his pocket and thumbs out a text before he heads for the door.

"When will you be back?" I ask. I don't know if I can do this, be alone with Jax. Doesn't Travis understand that?

"Don't wait up, sweets." Travis saunters toward the door and blows me a kiss before he disappears out the front door.

Damn it.

I look up and Jax is staring at me, the tension between us palpable. "Make yourself at home." I start heading back to my room.

He grabs my arm. "We need to talk. I need to apologize." His hands run up to my shoulders, and I stare at our feet. My fuzzy hot pink slippers look silly next to his black combat boots. I've never seen him in combat boots before, but he could wear a paper sack and look amazing. The boots make him seem edgy and dark. Intense.

Even though he looks tired and a little out of his element, he still looks incredible. His jaw is scruffy as he obviously hasn't shaved in a few days, and his lean muscular frame fills out his faded jeans and plaid flannel like he's some kind of Calvin Klein lumberjack.

Closing my eyes, I try to shake some sense into my head.

His finger tilts my head up, forcing me to look at him. "Danielle."

Hearing him say my name makes the few brain cells I didn't kill with alcohol scatter.

"Baby, I'm so sorry." His blue eyes are dark and intense. He grips me tighter. "You should hate me. I know that."

I pull out of his grasp and turn away, remembering all the ways he's hurt me. "What are you sorry for, Jax? For leaving me in your room after we almost had sex to run off with another girl? Or for thinking that I'm some horrible person who could be bought off?"

He steps closer until I sense him standing right behind me. "I had nothing to do with that non-disclosure. My mother is a bitch, and this is how she deals with anything that doesn't go her way. She buys people off. I swear I didn't know anything until that camp director thanked me for the donation."

I swallow even though my mouth feels like sandpaper. "You weren't supposed to find out about that. It was supposed to be anonymous."

He chuckles, but I'm not sure why any of this is funny. "Babe, you gave the man thirty thousand dollars and then caught a bus. That's not exactly how these kind of donations are made."

Right. Because I don't know jack shit about how to be a rich person. Crossing my arms over my chest, I shake my head. "Sorry, if I embarrassed you. I'm just the riffraff who doesn't know how to live among the elite."

I start to walk off, and he grabs me again. The next thing I know, he spins me around, and I'm caught between his arms as he braces himself against the counter.

"That's not what I meant, and you know it," he growls. He closes his eyes and stands there, still, and I watch his chest rise and fall. "Fuck, this is not going the way I intended." He steps back and runs his hands through his hair again and exhales. "Look, I am a dick. I have no excuse for anything I did, but I want you at least know why it happened."

The plaintive look in his eyes undermines my resolve, and I nod.

He takes a deep breath. "That morning when we were almost together, I remembered what happened at the club." He stops and looks down.

My conscience twinges. *I should have told him.*

He says, "I guess I freaked because I couldn't figure out why you wouldn't say something about that, especially after all the time we spent together. I started to think of you as a friend, and I don't have girls who are friends, so thinking you had this secret kind of threw me." He looks away. "I don't expect you to understand, but I have a long history of not being able to trust beautiful women."

He thinks I'm beautiful.

Shut it, Dani. Focus on what matters here.

He shoves his hands into the pockets of his jeans. "When I came back that day after Nick interrupted us in the kitchen, I thought we'd talk and I'd explain, but you were gone."

That snaps me back to reality. "Did you seriously expect me to stay when you left with another girl? Jax, that was so fucking humiliating." *Hello, I was basically spreadeagle on your table!* I scream in my head.

I stalk past him to the other side of the kitchen where I stare at the small stained-glass butterflies decorating the window frame. Those were my mom's favorites. What am I going to do with her butterflies? My stomach turns when I realize I have to go through all of her belongings.

Jax clears his throat. "Nothing happened with that other girl, Danielle. I swear. I was upset, and I overreacted. I guess I was hurt, and I wanted to hurt you."

I turn around, livid. "Sure, because those two situations totally equate." I huff out a breath wondering how my omission even compares to him leaving me the day we almost had sex in his kitchen. "I didn't tell you because I was embarrassed. You didn't remember me from the club, and nearly every time I saw you thereafter, you had a girl draped across you. And then there was your sister, and she hates everyone you date." I tighten arms over my chest. "I had just moved in with her, and all I heard was how you had a reputation for one-night stands with slutty girls, so forgive me if I didn't volunteer that I willingly stood in that line."

His eyebrows furrow. "But why didn't you say anything after the car accident?"

I bite my lip, not wanting to say what's been holding me back from telling him the truth.

"Dani?"

Exhaling loudly, I look up at him. He's standing in the middle of my mom's kitchen, and she's gone, and it feels so surreal, I want to smash something. "Have you looked at me lately, Jax?"

He frowns and starts to say something, but I cut him off.

"I almost told you on Thanksgiving, but I liked how well we got along, how you felt like a friend, how we laughed over sports and goofed around, and I didn't want to screw that up. Then after we started to mess around, I *really* didn't want to fuck it up. It was fun being with you. It felt like we clicked in so many ways."

I swallow, forcing myself to get to the heart of the problem. "Jax, you date tall, gorgeous women." Glamazons. "Models, actresses, heiresses. Blondes with big boobs and long legs. Girls who are aggressive and catty." Turning back to the window, I watch fresh snow begin to fall. "I'm not saying I'm ugly, and I'm not fishing for compliments, but it's hard not to be insecure and think maybe you were slumming it because I look like the exact opposite of the women you date."

"I don't date," he says firmly.

My eyes drop. *Ouch.*

I nod, realizing my mistake. Damn it. I bite my lip again. *I will not cry any more over you, Jax Avery.* I should be crying over my dead mother whose funeral I can't afford or the fact that I don't have the money to go back to school in Boston. Because even though my mom had life insurance, it won't pay out for a few months, and there's no way I can afford the mortgage and tuition with what's left in our savings after the funeral costs.

Forcing myself to finish this godawful conversation and be done with him, I take a deep breath, but then he whispers, "Or at least I didn't before you."

My heart beats a crazy rhythm in my chest as his hands come up and grab my shoulders, turning me to face him.

I focus my attention on his plaid flannel shirt. It's buttoned up wrong, and an extra button waves at the bottom of the fabric.

"Look at me." He tilts my chin up. "I didn't drive a thousand miles to have you insult yourself." He laughs and shakes his head. "Babe, I've had a crush on you all fall."

He laughs again when he sees the confusion on my face. "I couldn't understand why I wanted to kick Brady's ass when we went rock climbing and I saw him put his hands all over you. I couldn't get over how you felt like you were mine." He runs his hands up and down my arms until goosebumps prickle my skin. "But I guess what happened at the club would explain my possessiveness of you." He smiles, and it's so warm and sweet that it melts my anger just a little.

He tucks a strand of hair behind my ear. "And that was before we really spent time together. Before we watched scary movies and sports and laughed our asses off over Thanksgiving. Before we curled up on the couch together and I realized how much I loved waking up with you in my arms." He clears his throat. "Look, I know I've done everything wrong, and you have no reason to talk to me, but I want to make it up to you."

Part of me is jumping for joy at his declaration, but I

don't want to get burned again, and I have a hard time believing he'd be able to withstand the temptation of a tall, busty woman.

He must sense my reservation, and he asks, "Can we sit down? There are a few more things I need to say. If you still want to kick my ass when I'm finished, you can throw me out, and I'll never bother you again. Just so you know, I plan to grovel, so hopefully you won't toss me out into that fucking Arctic weather."

I let out a weak laugh and nod. He smiles, leans down and kisses my forehead, and it's so tender it makes me catch my breath.

CHAPTER FORTY-TWO

- Jax -

I take Dani's hand and lead her to the couch in the living room. She automatically sits as far away from me as possible. I can tell how much I've hurt her, and everything inside of me screams to make this right.

"I've never told anyone this story." I wonder where to begin as I rub the back of my neck.

She fidgets in her seat. "We don't have to do this now if you're uncomfortable."

That right there is why I adore this girl. She never pushes or pries. She lets me be me.

I shake my head. "I want to tell you, so you can see why I'm such a fuckup. I know my sister seems to think I've had a revolving door of women in my life, but I did once have a girlfriend."

That catches Dani's attention and her back straightens.

"During my senior year of high school, Giselle and I dated for several months." I take in the shocks of red hair that overlay Dani's dark mane. I want to touch her, run my hands through her thick locks. Instead, I lace my fingers together and let myself remember, something I never do except to harden myself. "By that spring, I thought I loved her, but we were going to different schools on the East Coast."

The memory is bittersweet, and I want to shut this shit down before it begins to hurt, but I want Dani to see me for who I really am. "We used to jump in my car and drive for hours and talk and listen to music and escape. Her parents were pretty strict, and my parents were never around, but when they were, they were assholes. And I needed to clear my head. Something about Giselle clicked for me. She was smart and beautiful, and she made me laugh and forget about how empty I usually felt."

Licking my lips, I get ready to slice myself open. "One day, she came over. She said she had some news. I thought she had gotten a scholarship. Her family didn't have a lot of money, and she was still figuring out how to pay for school." I rub my jaw, hating how the hurt still sits like a weight on my chest. "But she had been crying. Her face was splotchy and pale." I swallow, my mouth dry. "She told me she was pregnant."

Dani's eyes widen. "Holy shit. That's heavy."

"Can you believe I told her I wanted to keep it?"

She looks at me with warmth in her eyes. "Yes, actually, I can see that."

"I had some fucked-up idea that we could work it out, that we could be the family I never had." I roll my eyes, letting the anger settle over me. "I mean, it was my baby, my son or my daughter. How could I not want to keep it?" I stop and listen to the clock in the hallway and prepare for the worst part. "When she came to me a few days later, she looked so heartbroken." I clear my throat again, surprised that this still stings so badly after four years. "She told me she lost the baby."

Dani whispers, "I'm so sorry."

I know she means it, and I close my eyes, grateful that I can tell her.

A bitter laugh escapes me. "It was a lie. She had an abortion."

"Oh my God, Jax."

I tighten my jaw, waiting for the rage to subside. "I thought her parents had made her do it. That made sense, them wanting her to go to college and not be tied down. Except I don't think they ever found out." My stomach clenches at the memory. "A few days later, one of the rare times my mother was around, she asked about Giselle, which was so fucking weird. My mother never gave a shit about the girls I went out with. She was usually too busy running her company or making my dad's life miserable to pay attention to anything I did. I didn't even think she knew my girlfriend's name."

The only shit that ever reaches my mother's radar are things that affect her. I rarely make the top ten on her list.

"I'll never forget how she fucking ruined me over a cup of coffee. One of our housekeepers must have overheard me and Giselle talking about the pregnancy earlier that week and told my mom." I shake my head. "My mother said Giselle was lying, and it was like she was speaking another damn language. It didn't even occur to me that she was talking about the miscarriage."

I'd stood there like a total dumbass, at first grateful for my mother's time, thinking she must really care about me to talk. I must have been delusional. "She smiled. She fucking smiled at me when she told me she knew what was going on with me and Giselle. And then she said my girlfriend had an abortion."

"Jesus." Dani tenses next to me.

"That's not the worst part. No, that's when my mother said she paid for it along with Giselle's tuition to Georgetown."

Dani gasps, her hand covering her mouth.

"I still remember it so clearly. I was the jackass who wanted to tell Giselle I loved her and that we'd figure out a way to work this out while she lied to me and aborted my kid."

I hang my head, fighting to keep my shit together. Hate fills me. Hate for the woman who claims to be my parent, and hate for the girl I thought I loved. Hate for what they did and how I let all of that turn me into who I am now. "Then my mother had the balls to tell me I should thank her because Giselle would have ruined my life and ruined my family's reputation."

I don't know how long I sit there contemplating how much I fucking despise these people, Giselle for shredding my heart and my mother for handing her the knife.

Dani grabs my hand, and I shake my head at the memories. "That's when I totally went off partying. That summer after high school was the worst. I was a mess. And no amount of drinking or screwing around made it better. It wasn't until I was arrested for vandalism that shit got serious."

We sit in silence as I collect my thoughts. "You know what's fucked up? How each time I got close to the edge—got in trouble or got so wasted I passed out—a part of me wondered if this would be it. If this would get my mom to give a shit."

Dani's fingers twine through mine, but she doesn't say anything.

"My mother eventually got tired of the theatrics, but not because she cared. She had a merger coming up. She didn't want to look bad in front of her colleagues. Her answer was to throw cash at me to shut the fuck up. So we made a deal. I'd graduate from college and go to law school, and she'd never say shit about what I spent as long as I didn't get arrested again or embarrass her publicly. "

I swallow. "But there's nothing she can do to get me to forgive her for how she interfered with Giselle."

The wind blows outside, and the trees scratch at the house.

"Maybe your mother thought she really was helping you," Dani says softly.

"Like she thought she was helping me with that non-disclosure?" I turn to look at Dani, and she stills. She doesn't know how to make sense of my family because her mother actually loved her. *It's hard not to.* My heart squeezes in my chest, wanting to kick my ass for not chasing down this girl the moment she tried to leave my apartment.

Dani frowns, her lower lip pushing out slightly. "I was pissed when I got that contract, but in retrospect, I see why she did it. She runs a multi-million-dollar company, and you're her son, her heir. It's probably the smart move. It would keep you out of the tabloids and ensure your privacy."

"*Her* privacy," I correct. It never has anything to do with me.

"I wouldn't have said anything."

I turn to face her and brush her long hair off her shoulder so I can see her face. "God, I know. Dani, I'm so sorry. For leaving you that day, for the shit my mother made you go through, for your loss here at home. I'm sorry I wasn't here for you." I brush my thumb over her pale cheek.

Tears threaten to overflow in her eyes, and she blinks. "Thank you for sharing all of that with me, Jax," Dani whispers. "I know it must be difficult to talk about."

I nod, still feeling a little shellshocked. "I mostly blocked that whole thing from my mind."

"What happened to Giselle?"

"I never spoke to her again, so I have no fucking clue."

After a few moments of silence, Dani reaches for me. She drops her head on to my shoulder, and I automatically wrap my arms around her.

We stay like that for several moments, and for the first time in years, I feel like I can breathe.

* * *

Dani moves through the kitchen comfortably, knowing where everything is, reaching for pans and bowls and ingredients. Even though she's the one who just lost her mother, she's making me pancakes. But that's her. I hit her with a car, and she spent that weekend telling me it wasn't my fault.

I fight back a grin. Watching her—the way her small frame glides around the room, the way she frowns when she reads the recipe, the way she tilts her head when she's deep in thought—makes me want her more. I want to kiss her until our bodies are sweaty and tangled together and we can forget the whole fucking world, but I don't want to push her. I've crossed into all kinds of new territory with this girl, and the last thing I want to do is screw this up. Again.

As she stands at the griddle, waiting to flip a pancake, she bites her lip. I wait to hear what she has to say, but she remains quiet.

"Go ahead." I motion to her. "Say whatever is on your mind."

"Why doesn't your sister know about Giselle?"

I rub my cheek, the stubble on my face scratching my palm. "She was so wrapped up in Daren that spring that the Titans could have released the Kraken on her front door, and she would've been clueless. And I was pretty preoccupied with Giselle, which is how I didn't realize Daren was cheating on Clem until late in the game." Thinking about it now, four years later, still pisses me off. "Just before Clem found out that Daren was sneaking around with her best friend Veronica, Giselle told me she was pregnant."

When Dani nods, I remember one more thing I need to make right, and I grab the leather-bound notebook out of my bag and place it on the counter.

"I think this belongs to you."

Dani tenses when she sees it. I thought she'd be excited to have it returned. "Did you look inside?"

Not wanting to lie to her, I nod, and she tenses more. "It was on the kitchen table. I flipped through it."

"And?" She eyes me with a guarded look.

"Your artwork is phenomenal."

"That's not what I mean. You must have read the things I wrote in there. It's like a diary for me."

Shit. I run my hand through my hair. "I'm sorry." I shake my head. "I mostly looked at all the sketches you did about money." I say it because I want to hear her side without asking her to explain.

We stare at each other, accusation in her eyes, and perhaps the lingering doubt of suspicion in mine, one that I can't help.

"That was an assignment for class. We had to make a statement about wealth. That's why I drew twenty sketches on that topic." Her eyes narrow. "Not because I'm obsessed with money."

She's telling the truth. In fact, she's pissed that I doubt her. Hearing the conviction in her voice was all I needed.

"No, I wouldn't suggest that you are."

"Come on. You thought it. You still kind of do. I can

see it in your face. You think I'm like every other girl, that I only care about your trust fund."

The smell of burning food gets her attention, and she curses as she scoops a charred pancake into the trash.

"Dani, if I thought you were like every other girl, I wouldn't be here. If I thought that, I wouldn't have nearly knocked down Travis's door to get him to come with me." Especially since he kind of hates me. "But to be honest, yes, I wanted to hear your explanation. I'm sorry I'm wired this way, but I was raised to be suspicious of people and their intentions. It sucks that I needed to hear you say it, but I did."

She stares at me she might hit me over the head with the griddle in her hand.

"Are you planning to kill me with that?" I ask.

She blinks a few times and then laughs. "I might. Don't get any ideas." Returning to the stove, she pours another pancake. "Now shut up, or I'm never going to finish these, and you'll starve."

With that, I think I'm forgiven. For now.

CHAPTER FORTY-THREE

- Dani -

We talk about our finals and the last few weeks of school, avoiding anything awkward. I stuff him full of pancakes, and as I'm gathering our plates, Jax stands up and holds out his hand.

"I think we need to start over." He bats his eyelashes and shoots me a sexy smile. "I'm Jackson Avery."

What a goofball. I smack his hand away. "Get over yourself and help me do the dishes."

He grins and follows me to the sink. "So we're friends again?" he asks in my ear.

Ignoring the shiver that runs through me, I nod curtly and shove him with my elbow so I can get some space. The last thing I need right now is Jax clouding my head.

After we get the kitchen clean, I settle at the table with my laptop and my mom's bills.

"So what's the plan for next semester?" Jax asks.

Keeping my eyes firmly planted on the bills in front of me, I say the words I've been dreading. "Can't afford to go back. Not right away at least."

"Did your mom have any life insurance?"

I nod and explain my cashflow problem. But regardless of the bills or tuition, my mom's funeral is my priority. My eyes well up for the millionth time this week.

Jax reaches for my hand as someone knocks on the front door. Susan doesn't wait for me to answer it. Instead, she pokes her head in.

"Dani?"

"Back here," I call out as I blink the tears away.

My mom's best friend is bundled in a thick coat, hat and scarf. After unwrapping a few items of clothes so I can see her face, she digs into her pockets and pulls out my credit card.

"Tomorrow is all set, honey," she says. "The memorial starts at eleven, and the funeral procession starts around noon."

"Thanks, Susan. I don't know what I would have done without you this week."

She smiles sadly and pats me on the shoulder. "That's what friends are for."

I glance down at the white piece of plastic in front of me as anxiety coils in my belly. "Am I maxed out yet?"

"Nope."

My head tilts as I look at her sideways. "Really? I thought you said it would cost about nine grand."

She shrugs. "Honey, sometimes things just have a way of working themselves out." She looks to Jax and grins. "Son, are you enjoying our fine weather?"

He smiles back, and they chat like they've known each other a lifetime. I'm still scratching my head about the cost of the funeral when she leaves. With a trace of a migraine still spotting my vision, I decide to worry about it tomorrow.

It isn't until morning that I realize I don't have anything appropriate to wear to my mother's funeral. Travis finds me sobbing on the floor of my closet, and he tucks me under his arm, sets me down on the love seat and riffles through my clothes until he finds a black wrap-around dress.

I hiccup. "That's not mine."

"Sweetheart, it was in your closet, and it's your size.

I'm not good at math, but I'm guessing two and two equals four, so that must mean it's yours."

"Your folksy logic is pissing me off."

He smirks and throws it at me. "Put it on." It lands on my head, and I roll my eyes.

Twenty minutes later, I'm dressed. I leave my hair down because I don't have the energy to do one more thing. "Is this okay?" I ask.

Travis looks me up and down. "Yeah. You look hot."

I stare at him dumbly. "I'm dressed for my mother's funeral."

"Trust me. She'd think you looked hot too."

I shake my head at him. My typical responses—a laugh and a sarcastic remark—are a distant thought as I walk downstairs. When Jax sees me, he stops mid-step, and his eyes widen.

"What?" I ask, self-conscious now.

"Nothing. You look beautiful."

I bite my cheek, unsure how to respond to compliments on a day like today. I frown, feeling like I can't make sense of the world anymore.

As though understanding my inability to function, Jax walks me to the closet and helps me put on my coat. I go through the motions. One arm, then the other before we walk to the car. I watch the muted world outside as we drive to the funeral home.

I'm burying my mother today.

Funerals are done for the living. It's a way to deal with the passing of a loved one because my mother can't appreciate the color of her casket, the bouquets of flowers I bought to decorate the room, or the headstone I had engraved.

She'll never know I can't afford to go back to Boston.

As we walk through the front door of the funeral

home, I choke back a sob at the thought that I lied to her and can't finish my degree at BU.

"Come on, sweetie," Travis says as he hands me a tissue.

He wraps an arm around me and holds me in a hug. Jax walks ahead to talk to Susan, who is congregating with a dozen of my mom's friends. I eye the podium, and the blood drains down my body as I realize I should have prepared something to say. At some point during the last few days, Susan mentioned something to that effect, but between the booze, Travis and Jax shocking the hell out of me by visiting, and the trauma of waking up on Christmas morning to find my mother cold and stiff in her bed, I forgot.

Panic overwhelms me, and suddenly I can't breathe. Blood is pounding in my ears.

"Honey, sit." Travis guides me to a chair in the front row, and I feel him motioning to someone. Jax approaches on the other side and pulls me to his chest.

"Breathe, baby. It's going to be okay."

Thankfully, Susan gets up first and talks about how brave my mom was in the face of cancer. She shares beautiful stories about their time together as neighbors for twenty years. I tune out, the ache of hearing so many painful memories overwhelming.

When it's my turn to speak, Travis walks me to the dais and holds my hand until I grab the podium. Taking a deep breath, I decide to ignore all the people who have come, and I just start talking from the heart.

"One of my mom's favorite quotes was by Hemingway, who said that 'the world breaks everyone and afterward many are strong at the broken places.' The rest of the quote is actually atrocious—something about how those the world doesn't break, it kills—but my mother, the eternal optimist, preferred to ignore that."

People in the crowd nod, offering sad smiles. Jax sits in the front row, his elbows resting on his knees, his hands clasped in front of him, his head bowed.

"I can't say anything about her life that would do her justice except that despite all the hard times we had, and there were many, I never felt the pressure of the world—the weight of what stood to break her, to break us—because she protected me. Until this last bout with cancer, I honestly felt that each battle she faced made her stronger. Even cancer made her this incredible life force."

I wipe away the tears coating my cheeks. "She and I are different in so many ways. Where I am scared, she was brave. Where I want to hide, she took chances. Where I hate being hurt, my mom said the hurt made her feel alive."

Bringing the tissue to my nose, I sniffle.

"She thought I was brave for going to Boston for college, but I could take that chance because I had her in my corner. I had her to cheer me on, to push me to be better, to help me find my way, and I know not everyone is as fortunate."

Jax raises his head, and we stare at each other.

Looking away, I clear my throat. "I guess I hope to embrace the challenge of life and love the way she did even though it's easier to run and it's easier to hide."

Turning toward the casket, I stare at the large framed photo Susan had printed. "Mom, thank you for taking the risks and feeling the breaks and letting yourself be strengthened by all the bullshit in this life." I cover my mouth, unable to speak. I can't see anyone through the tears in my eyes. I take a shuddering breath. "You've been telling me lately that if I'm going to curse, to say it like I mean it." I laugh as I think about what I want to say. "You were the best fucking parent. I love you, and I hope to make you proud."

Travis helps me walk back to my seat as everyone applauds.

"Why are people clapping?" I ask Travis. It's a funeral. Who claps at a funeral?

"Because that was fucking incredible."

CHAPTER FORTY-FOUR

- Dani -

All I can do is stare at the headstone.

I had ordered a simple, flat grave marker because three hundred dollars was all I could afford. The one in front of me is an upright stone in two tones. On the polished black side, it says, "Beth Hart, beloved mother and friend." On the polished grey side, a cutout butterfly perches as though it is about to take flight. It's lovely, but astronomically out of my price range.

I glance around at the stones nearby, which are all flat, like the one I thought I had bought. My mother's gravestone is enormous in comparison, like it belongs in the other lot with the family plots and expensive mausoleums.

"This has to be a mistake," I whisper to Susan, who has her arm looped through mine. "This one costs like three grand. And they told me it wouldn't be ready for a week unless I paid extra." I remember flipping through the brochure and being aghast at the prices. "I… I can't afford this."

She pats my hand. "It's all taken care of, honey. Stop worrying."

"Did you pay for this? It's beautiful. I know she'd love it. If you can wait until this summer, I'll pay you back."

Susan turns to me. "You don't have to because I didn't pay for it."

Now I'm confused. "Okay," I say slowly. "Who did?"

Maybe Mom's friends in her book club pooled their money together.

She turns me around until I'm facing Jax who is standing on the other side of the tent, talking quietly to Travis. "That's who you should thank. Jax paid for everything today. He wanted you to think I covered these expenses, but that wouldn't be right. You should know that lovely boy did this, and he picked the headstone, specifically requesting the butterfly after he saw your mother's stained glass in the kitchen. He paid extra to have it ready today." She nods toward him. "He's a keeper."

Then she walks off, leaving me with my mouth gaping open.

I wait until we're in the car to freak out. What the hell is wrong with him?

"Jax, you said we'd be friends. How can you lay down twelve grand for my mother's funeral? Wasn't money at the heart of our little misunderstanding?" The irony of the situation is not lost on me. "Would you do that for any friend?"

"I don't know about *any* friend." He looks at me sideways as he pulls onto the highway. "But I would for my girlfriend. In a heartbeat."

I still, not knowing what to say. Behind me, Travis kicks my seat, and I shake my head. "I thought you don't date. I thought you don't have *girlfriends*." Or at least not anymore. "I mean, not since Giselle."

"I don't. But I'd like one."

"Just one?" I look over at him, almost afraid of the answer.

"Just one. Just you."

Numb from the funeral, I can't seem to process his words. We're quiet the rest of the drive. Even Travis is silent. When we get to my house, Travis immediately disappears upstairs, but I'm not quick enough to do the same. Jax grabs me the moment my coat is off and wraps me in a hug, pressing me to his hard body.

"I'm so sorry you had to bury your mother," he whispers. Feeling his arms around me makes me relax. "She sounded like an amazing woman." I press my cheek to his shoulder and brace myself so I don't cry. "Guess the apple doesn't fall far from the tree."

I swallow back tears and focus on taking deep breaths.

Jax strokes my head. "Let's do this, Dani. We'll go slow. But I want you in my life, and I think you want me too."

He nuzzles in my hair, and I close my eyes, surprised by how good it feels to be in his arms. He runs his nose against my jaw, and I inhale his scent. I could get lost in the way he smells and how he holds me. So lost.

That thought alone makes me stop. I put both hands on his chest and push him away so I can look him in the eye.

"I appreciate everything you did for me today, but if we're being honest, I don't know if I can trust you."

He stares back, not flinching.

"I'm okay needing to prove myself to you." Ignoring my hands, he tugs me closer until we're nose to nose. "Let me prove it. That I can be yours and only yours." He leans forward, pressing his forehead against mine. "I can't promise I won't hurt you because I know I'm an idiot sometimes, but I want to try, and maybe if you help me, I can be more for you." He takes a deep breath. "I want to be more for you."

I'm at a loss for words.

He stares like he's trying to memorize my face. "I swear you're the only woman I want. Even when we were apart, you're the only girl I've thought about."

I wiggle out of his grasp. "You slept with other women." My eyes dart down as I remember his date in the limo.

"I haven't slept with anyone in months. Yeah, I've gone out with other people, but I swear I haven't slept with anyone."

I find that hard to believe, and I half laugh. "So you haven't slept with anyone since Thanksgiving?" I stare at him, daring him to answer.

He doesn't look away, he doesn't pause, he doesn't flinch. "No. No one." Seeing my expression, it's his turn to laugh. "Have some faith, Dani." His eyes pass over me. "What about you? How many people have *you* been with since then?"

I glare at him. "What kind of girl do you think I am that I'd go from nearly having sex with you to jumping in bed with someone else?"

"What about Brady?" he asks, starting to look pissed.

"What about Brady?" Is that really who concerns him?

"Did you sleep with him?" The anger in Jax's voice is unmistakable, but there's something else there too. Hurt?

"Come on, Jax. Get serious. He and I aren't like that. I told you that over Thanksgiving."

"Yeah, but I saw those pictures of the two of you."

"That was just a photoshoot."

"You two looked pretty intimate." Jax gives me a pointed look. "You were naked, and he was wrapped around you."

"I was not naked. Just topless. And it was for an art class. Besides, as you should know, looks can be deceiving." I can't help but think about that girl in the limo and the breathy way she said his name like she was two seconds from going down on him. The thought of him with her pisses me off, so I say something to turn the tables. "Why? Are you jealous?"

"Fuck, yes, I'm jealous." Now it's his turn to glare at me.

I laugh. Yes, to think I'd be with Brady like that makes me laugh. "Jax, I don't know if you realize it, but you kind of ruined other guys for me, so no, Brady and I are not like that. At all. And anyway, he has a girlfriend. Those photos were for an assignment and nothing more."

Can I do this? Can I be with Jax when everything about him threatens to destroy me if he changes his mind?

Stronger in the broken places… I hear the words, like my mother is reminding me to give him a chance. He drove across the country not even knowing that she passed away. Just because he was sorry about what happened. Just because he wanted to see me.

"How did you see the photos?" I ask quietly.

He relaxes a little. "My sister texted them to me to show me I'm a dumbass."

I feel the wall I've built around me start to crumble. Taking a deep breath, I decide to take a chance.

"Remind me to thank her," I say with a small smile, enjoying the annoyance in his eyes. "So you want to prove yourself to me, huh?"

"More than you know." He wraps his arms around me again.

"I'm not going to sleep with you."

I stare at him, trying to be convincing. Inside, I'm doing my damnedest to focus on all the reasons it would be prudent to wait.

"I wouldn't expect you to." He grins. "Yet."

It's tough to ignore the lust that pulses through me at

the prospect of being with him. "You're going to have to earn it."

He growls against me and presses my back against the counter, his hard length wedged against my belly.

"I might die in the process, but I'll do whatever you want." He kisses me softly. "Besides, you playing hard to get is hotter than fuck."

I look down between us and laugh. "I can tell."

CHAPTER FORTY-FIVE

- Dani -

Travis, Jax and I hang out the next day, drinking beer and watching football as I start sorting though some of my mom's stuff. Travis flies home on New Year's Eve so he can see his family. Jax gets him a first-class ticket.

Aside from the big boner he pressed into me the other day, Jax keeps a certain distance. I get the feeling he senses I'm too fragile right now, which is probably true.

While we have a good time hanging out, the elephant in the room gets too big to ignore, especially after he sends Travis home.

"When are you going back?" I ask, unable to avoid it any longer. He does live in Boston after all, a fact I was too willing to ignore on the day of my mother's funeral.

He twists on the couch so he can face me. "The same day you go back."

On the TV, the announcer says it's ten minutes until New Year's.

"What do you mean?"

He rubs his palm over his jaw.

"I brought my SUV to drive you back East, so we could move whatever you wanted. I can store furniture or any other belongings if they don't fit in your dorm room."

What? I stiffen in my seat. "I told you I don't have the money."

The left corner of his mouth tilts up. "Yeah, you do.

The rest of the semester is covered. You're coming back to Boston when I do."

My face burns from embarrassment. Does he really want me to say this again? "Jax, I don't have the money to pay for my second semester."

"You don't need money. I covered it."

My eyes narrow. "You can't go around paying for everything, Jackson." I gear up, ready for a fight.

He grins. Why the hell is he smiling? "Fine. Then pay me back when you get the insurance money."

Huh. The anger starts to deflate in my chest. "So this is a loan?" If I borrow the money, I can keep my promise to my mom and go back to BU.

"If that's what you want, sure."

I chew on my lip, trying to keep my emotions in check, and his grin widens. "Why are you smiling?"

"You."

I quirk up my eyebrow. "What does that mean?" Is he laughing at me?

"It means you're fucking adorable."

Ignoring him, I huff. "This has to be a loan, Jax. I'm serious."

He smirks, and I squeak when he reaches across the couch, dragging me to him. He lies back and pulls me on top of him. "Fine."

I stare down at him. My hair falls around us as he nudges my knees open with his leg until I'm straddling his thigh.

Jax's expression burns my cheeks for an entirely different reason. Forgetting my anger, I look down at this gorgeous guy who helped me with my mom's funeral and is loaning me a buttload of cash so I can go back to school. And he's lying underneath me, hard as a rock and sexy as sin.

Sweet Jesus, I want him. Remembering the other times we've been together only fuels my desire.

In the background, the crowds cheer for the countdown to begin.

"What do you say we ring in the new year together, Dandelion?"

He doesn't wait for me to respond. Instead, he grabs a fistful of my hair and pulls me closer until I'm pressed against him, belly to belly. Instantly, heat roars between my legs. He rolls his hips until there's no doubt what's nestled against my hip.

"I… I thought we were going to go slow." I can barely speak.

"Ten, nine, eight…"

"We can go as slow and soft as you want, babe." His lips brush against mine in a feather-light touch. "Or we can go hard and fast," he says against my mouth as he deepens the kiss.

Oh God. Hard. I'm definitely thinking hard.

"Three, two, one."

My brain shuts down as my body takes over.

I moan into his mouth and grip his shoulders as his hands run down my back and over my rear. I lift my leg up over his so he's planted firmly between my thighs, and then I disentangle myself from his arms and sit up.

I don't know what possesses me, but I want to make him as crazy about me as I am about him. I stare down at him as I slowly rotate my hips, pressing our needy parts together.

"Is this what you want?"

He sucks in a breath. "Fuck, yes, Dani."

He feels huge and thick against me. I give him a wicked smile as I say, "Happy New Year, Jax," and climb off him. He looks confused, but then I lean over and whisper in his ear, "I choose hard and fast," before I race to my room.

His footsteps behind me make me giggle as I run up the stairs. I barely make it through my door when I'm jerked backwards. Laughing, I fall into Jax's arms as he slams us both up against the wall.

He lifts me up and my legs wrap around his hips. He pushes hard against me and we both gasp as our bodies align.

We kiss, desperate and hungry. His tongue stroking against mine sends pulsing need to my core. His hands are everywhere—my back, my breasts, my thighs—and just when I think I'm going to implode from lust, he stops.

It takes me a second to catch my breath.

"What's wrong? Why did you stop?"

He swallows. "I want you to know you mean more to me than just sex. I can't get enough of you, Dani. I've… I've never felt this way. Even with Giselle."

Before I can process what he just said, his mouth is on mine, and all I know is I'm on fire. He sets me down on the floor one second before he rips off my sweater. I shimmy out of my jeans until I'm standing in a hot pink bra and boy shorts.

I'm ready to collide with him again, but he takes a step back, his eyes traveling slowly over my exposed skin. He looks like he wants to devour me. I give him a coy smile, grab the clasp on my bra and let it tumble off my shoulders.

He groans. "Goddamn. Danielle, you're gorgeous."

I shake my hair forward, so it covers my chest, and then I cock my hip and stare back. "Get naked, Jax. Now."

His clothes are off in a nanosecond so we're both

standing in underwear. His erection is about to poke a hole in his boxers. I reach out and grab him firmly, stroking until he collapses against me with my back to the wall.

I'm contemplating going down on him when he moves my hand away and drops to his knees. He stares up, eyes heavy with desire, his hands tracing invisible patterns on my thighs. And right now, with one of the most beautiful men I've ever seen kneeling before me, looking at me like he wants to eat me whole, I feel totally and utterly worshipped.

I thread my fingers through his hair as he plants his mouth on my breast. He sucks hard, and a desperate gasp leaves my mouth. He tongues my piercing, and I arch my back, reveling in the sensation.

He breaks away briefly to grab hold of my other ring between his teeth. As he stares up at me, I pull him to me, tighter, wanting more.

When I think I might collapse on the floor from the attention he gives my piercings, he dips his finger into the waist of my underwear and tugs them down. We stare at each other, my heart in my throat as my girl parts have a nuclear meltdown.

Then his mouth is on me, pressing a gentle kiss on my thigh. He grabs my ankle and wraps it over his shoulder, completely exposing me. Of course, he takes a long heated look between my legs before his eyes travel up my body. His expression alone threatens to melt me.

When our eyes meet, he growls as he opens his mouth and nips my thigh. Holy shit. I decide right then and there he can bite me any time he wants.

His lips mark a trail of fire as he teases closer and closer until his tongue dips into me. Neither of us look away. And I see it in his eyes. How I mean more. And I hope he sees the same in mine.

I moan loudly, unable to contain it any longer. Gripping his hair, I tilt my head and arch my back, trying to get closer.

Around and around he goes, massaging the most delicate part of me. But then he stops, sinks down lower and presses two fingers into me, and I fall apart, the rush of blood and all sensation to my core unhinging me.

I pulse around him, and I can see him grinning against my skin.

When I finally stop shuddering, he sets my leg down. He must sense my inability to function because he grabs my hips and pulls me to him. Welcoming the warmth of his naked torso, I press a kiss against his muscular chest and breathe him in.

Jax holds me tightly and kisses me on the top of my head. I feel him hard against my belly, and I whisper that it's his turn.

"Babe, are you sure?" His throat is raspy and deep.

I close my eyes and nod against him. "Yes, I'm sure. I'm *so* sure."

He moans his approval as he squeezes me tighter. "Can I tell you I've been dying to fuck you senseless for the last four months?"

Laughing, I stand on my tiptoes and let my lips linger against his. "Can I tell you I've been dying for you to fuck me senseless for the last four months?"

Grinning, he lifts me up and the next thing I know, I'm on my bed and a very naked Jax is crawling toward me like a predator, all hard muscle and chiseled sexiness. He tears open a condom and suits up.

I drop my legs open for him and feel the length of him drag against my sensitive skin. I close my eyes, shivering.

"You feel so good, babe," he murmurs against my neck.

Up, down, up, down he goes, teasing me with his erection until I'm so racked with lust I could scream.

"Jesus, Jax," I breathe, dying to feel his full weight pressed against me.

My blood hums in my veins, desperation clawing its way to the surface. He presses gently at my entrance, and I feel like I've been waiting for years to be this close to someone I really want, someone I lust for, someone I love.

And just like that I realize it. I love him. Deep down, from the bottom of my soul, love. My other boyfriends were like warm blankets on a cool day. Jax is fire, an inferno that burns me inside and out.

My other lovers fade away as Jax's eyes pin me.

Linking my legs behind him, I press my heels into his back and bring him closer, his crowned tip surging just a little deeper.

I moan and wiggle beneath him, but he stills. Narrowing my eyes, I huff out a breath. "Are you deliberately trying to torture me?"

He laughs against my neck and then pulls out. Pulls out! I groan, and I sound loud and needy, but I don't care. I'm about to toss him out of my bed when he rubs himself all along my wetness again, and I nearly lose my mind.

Finally, finally, he sinks into me.

I gasp, barely able to think as he stretches me to the brink.

"Oh, fuck," he groans. "So tight. So good, babe."

When our thighs meet and he's fully seated and I think my eyes are going to roll back in my head, he stills, and I'm guessing it's because he's as turned on as I am.

I've never come before from rocking out the missionary position, but holy hell, he feels amazing.

Sighing, he pulls back and gently returns, slow and steady, soft and gentle. It's sweet for our first time together, but remembering his words downstairs, I pull his earlobe between my teeth and tug before I remind him, "Hard and fast."

Jax gives me a devilish grin. "You are the perfect fucking girl."

He pulls out languidly, dragging against my skin, and I'm about to beg for more, but then he slams into me. Both of us groan, and the room is awash in moans and grunts and the slapping of naked skin as he keeps a steady rhythm. I open my legs wider and tilt my hips to take him deeper. He nips my shoulder, and I press my mouth to his neck and taste his sweaty skin.

Rearing up on his knees, he yanks my legs toward him so my ass rests on his thighs. Looking down at where we join, he resumes the pace, and I feel myself chasing the high, reaching for the light at the end of the tunnel, the one I've never achieved with any man other than Jax.

Just when I think I can't take it any more, the intensity of him filling me, he brings my legs up in front of me, folding me in half so that my thighs rest on his chest.

"Jax!" I scream at the new depth, my nails raking down his arms. He whispers into my ear, deliciously naughty words that make me shudder, setting fire to my skin.

My heart thrums wildly in my chest as our naked bodies meld together. I can feel myself coming apart, disintegrating underneath him, but then his hand trails slowly between my breasts, down my belly, across my hip, reaching down between us, brushing ever so gently on the only part of my body that now seems to exist.

Another soft brush of his finger, and I scream as I come. I writhe beneath him as he throbs inside of me, hot and thick, stretching into me as he finds his release.

He groans my name as we rock together. And nothing has ever felt as right as the two of us locked together like this.

For a while, we lie there, connected and panting and sweaty. When we can finally breathe again, he presses his forehead to mine and smiles.

"There's one more thing you should know." His voice is scratchy and deep. Post-sex Jax is even sexier with hair that goes every which way and skin that glistens along the ridges of his hard muscles. But really, that adorable smile on his face and the way he looks at me like I'm the center of his universe are what do me in.

I lick my lips, trying to focus on what he's saying. "What's that?"

"I think I'm in love with you."

I arch up and kiss him, stopping to nibble on his lip. Then it's my turn to smile. "It's about time."

CHAPTER FORTY-SIX

- Dani -

Jax is quiet on the ride to the mall, but he wound his fingers through mine the moment we jumped in his SUV, and he's been stroking my palm with his thumb for the last twenty minutes. And it's driving me damn near insane with lust.

By the time we reach the parking lot, I have half a mind to jump him in his seat, but I don't want to ruin his plans. He wants to hang out in all the places my mom and I enjoyed, so I've brought him to our number one spot. The Old Orchard Mall.

"Are you sure *this* is what you want to do today?" I ask skeptically as we mill about by the indoor fountain.

"Yup." He tucks me under his arm and kisses my forehead. "But you need to narrate our trip. Tell me where you two went. What you loved. What made you guys laugh."

Tears prick my eyes, and I blink them back. I'm not sure if they're from the sudden rush of emotion I get from remembering my mom or how my heart fills with love for Jax, but I'm overwhelmed nonetheless.

We haven't had sex since New Year's Eve a week ago. But it hasn't fazed him. He's been nothing but amazing. Cleaning the house. Helping me go through my mom's stuff. Calling Susan for recipes and attempting to make me dinner. And as hard as it's been, I haven't slept with him since. I wanted space. I wanted to give him the opportunity to back away from this if he had just gotten too caught up. Because people make mistakes. And I don't want to be one of his. Nor him mine.

So each night I've slept nestled against him, and we talk until exhaustion overpowers us. And each morning I look into his eyes and wonder if he'll view at me differently, maybe with regret or indecision. But he wakes with a grin on his face and my name on his lips. With his hands in my hair and his breath on my skin. Like he can't get enough. Like he misses me even though we're snuggled together under the covers. Well, like he loves me.

I sniffle, and he turns me in his arms. "Dandelion, I'm sorry. Maybe this is a bad idea." He wipes an escaping tear as he holds my face. "I wanted to learn about your mom. To learn more about you. I love seeing you in your home so much, I thought if you showed me places you enjoyed growing up, I could—"

"Oh my God. Stop." I place my lips on his for a soft kiss. More tears fall while I wrap my arms around his neck and rest my head on his chest.

He strokes my hair, and we stand in the middle of the mall as people pass around us. I close my eyes and breathe him in.

"I love you too, Jax."

A part of me feels bad that I haven't told him yet, but I wanted to make sure that he meant what he said the other night. That it hadn't just slipped out because we were naked.

But now I know he means it, and I want him to know I've never loved another man more.

At first, I don't think he hears me, but then he laughs, squeezing me tighter before he leans down and brushes his lips against mine. "Thank God."

I giggle, and he kisses me deeper before some guy barks, "Get a room!"

We pull away from each other and laugh, and I dare say Jax's cheeks look flushed.

"Are you blushing, Jax Avery?" I ask as I tuck my arm through his.

"Nah. It's hot in here. I'm wearing layers." He keeps his eyes trained straight ahead, but his lips curl up.

"Hmm. I'm going to call bullshit. I think you blushed."

"Men don't blush, babe."

"You'll forgive me if I have to test that theory." I lead him around a pack of sorority girls who stare at my boyfriend like he's a steak and they've been on a steady diet of twigs and berries. The best part? He never glances their way. Ha! #BiteMeBitches

"Be my guest, Dandelion."

I grin to myself as I spot the store I need because I'm going to need some good ammunition to make this boy blush. I pull Jax to a stop and turn him toward the mecca of sugary goodness.

"I need to do a little shopping, sweetie pie." I peck him on the cheek. "So while I make a quick stop, you need to stand in that line over there and get us two caramel Pecanbons, which were my mom's favorite."

"Cinnabon, huh? I like this plan."

"I like you." I lean up to kiss him.

"No, you love me." He's joking, but there's something in his eyes that completely melts me.

Grinning, I pull away. "I do. And I plan to show you just how much."

He tries to grab me, but I dart away, laughing. Tonight is going to be epic.

* * *

Peeking around the corner, I see Jax sprawled on the couch, watching a basketball game. The room is dark, illuminated only by the flickering light from the TV.

I know he must be tired. After our trip to the mall, he shoveled the remaining snow out of the driveway and trimmed several branches in the backyard that looked like they might collapse on the porch. Then, right before we sat down for dinner, I found a present on the kitchen counter. All it said was "To Dandelion" in Jax's blocky handwriting. Beneath the pale pink wrapping paper, I found a new leather journal.

When I glanced up, I found Jax watching me. "I didn't mean to look in your journal. I'm sorry I had it all this time."

My heart beat in a crazy rhythm as we stared at each other, but then Susan knocked on the front door, so all I did was give him a quick hug to say thanks.

But now we're alone. And now I can't wait to show him *his* present.

Jax just took a shower, and his damp hair is sitting at crazy angles. I can't help but think of the one we took together at his apartment. How he let me cry on his shoulder. How he held me and whispered soothing words to calm me down before he sank to his knees and placed his mouth on me.

The memory makes my heart race. As I stare at him, the longing in my chest becomes almost unbearable. I tiptoe farther into the living room, and he looks up. His eyes widen as he takes in the fact that I'm only wearing a t-shirt.

"Jax, do you like lingerie?"

He clears his throat. "Babe, I'm a guy. All guys love

that stuff. But you don't need lingerie. You're rocking out the t-shirt just fine."

I frown. "Oh, well, then maybe I didn't need to get this." I pull off my shirt, and Jax sucks in a breath.

The lacy black baby doll barely comes to the top of my thighs. The room is cold, and my nipples tighten, and I know he can see the silver hoops beneath the thin fabric. My fingers toy with the hot pink bow between my breasts as I wait for him to say something. When he doesn't, I chew my bottom lip. The back! He needs to see the back!

I twirl around and then bend over slightly so he can see the frilly panties. Glancing at him over my shoulder, I put on a pout. "So… You'd rather I wear the t-shirt?"

"Get over here."

Laughing, I shake my head. "I don't know. As I recall, you've kept me waiting a time or two." I rest my hand on my hip as though I really mean to scold him.

"Right the fuck now, Danielle."

Before I can come up with a witty reply, he reaches out and yanks me onto his lap so that I'm straddling him. He leans up to kiss me, but I pull away. "Impatient, are we?"

"Babe, you're asking for it." A growl escapes his lips. "I'm going to fuck you six ways from Sunday if you're not careful."

I had intended to use this moment to prove my theory that guys can blush. Instead, my breath shallows, and my body feels feverish from the way he's looking at me. I press my hips down and grind against the hardness beneath me. "Promise?"

His devilish grin makes me throb harder. "Boy Scout's honor."

I smack his shoulder. "You were never a Boy Scout."

He laughs and pulls me closer. "Wanna bet?"

Jax dips his head to my chest. Before I can blink, one hand is fisting my hair and the other is plumping my breast into his mouth. But what kills me, what sets me on fire, is how he keeps his eyes trained on mine.

His tongue flicks at the metal hoop through the fabric of my nighty as my hands grip his biceps.

When I can't take it any longer, I tug on his t-shirt, which he whips off before he reaches for the hem of my top. He flings it off me, and I reach down to unbuckle his jeans. My fingers tremble as they unsnap the button, and I'm surprised when his big hands wrap around my wrists to still me.

"Baby, as much as I want this, we don't have to. If you want more time, if this is too much, we can wait." He closes his eyes, and I'm struck by how his whole body is taut, like it's taking everything in him to stop our momentum. "I shouldn't have pushed you the other night. I'm sorry. I got carried away, and—"

I answer him with a kiss as I push him down on the couch and press my body along the length of his. "I'm ready." I run my tongue along the seam of his lips. "I love you. I want this. Just as much as you do."

"I love you too, babe." He groans as our mouths fit together, and he fists my hair again. I reach down between us and stroke him over his jeans as I suck his tongue to the same rhythm. And just like that, we're feverish to get the rest of our clothes off. He tugs down his pants, and I kick off my undies until there's nothing between us.

Tilting my head, I let my long hair tumble to the side. His name falls from my lips as I widen my thighs and press myself down until he is wedged perfectly against the apex of my thighs. I rub against him slowly. We stare down where our bodies meet, and the sight makes me grind down harder.

His fingers grip my hip to still my motion before he reaches over and pulls a condom from his jeans. Once it's on, I angle him toward me.

As I sink down, he moans. "Fucking fuck, you feel good." I'd love to revel in the fact that I'm making him fall apart, but all I can mumble is "mmm."

I still to get used to his invading size, but after a minute, I want more and sink down as far as I can go, and we both groan at the sensation.

My skin is flushed and damp from sweat as our bodies begin moving against each other. Leaning down, I kiss him, and his hands tangle in my hair.

And it's at this very moment that my head decides to freak out.

I still have another year of school to go, and Jax is graduating in a few months. Doesn't that kind of thing screw up relationships, especially since he's been talking about signing with a professional soccer team?

The words come out of my mouth before I can stop them. "What happens after you graduate? If you sign with a team, you'll go on the road."

Jax stills beneath me and reaches up to tuck my hair behind my ear. "You know that answer." He stares long and hard into my eyes before he pulls my mouth to his for a gentle kiss. "We stay together." He holds my face with both of his hands. "Because you're what makes me want everything else."

Tears fill my eyes and I collapse on top of him and bury my face in his neck. His arms wrap around me, and we lie there entwined.

"I'm sorry," I whisper as his hand rubs up and down my back. "It's is a stupid time to talk about this."

"Sweetheart, being together is the only thing that matters to me. We'll figure out the rest."

I turn and kiss him, for minutes or hours, I can't tell. All I know is I get lost in the way he tastes, in the way our bodies meld together. And then he flexes his hips, and the swelling sensation between my legs has me desperate all over again. Even though I just had this weird emotional break down and I should probably be embarrassed, when I look in Jax's eyes, all I see is his love for me.

He holds the back of my neck as he shifts so we're on our sides. His hand wraps around my thigh as he tugs it up over his hip, and he presses deeper into me.

His thigh slips between mine until our legs are scissored together, and my breath catches. I've never had sex like this, twisted around another person so intensely that I can't tell where I end and he begins. Everything—from the way our breaths mingle to how his fingers are twined through mine as he looks into my eyes—tells me this is love.

I'm pinned by his stare, the intensity unraveling the part of me that's been afraid. All week, I've been waiting to be disappointed. Waiting for him to change his mind. But right now I feel anchored to him, like he's my mooring. Like I'm his. And just like that, my fears melt away. I don't know what's going to happen, what the future holds, but I do know I want to take this journey with him.

Jax nips my shoulder as he slowly pushes in and out of me. His arm wraps tightly around my thigh, hugging me to him, and I can't get close enough. The drag of his skin against mine is so exquisite, the throb between my legs intensifying until everything inside of me tightens and pulses, and I'm falling apart. With a scream, I gasp, and a moment later, he tenses as he comes.

The room is quiet but for the sound of our heaving breaths. Jax runs his hand along my back in a slow drag, pressing the tips of his fingers into my skin. Although exhaustion weighs all of my muscles, I reach up and thread my fingers through his sweaty hair, and he murmurs his approval.

"Jax," I whisper, "thanks for coming to Chicago to find me."

I close my eyes as he pulls me closer, and I nestle my head against his chest and listen to his heartbeat.

"Dandelion, I'm starting to think you're the one who found me."

CHAPTER FORTY-SEVEN

- Jax -

If the truth be told, I have a hard time concentrating when Dani is sitting so close. She may be in the passenger seat as I drive, but the scent of her hair and skin and clothes make me want to pull over to a rest stop and pin her underneath me.

She said it again this morning, and it's all I can think about.

We were loading my SUV with her luggage and a few boxes, and as I slammed the back hatch closed, she grabbed my jacket with both hands and yanked me to her. When our lips touched, she said it.

"Jax, I love you. So much."

She reaches over and laces her fingers through my free hand. "What are you smiling about?" she asks.

"You and all the love."

She giggles. She fucking giggles. I love that sound.

"Babe, you need my new number." When she doesn't say anything, I glance over to find her frowning. "Your phone. Get it."

She reaches for her cell, still looking confused. I call out my digits as she punches them in. "What happened to your old number?"

"Too many unwanted callers. I changed it last night."

I don't get a chance to look over again because her arms wrap around my neck. "So no more sexts from random girls, huh?"

"What girls? I only have one, and she's the best sexter I know." It was comical how fast I moved yesterday afternoon when I got that text from Dani, who was parked out in the living room as I cleared out boxes in the garage.

She places a sweet kiss on my cheek before she settles back in her seat. We drive in silence for a while. But she's quiet for too long.

"What's going on?" I ask.

She nibbles on her lower lip. "I'm worried about how all of this is going to affect your relationship with your mother. I hadn't really thought about it with everything going on in Chicago, but I don't want to cause any problems, and I—"

"Stop right there." I grip the steering wheel. "I've already been offered two contracts with pro teams and a few endorsements."

I've never been into the whole modeling thing, but it's a smart move business-wise. After I found out what my mother put Dani through with the non-disclosure, I decided I'd had enough. If I can put my face on a few ads for athletic wear or underwear to pay the bills, then so be it. My sister's book is selling well, so I'm not as worried about her as I was a few months ago.

"If my mother chooses to cut me off financially, that's on her. I'm not going to law school anyway, so I doubt any fallout will have to do with you. I'm doing what's right. I love you, and I'm not going to sit in Boston while you're in Chicago. Fuck that. I finally found the right woman, and I'm not letting you go."

When I look at her, she has tears brimming in her eyes. "So I'm kinda stuck with you, huh?"

I smile. "Fuck, yes."

She kisses me on the cheek, and damn it if my heart

doesn't do silly little backflips. Yeah, I'm totally fucking whipped, and I wouldn't have it any other way.

Dani reaches over and wraps her hand behind my neck, massaging my sore muscles. "Are you getting tired? Do you want to swap and I can drive while you take a nap?"

"I'm good for a while." I peek over at her. She has her hair tied up, and red swaths of color come tumbling down over her face. I love her hair, whether she's dyed it red or pink. I imagine just her normal dark brunette hair is gorgeous too.

"Why are you looking at me like that?"

I grin. "I'm counting the minutes until we can stop for the night and I can get you naked."

Her eyebrow pops up. "You know… we could always take a break at a rest stop."

My foot comes off the gas as the thought of ripping off her clothes overpowers my brain. I have to clear my throat to speak again.

"A girl after my own heart," I say, eyeing the next exit.

When we eventually reach Boston, it's two days later than I expected, but a guy can't stop that frequently and not expect to get behind schedule. As I eye Dani, who is sleeping in the passenger seat next to me, I think school be damned. Every extra stop was worth it.

I unbuckle my seatbelt and reach over to brush the hair out of her face. Her eyelids flutter open and she smiles.

"Hey," she whispers.

"Hey back."

She sits up and kisses me. It doesn't matter that the moment I turn off the ignition I can see my breath or that I should be moving her stuff into her room because I don't want to remove my hands from her body.

A knock on the window jars me.

"Hey, loser, do I get my roommate back anytime soon?" my sister yells, a huge smirk plastered on her face.

Dani's cheeks ignite in embarrassment, and I grin. "How about we unload your stuff and then stay at my place tonight?"

She nods, still looking sheepish.

I make her hang with her roommates while I bring her luggage up. When the last box is unloaded, I reach for Dani's hand.

"You ready, babe?"

Clementine cuts me off. "You're taking her?" I give her a look that she should understand, and she rolls her eyes. "Fine. Go have obnoxiously loud sex somewhere else."

She hugs my girlfriend who looks mortified again, and Clem laughs. "Let's do lunch later this week. I miss you. Jax is going to have to share custody of you."

Dani smiles. "I've missed you too."

My sister shakes her head. "The girl who tamed my brother. Maybe it's the sign of the apocalypse."

I put her in a headlock and she screams, "Dani, I'm not taking him back. I have a no-return policy on my dipshit little brother."

"You're three minutes older," I remind her.

"Exactly. Older. Wiser. Smarter."

I give her a noogie, and she squeals.

A small hand wraps around my wrist, and I look down as Dani stands on her tiptoes. She leans over and whispers in my ear. Two seconds later, I have my jacket and my girlfriend, and I'm dragging her down the stairs. Clem's laughter echoes behind me.

"I don't even want to know what she said to get you to leave that fast," she yells after us.

I look over at Dani who licks her lips like a little vixen. "Dandelion, I have plans for that tongue, so you'd better put it away for now."

She grins as she gets in my SUV. "I can't wait."

I adjust myself in my seat, straining against my jeans. She's reduced me to a horny teenage boy.

She reaches over and threads her fingers through mine. "If you're going on the road with your team this summer, I might need to give you a few good memories to take with you."

I laugh. "Hell, yes. Bring it, baby."

EPILOGUE
(SIX MONTHS LATER)

- Jax -

This never gets old.

I give the row of kids high-fives as we wrap up practice. The straggler at the end stops in front of me. "Jax, thank you so much for the scholarship."

I look down at Alejandro, who is ten and a natural-born soccer player. "No problem, buddy. Work on those drills I showed you today until I get back next week."

He grins ear to ear. "Coach is putting all of your games on the projector so we can watch them."

"Awesome. I wanna get your feedback. Let me know if there's anything I should work on, okay?"

That grin gets wider. "You got it!"

He jogs off to his friends, and I grab my gear as Coach Patterson strolls up and pats me on the back.

"Jax, I'm proud of you, son." He motions toward the pack of kids headed toward the locker room and smiles. "These kids will never forget what you're doing for them. Plus, it'll give the BC boys something to keep them out of trouble this summer. I'm glad you coordinated this camp."

"Sure thing, Coach."

"How are your practices going?"

I started playing with my new pro team this spring, and I've never had more fun. I feel like a kid again. But the best thing? Looking up at the stands and seeing my girl.

"I'm having a blast, and the soreness I had in my quad is gone. My trainer says I'm cleared for Thursday's game."

"That's what I want to hear." He taps his clipboard. "Kick ass out there next week. You've got thirty kids here cheering you on."

"Thanks. I'll do you proud."

"I know it," he says with a smile as he heads off the field.

A few more boys come up to talk, and we chat for a while, but I'm starting to get anxious. We can't be late tonight. Finally, I see my girl and take off in her direction.

"Those kids love you," Dani says as I wrap her in a sweaty hug.

Her tank top dips down, and I spot her tattoo. I love that ink. It couldn't be more fitting because that's what she is to me, my North Star.

I wipe my face on her neck and she laughs. "You stink."

"I'm giving you something to remember me by when I leave for my game in a few days."

"Don't remind me." She pouts, jutting out her lower lip. Glancing around to make sure I'm not giving anyone a show, I lean down and nibble on that little morsel.

She smacks me in the chest for being unable to control my public display of affection. Shit, she should be used to this by now.

Sighing, she says, "Thank God you're playing for New England. I don't know what I would've done if you'd gone to Los Angeles."

I frown.

"Do you really think I would have accepted an offer

from a team across the country when you're here?"

Her head tilts up, a small smile playing on her lips. "No, I guess not."

"Besides, we have to finish up our business plan for the GoPro ski helmets."

"Not ours, Jax. Yours."

She can't be serious. "Babe, that was all your idea. You took that silly contraption I made when I was screwing around on vacation and made a real business out of it."

She saw the promise of my helmet and found there was a huge demand for it. She lined up orders before we even got the prototypes back, and when she talked to her professors about it, they were so impressed they convinced her to stay a business major and double-degree with art.

I hug her tighter. "So yes, it's *our* plan because it's *our* business."

I want to say it's also our money, but I don't want to freak her out. After last winter, she's sensitive about what I spend on her, which pisses me off because I want to buy her things. Lots of things.

But I have a plan.

She blows out a breath, not wanting to get into this with me again, and I run my nose along her jaw because I know I've won this battle.

I smack her on the ass, and she jumps, laughing. "Let's go. We need to get to the restaurant by five if we want to make the game."

"I can't believe you got me playoff tickets to see the Celtics play the Heat. I'm so psyched!"

That's not all she's getting, but I have to keep my shit together if this is gonna be a surprise.

Even though I've been trying to save up some cash

for our business, I wanted to splurge tonight.

Doing this on my own feels good. No, it feels fucking incredible.

My mother lost it when I told her my plans. But it doesn't matter. I won't let her control me anymore. Even though I could've asked my father for help, it doesn't seem right. If he had wanted to help, to be part of my life or my sister's, he'd have been here.

I sold off all of my expensive toys and cars, and my modeling gigs have been paying well. I've made enough to get Dani and me through for a while and still have something left to invest in our business.

She hasn't decided what she wants to do with her mom's house in Chicago, and I don't want to rush her. We've talked about staying there a few weeks this summer to help her finish packing. I want her to have all the time she needs to make peace with her mom's passing.

By the time we get to the Garden, Dandelion is decked out in green. I had to put my foot down and hide her Heat jersey. Privately, I don't mind her Miami fanaticism, but I can't very well let her walk the streets of Boston in anything but Celtic colors.

Her eyes widen as we get closer to the players. She turns to me. "You got us courtside seats?"

I kiss her. "It's your twenty-first birthday. I wanted to make it memorable."

Her hands reach up and cradle my face. "As long as I'm with you, I wouldn't care what we did. You know that, right?"

Fuck, yeah, I know that, which is why she's the girl for me.

We find our seats, and a few minutes later, she jumps out of her chair to hug Clementine, Gavin and Travis.

"Did you know your brother was doing this?" she asks Clem.

My sister gives me a playful shove. "He's been planning this for ages. He wouldn't shut up about it. I'm shocked this is an actual surprise for you."

My sister is her usual ornery self, but I've already told her how to play it tonight, so I know she won't let anything slip.

Travis gives me a half smile and leans over to whisper, "Don't fuck up."

"Thanks, man. Really." I place a hand over my chest to feign sincerity. He laughs, turning to the birthday girl to pick her up in a hug.

Nick and Daren join us, and after a few bro hugs, we take our seats.

"Dude, you okay?" Daren asks. He snagged me the tickets.

"Never been better," I say with a wide smile. He looks at my leg that's nervously jiggling and then back at me with a smirk. "Is everything all set at Ryan's?"

He leans a little closer. "Yup. Sammy and Jenna have it covered. Everyone will be there by the time the game is over." He slaps me on the back. "Good luck, Jax. Don't have a heart attack first."

"Thanks, brother." I glance around. "Where's Veronica? I thought she was coming tonight."

He shrugs, his brows furrowing into deep grooves on his forehead. I don't need to ask anything else. Maybe he's figuring out what everyone else has always known, that they're not right for each other. Because Daren and Veronica never really had that kind of connection. The kind I have with my girl.

I spend the game watching Danielle. She's smiling and laughing, and I can't wait to surprise her.

Her hand twines around the locket her mom gave her for Christmas. Last week she put a small picture of me in it, and nothing has ever meant more.

By half time, my palms are sweaty, and my heart is beating out of my chest. Who knew I'd be such a fucking pussy when the time came?

Clem catches my eye when Dani isn't looking and gives me a wink of encouragement that only makes me more nervous.

Finally, the kissing cam goes up on the big screen during half time, and I wipe my forehead as I wait.

When the camera reaches us, Dani gasps in surprise before she grins and leans over to kiss me, but the sudden cheering gets her attention, and she looks back up at the jumbo-tron to read those four little words that will change our lives forever.

"Jax?" she asks, her eyes bugging out as I get down on one knee.

"Danielle, I love you more than life itself. Will you marry me?" I put the rock on her finger. She looks at it, blinks a few times and smiles. It's not as big a stone as I'd like, but I know she doesn't care about that.

"Oh my God. Yes, yes, yes!" She leaps up, and she's in my arms, and the crowd goes crazy. My sister is crying, and the girls hug each other and laugh as the giant screen above our heads plays our special moment for the entire arena.

Finding Dandelion is the best thing that's ever happened to me. I know she still has a little more school, and my soccer schedule is hectic, but when we're apart, I want her to know that she is mine and I am hers. Forever.

She turns to me, and I lean over to kiss her, the first of many yet to come.

See, there are happily ever afters. Even for assholes like me.

TO MY READERS

Thank you for reading *Finding Dandelion.* I would love to hear what you thought of my novel and hope you'll consider leaving a review on Goodreads and Amazon.

If you enjoyed Dani and Jax's story, Daren will get his own book later this year. Look for *Kissing Madeline,* the third novel in the Dearest Series, in early 2015. (Each is a standalone.)

ORDER OF BOOKS

Dearest Clementine, #1

Finding Dandelion, #2

Kissing Madeline, #3 (Expected publication - Early 2015)

KISSING MADELINE

After walking in on her MMA fighter boyfriend in the arms of another woman, Maddie McDermott learned her lesson about dating athletes – don't do it. Ever. Not even if he's the "it boy" of football and her hot-as-hell new neighbor.

NFL's newest star, Daren Sloan, kicks ass in every area of his life – football, school, family – every area, that is, except relationships. Newly single after almost marrying one of the worst mistakes of his life, he plans to take full advantage of all the benefits he's worked so hard to achieve. For now, those perks include no strings, and fortunately, no woman can resist his charm. Well, no one except his feisty neighbor.

When their jobs collide, Maddie and Daren can't seem to avoid each other or their undeniable attraction. So they keep things casual… until they quickly realize "friends with benefits" is not enough.

Although they do their best to keep the nature of their relationship under wraps, the media loves a good story. And so does the person scheming to break them up. Will Daren convince Maddie she can trust him? Or will the media storm brewing tear them apart before they even get started?

(Release date - Early 2015)

DEAREST CLEMENTINE

Before the drama of Jax, there was Clementine. Have you read her story yet? It's available now if you haven't.

Twenty-year-old Clementine Avery doesn't mind being called bitchy and closed off. It's safe, and after being burned by her high school sweetheart and stalked by a professor her freshman year of college, safe sounds pretty damn good.

Her number one rule for survival? No dating. That is until she accidentally signs up for a romance writing class and needs material for her latest assignment. Sexy RA Gavin Murphy is more than happy to play the part of book boyfriend to help Clem find some inspiration, even if that means making out…in the name of research, of course.

As Gavin and Clem grow closer, they get entangled in the mystery surrounding a missing Boston University student, and Clem unwittingly becomes a possible target. Gavin tries to show Clem she can handle falling in love again, but she knows she has to be careful because her heart's at stake…and maybe even her life.

DEAREST CLEMENTINE is a stand-alone New Adult romance with two companion novels. The Dearest Series is recommended for readers 18+ due to mature content.

ACKNOWLEDGEMENTS

The person who deserves my biggest thanks is my husband and best friend, Matthew. Without his constant support, I never would have had the balls to do this. Matt, thanks for believing in me and for being such a kick-ass dad to our girls. I don't know any other four-year-olds who know the difference between Mozart and Beethoven. You're seriously cool as shit, and I love you. Girls, thanks for being so patient with me while I write. Wub you, little bears.

To my Texas family, thanks for giving me the courage to venture far from home. Dad, I appreciate you buying my books even though I won't let you read them. You're the best!

I also have an amazing writing family. AJ Pine, Megan Erickson, Natalie Blitt and Lia Riley, I'm so grateful to have such fantastic critique partners and honored to get your input on my work. *cue cheesy music* You complete me!

Thanks, of course, to my fantastic editor, RJ Locksley. She keeps me from looking stupid. RJ, everything I write is better after you do your magic.

My new bestie Kimberly Brower also gave me killer input on *Dandelion*. Kimberly, I love that I can send you emails in the middle of the night and you write me back at one a.m. You're awesome!

You should know I'm a total fangirl. I have authors I adore like groupies love rock stars. So when those authors respond to my emails and offer advice in return, they get my undying love and affection. You might have noticed I give away a lot of other people's books on my

Facebook. This is why.

The first two authors in that "I love you like a love song, baby" category are Becca and Krista Ritchie. They helped me get my feet wet with my first release and walked me through many big steps. Becca, you should be sainted for having so much patience with me and all of my questions. Krista, dear lord, thank you for my gorgeous covers and for mocking up a dozen different options until we nailed down the right ones. #LuvYouGuys4Life

JB Salsbury is another writer whose success as an indie author inspires me like nothing else. No one deserves it more because she is such a talented and sweet person. Jamie, thanks for your support and optimism and for introducing me to your hot MMA boys!

I have huge hugs for M. Pierce, whose work I deeply admire. M., seriously, you're awesome. If I follow you like a puppy, it's because the fangirl in me won't shut up. Thanks for the encouragement and tough love. And to StudBun, my favorite tweeter of all time. Don't let M. work you too hard.

Self-publishing comes with some serious ups and downs, but I always know I can turn to my friends in FebNo and NAAU for advice. I'm so grateful for those relationships. When I have a crisis in the middle of the night, someone there always comes to the rescue.

Another person who has saved my ass many times is Brandi Leigh Hall. If you buy a print copy of one of my books, she's to thank for helping me survive the formatting process. Brandi, you rock, girl. Love you!

To my friends Taylor Hyslop, Barbara Ransom, Doris E. Gray, Jullie Anne Caparas, and Sheri Thompson-Gustafson. Some of you read early copies, offered feedback, made me graphics, or helped me pick my covers. Thank you for your endless kind words. Taylor, I'm so glad you encouraged me to write Jax's story after Clementine's.

I've also received amazing support from bloggers who picked up my books to review or promote. Thank you for giving a new author a shot. *insert big hugs here* I know I'll never be able to mention everyone, but there are a few who went out of their way for me, including Aestas at Aestas Book Blog, Becs at Sinfully Sexy Book Reviews, Jen at The Sub Club, Lanie and her fairies at The Bookaholic Fairies, Sue at YA Hollywood, Christie & Patryja at Smokin' Hot Book Blog, Ellen at Book Bellas, Kawehi Reviews, Book Worms, The Insomniac Book Hoarder, Book Reader Chronicles, Leann at Twin Opinions Review, Lesley at Let's Get Lost in a Good Book Blog, Linda at True Blood Diaries, The Little Black Book Blog, Jovana at Rumpled Sheets, Michelle at The Romance Vault, Cathy at Forever Reading Book Blog, Renee at Book Happiness, Jen at Romance Obsessed Book Blog, United Indie Book Blog, the Concupiscent Bibliophile, Doris at Owl Always Be Reading, and Jullie at Teacups & Book Love.

A special shout-out goes to Natalie at Love Between the Sheets for all of her awesomeness. She does a killer job coordinating my cover reveals, blitzes and blog tours.

Lastly, to my readers. Thank you for picking up my books. I LOVE getting your emails, tweets and reviews. And when you create amazing graphics for my stories, seriously, I die. I hope you weren't too pissed at Jax and that he found redemption in your eyes. Speaking of redemption, stay tuned for Daren's story. Thanks for coming on this ride with me!

xo,
Lex

CONTACT LEX

Email: lex@lexmartinwrites.com
Blog: www.lexmartinwrites.com
Twitter: @lexlaughs